You Were Almost Home

Book Cover by L.M. Bennett

ISBN: 978-1-7378154-5-7

1st edition 2025

Contents

Suggested Playlist

Zero 7 – Distractions [feat. Sia]

Fleetwood Mac – Dreams

Coldplay – A Warning Sign

Doechii – Anxiety

Ne-Yo – Stay

Radiohead – Planet Telex

Sade – Somebody Already Broke My Heart

Fiona Apple – Left Alone

The Pharcyde – Runnin'

Atoms for Peace – Stuck Together Pieces

Tupperware – My Lucky Stars

Kendrick Lamar – Complexion (A Zulu Love) [feat. Rapsody]

Case & Joe – Faded Pictures

Stevie Wonder – Another Star

Janet Jackson – I Get Lonely [TNT Remix feat. Blackstreet]

Erykah Badu – Green Eyes

Mary J. Blige – Memories

Kate Bush – Hounds of Love

Coldplay – Amsterdam

Stevie Wonder – As

Brandy – Almost Doesn't Count

Janet Jackson – Come Back To Me

Luther Vandross – A House is Not a Home

Amy Winehouse – Love is a Losing Game

Coo Jones – I C U

Maxwell – Lifetime

Cleo Sol – Sweet Blue

Listen to the playlist here:

spotify playlist qr
code for playlist

To my wife, who loves me

even when I'm obsessing over whether

my fictional lesbians are communicating properly.

Love you.

Preface

Shaye's story continues in *String Theory*.

So, This Is What Rock Bottom Tastes Like (Hint: Extra Hot Sauce)

BG

2023

THREE DAYS AFTER THE record came back with Riley's note attached like a tiny paper grenade, I was still bleeding out in slow motion.

I don't want anything from you.

Six words that basically translated to: *You are nothing. You were always nothing. Delete yourself from my life, post-haste.*

Cool. Very cool. Totally fine. Just your average Saturday morning emotional evisceration, no big deal.

I pushed through the bodega door, the little bell announcing my arrival like some cheerful funeral march. The familiar smell of Café Bustelo and plantain chips should've been comforting, but everything felt wrong-sized now. Like I was viewing my life through a funhouse mirror.

"Buen día, Mrs. Rosario," I called to the woman behind the counter, forcing my voice to sound normal instead of like I'd been gargling gravel for three days straight.

"Ay, Mija, you look tired," she said, already reaching for the coffeepot without me asking. God, I loved this place. Predictable. Reliable. Unlike literally everything else in my life.

I made my way to the back where Mr. Hector was slicing ham behind the deli counter, his hands moving with the efficiency of someone who'd been doing this for decades.

"The usual?" he asked, not looking up from the slicer.

"Yeah, extra hot sauce, though. I'm feeling kinda destructive today." I tried to keep it light, joking, but even I could hear the brittle edge in my voice.

Mr. Hector glanced up, his dark eyes taking in my disaster appearance with the bluntness only bodega owners possess. "Rough night?"

"Rough life," I said, attempting a laugh that came out more like a wheeze. "But hey, that's what coffee's for, right?"

He nodded sagely, like this was profound wisdom instead of basic millennial survival strategy. "Coffee fixes many things. Not everything, but many things."

I watched him build my sandwich with practiced ease. Baconeggandcheese, enough hot sauce to strip paint. He rolled the sandwich in parchment and sliced the poppy seed hard roll in half. The mundane ritual felt like the only stable thing in my universe right now. He wrapped it in foil, grabbed a black marker, and scribbled "$4.50" on the side before handing it to me.

"Have a good one!" I called behind me with a wave.

I clutched the warm foil package like a life preserver and headed back to the front. Mrs. Rosario had indeed prepared my café con leche, the perfect shade of brown in a blue paper cup. Benito had materialized from where cats disappear to, his little tuxedo chest puffed out importantly. At least someone in this place was thriving. I crouched down, letting him headbutt my palm while I tried to remember how to breathe like a normal human.

"Hey, handsome," I whispered, scratching behind his ears. "You're the only man who's never disappointed me."

Benito purred, completely unbothered by my existential crisis. Must be nice to be a cat. No ex-girlfriends returning your gifts. No complicated feelings about commitment. Just naps and tuna and the occasional bodega mouse to terrorize.

Almost home free. Just pay for breakfast, pet the cat, and escape back to my new apartment where I could continue my scheduled emotional breakdown on an air mattress.

The bell jingled.

I was mid-reach for my wallet when she walked in, and the sight of her sent my entire chakra system into emergency shutdown mode. No warning, no time to brace, just Riley suddenly filling the doorway like she'd materialized from my worst nightmares.

She looked terrible.

That threw me completely off guard, because I'd expected her to look...fine, I guess. Maybe even relieved. Like, finally got rid of that chaotic mess of a human, you know? But this was something else entirely. And somehow that made everything worse. Her short curls were roughed up like she'd been tossing and turning all night, and her eyes were rimmed with the same red exhaustion that had been haunting my mirror for three days. The lighting wasn't helping that yellow undertone hue, either. Was that a stain on her hoodie? She was wearing those ratty plaid pajama pants she reserved for her most depressing weekends, the ones that made her look like she'd given up on life entirely. Dirty socks and Nike slides.

Wait. Hold up. Those weren't just any pajama pants. Those were her "I'm embodying every breakup anthem SZA ever wrote" pants. The ones she'd worn after her grandmother died. The ones from when she got passed over for that promotion. Riley, who treated her wardrobe like a masc-leaning Instagram style feed even on her laziest days, was standing in a bodega looking like she'd been stress-eating ice cream and watching "happy, hopeful, heart-warming" small town Netflix rom-coms for 72 hours straight. (Not that I'd been doing the same thing. You can't prove I was, either.)

And suddenly my brain started doing that annoying thing where it whispers unhelpful truths: People don't fall apart like this over someone who never mattered.

Shut up, brain.

She stopped short when she saw me, her whole body going rigid. For a heartbeat, we just stared at each other across the tiny space. Two train wrecks in house clothes, separated by three feet whatever the hell this mutual destruction was that we'd both apparently been living in for three days straight.

Because looking at her now, I had to wonder if maybe I'd been writing the wrong story this whole time. Maybe this wasn't just Riley being dramatic or pulling some reverse psychology bullshit. Maybe she actually...

Nope. Hard pass. I'm not doing this. I'm not turning into one of those people who analyzes every micro-expression like they're decoding the Da Vinci Code. That way lies madness and endless YouTube deep dives about body language.

Her face cycled through emotions in real time. Shock, then something that looked like it might have been regret, then her expression flattened into nothing. Like someone had just shut off all the lights behind her eyes. The same expression she'd probably worn when she wrote that note, when she decided I was worth exactly nothing to her anymore.

Except she'd never used that face on me before. Not once. Not even when I'd been at my most insufferable, which, let's be honest, was a pretty high bar.

But wasn't that what I'd taught her? That I wasn't worth fighting for?

Mrs. Rosario cleared her throat softly. "Seven fifty, Mija."

Right. Money. Normal human behavior. I could do this.

My hands were shaking as I fumbled for bills, grabbing the first thing I found—a twenty that was way too much, but whatever. The math part of my brain had apparently evacuated the building the second Riley walked in.

Riley moved toward the newspaper rack like we were two magnets with the same charge, automatically creating distance. She grabbed the Times without really looking at it, her movements jerky and uncertain. This was the woman who used to plan our entire weekends with the precision of a NASA launch sequence, who had strong opinions about which bodega had the best coffee-to-price ratio. Now she looked like she'd forgotten how to human in a space she could navigate blindfolded.

Like she was just as wrecked as I was.

Which was...unexpected. And kind of terrifying. Because if Riley—Riley, who bounced back from everything like some kind of emotional Energizer Bunny—was this destroyed, then maybe...

No, Becks. Not going there. That way lies rom-com thinking and showing up at her apartment with boomboxes, puppy eyes and apologies. She wrote those words. She sent back my gift. Case closed, file sealed, end of story.

"Keep the change," I choked out, practically throwing the money at Mrs. Rosario.

I had to get out. Had to move before this awkward standoff killed us both. But Riley was still between me and the door, and the space felt smaller than a coffin, pressing in from all sides.

I clutched my breakfast like armor and made my escape, squeezing past her without making eye contact. Our shoulders almost brushed, and I swear the air between us crackled with everything we couldn't say. Everything I'd been too scared to say when it mattered.

Behind me, the weight of Mr. Hector's disappointed gaze burning into my back. "Ay, Mija. What did you do?"

The bell announced my frantic exit, and I was already halfway down the block before I realized I was literally running. Foot to ass. Rogue coffee splatter all on my pants.

And the worst part? Seeing her like that: destroyed, falling apart, wearing her grief like those stupid pajama pants, it made me wonder if maybe I'd been the villain of my own love story this whole time. Maybe she hadn't been looking for an exit strategy. Maybe when she talked about our future, she'd actually *meant* it.

Because here's the thing I keep trying not to remember: I'd gotten so deep with Riley that I couldn't breathe, couldn't think, couldn't function. Too giddy from dancing in kitchens and wheezing watching weird historical docs with her while listening to her snarker deadpan commentary and making out like teens and talking about future plans. For a few months there, I'd actually started believing she might choose me. Really choose me. Forever. I'd been deliriously, stupidly happy, walking around like someone had handed me the universe wrapped in a bow.

I'd always been too much for everyone else. Too intense, too loud, too chaotic. The girl who loved too hard and burned too bright until people got tired of the heat.

So I'd convinced myself it was temporary anyway. That eventually she'd wake up just like the rest of them and realize I wasn't the kind of chaos you tried to build a life around.

But what if I'd been wrong? What if seeing her like this meant...

Jesus, Becks. Listen to yourself. Next you'll be analyzing her grocery list for hidden meaning. She made herself crystal clear: she didn't want anything from me. And maybe that was exactly what happened when you showed someone your true colors and they turned out to be commitment-phobic red flags.

Riley could have the bodega. The neighborhood. She could have the whole damn Bronx, if she wanted.

I was out.

Gravity

Riley

2025

I COUNTED THE HOURS until I wouldn't see her.

My tea settled on the desk with barely a sound as my focus drifted between the patient charts and the party looming tonight. The indoor fountain trickled in the corner of the reception area, each drop like a tiny clock tick counting down to Harlem. Water hitting water. Time slipping away.

Dr. Riley Benson. Focused. Professional. The nameplate on my desk gleamed under the soft lighting. Someone who didn't let personal drama interfere with patient care. Someone who had moved on.

Outside my window, January sun struggled through winter clouds, casting the kind of half-light that made everything seem less real. Less immediate. I traced a finger along the rim of my mug, the ceramic smooth and warm against my skin. Then wrapped both hands around it, the heat from the lemon ginger tea anchoring me back to now. The slight bite of ginger on my tongue. The bright sweetness coating my throat. Just a few more charts, then plenty of time to convince myself that tonight wasn't a mistake.

My phone buzzed across the wood, demanding attention. The screen vibrated against the polished surface, each buzz a tiny earthquake in the quiet office. Tangi's name lit up the display: *'You coming tonight? Need moral support if I have to hear about wedding colors for 3 hours.'* The words stared back at me, her perfect bait dangling.

I opened Mr. Liu's file, catching up on his last imaging studies. Last visit: neck subluxation, mild lumbar pain. The phone skittered again, interrupting my concentration. My stomach tightened before I even read the text.

'You probably won't even see her. She's never on time for anything.'

Even the mention made my whole body tense up. My leg bounced underneath my desk.

Beyond the screen, my reflection in the window looked back at me: jaw tight, eyes wary. I rubbed my hair over tight curls grown out too long, time for a trim. The calendar app notification blinked in the corner: Deena & Taj's Party, 7PM. My pulse quickened as I mentally traced the route to Harlem, calculating traffic patterns, snow possibilities, the exact minute I could arrive and leave without drawing attention. Every breath felt like preparation for a moment I'd rehearsed avoiding. I typed my response before I could change my mind.

I inhaled lavender from the diffuser, my lungs filling slowly, expanding against my ribs in the controlled breathing pattern I taught anxious patients. Closed my eyes. Counted three beats. Then typed: *'I'll be there. Someone has to save you from yourself.'*

The words appeared on screen, a promise I'd have to keep, under penalty of never-ending guilt trips from Taj. My finger hit send, and instantly I wanted to take it back. But it was done.

Before I could return to work, another notification flashed. Different tone, different vibration. My dating app. Shaye's name appeared with a simple *'Have a great day, Doc.'* A smile formed, brief but genuine. Two days of messages with someone new. Someone who liked hiking and jazz. Someone who wouldn't demolish my composure simply by entering a room.

I set the phone down, screen-side onto the desk, letting Shaye's message settle inside me. January. New year, new start. The mantra I'd been repeating since the ball dropped in Times Square. Maybe this time...

Mr. Liu lay face down on the table as I positioned his arm with slow, exact movements. Quiet enveloped the office, ambient music threading through the stillness, harmonizing with the sound of my working hands. My voice stayed low, steady. I lifted his legs carefully. Left side was still short.

His head nodded slightly in the cushioned rest. I gently lifted his legs first, checking how his heels aligned. Left slightly higher—the subluxation was still affecting his posture.

"Look left for me, please."

As he turned his head, I lifted his legs again, noting how the rotation of his skull affected the alignment. The left heel drifted higher. I set his legs down and moved to his upper back, fingers tracing along his spine, searching for that telltale resistance. There. C5 vertebra, slight rotation. I picked up the activator from the side table, its familiar weight settling into my palm.

Tension gathered in his shoulders, breath held before the adjustment.

"Breathe in for me," I instructed, placing my hands on his spine. I felt for the telltale knot, noting with satisfaction that it was smaller this time. As he exhaled, I made the first adjustment with a smooth motion. "Perfect. Let's do that again."

My finger moved with precision born from years of practice, but my mind

11

wandered to the party, to Tangi's expectations, to her. The possibility of her presence shouldn't matter anymore. But it did.

I refocused on Mr. Liu, the activator's soft click drawing me back. After the adjustment, I checked his legs again, gently pushing his heels together. Better alignment. Even as I healed his body, mine tensed at what tonight might bring.

"Nice work, Mr. Liu. You've been keeping up with the exercises?"

"Every morning," he replied, voice muffled against the table.

"Good." I guided his arm to the next position.

New Year's Eve played through my mind. Two years ago. At another party like tonight's. Her hand on another woman's arm, a bright-smiled someone with a room-filling laugh. Their easy connection, the casual intimacy. Too familiar. Too fucking *soon* after she ripped my heart out. Midnight approached, but I'd already gone, their flirtation ringing in my ears.

My grip loosened for a split second, my rhythm broken. A deep breath pushed the memory away.

"Last one," I announced, voice unnaturally steady. "Ready?"

The final adjustment finished with a hard twist with lots of pressure—the kind that kept Mr. Liu returning month after month.

"Thank you, Dr. Benson," he said, sitting up and rubbing his neck.

"See you in a month, Mr. Liu." I helped him off the table, my hands firm, professional.

He left with a satisfied nod, and I remained alone with thoughts of tonight. Of maybe seeing BG. At least here, in my office, control still belonged to me.

Keisha's head appeared in my doorway as I packed up. "Night, Dr. Benson."

"Goodnight, Keisha." Tangi's texts weighed down my pocket. "See you next week."

The parking lot greeted me with cold air that bit through my coat. Shaye's message warmed my thoughts again. Something new. Something uncomplicated.

The drive to Mott Haven passed quickly beneath threatening skies. Radio silence filled the car as my mind sorted through jumbled thoughts. The memory of that hesitation during Mr. Liu's session nagged at me.

Maybe I should just cancel. Tell Tangi the weather looked too dangerous. She'd understand. My couch beckoned: wineglass in hand, under warm blankets, watching the city disappear under white.

But bailing again wasn't an option. Tangi was probably right—*she* might not even show up on time. And if she did? After two years of distance, I wouldn't let her ruin my evening.

My car pulled into the driveway under gray, heavy clouds. Forty-five minutes to shower and reach Harlem by seven.

"One hour," the words fell into empty space. I'll go for exactly one hour, show my face, grab a drink, drop off my gift, then I'm throwing up the deuce on my way out.

Hot shower water washed away lingering doubt. She didn't get to take my friends too. We were both too stubborn to give up this circle we'd stitched together, so we'd settled for a game of chicken instead—her showing up only when I wouldn't be there. Me finding something else to do when I knew she would be there. Hell, even my family had stopped asking about her.

By the time I dressed, snow flurries had started their dance outside. They swirled around me on the drive to Vine & Oak, roads still mercifully clear. A little snow wouldn't stop me now.

Three blocks from the venue, I parked and stepped into the gentle snowfall. Flakes melted on my shoulders during the short walk. Outside the club, my lungs filled with sharp, cold air. Deep breath. Shoulders back. The night wouldn't defeat me before it began.

Inside, energy buzzed throughout the space. Deep emerald walls embraced low leather banquettes. My pulse slowed as my eyes swept across faces. No her. Maybe Tangi called it right.

"Ry!" Sakia's voice cut through the crowd, her hand waving me toward the bar.

I navigated through clusters of people, pretending casualness while scanning every corner. The room pulsed with conversation and laughter, bodies shifting like currents I had to wade through. Each face I passed wasn't hers, a small relief that accumulated with every step.

"Hey, Kia," I accepted the drink she extended, cool glass against my fingertips. "Thanks."

Sakia's eyes met mine, warm and knowing with that intuitive depth that made her such a good friend. And probably why her clients trusted her so easily. Her gap-toothed smile was gentle as her gaze lingered a beat too long, blonde locs catching the bar's dim lighting as she searched for something on my face. "Glad you made it. How long you staying?"

"One hour, maybe two," a smile teased at the corner of my mouth, but never fully formed. My free hand brushed at an invisible wrinkle on my shirt. "Got a lot of charts to finish."

Familiar faces filled the room—Cruz by the DJ booth, Taj's cousin near the window, Deena's coworkers clustered by the bar. Each greeting became a small victory, a moment where I thought about something other than her. Her absence was an unexpected gift I held carefully, afraid it might disappear if examined too closely.

Tangi caught my eye across the space, drink tilted slightly in my direction. Her look knowing and slightly smug, the silent told-you-so hanging in the air between us. She mouthed, "You good?"

My smile never reached my eyes, the motion mechanical and practiced. "So far." The words tasted like tempting fate.

Time warped. Too fast and too slow simultaneously. My watch became a talisman checked repeatedly, each glance confirming I was closer to escape. Conversations stayed brief, deliberately light, exit strategy always in mind. I absorbed nothing, kept less. Deena and Taj—tonight's celebrated couple—basked in their friends' attention across the room, their happiness almost too bright to look at directly. Deena beamed, showing off her new ring. I waved from safety's distance, my body angled toward the door.

At the fifty-nine minute mark, I drained my glass and set it down on a nearby table. "Alright, y'all," my voice lifted above the music, pitched to sound casual rather than relieved. "Aiight, I'm heading out. Congratulations again to the happy couple."

Coat in hand, tension drained from my shoulders like water. My spine loosened for the first time since arriving. One hour, as promised. Mission accomplished. I'd dodged the ghost I'd been dreading all night. My breath came easier as I reached for the door, the night air already calling to me. Freedom waited just on the other side, and I'd earned it.

The door swung open just as my fingers brushed the handle. The music, the laughter, the clinking glasses—all of it faded in an instant. The world collapsed to a single point.

Beckham Grace, in the flesh.

My lungs forgot how to work. My skin prickled with awareness. Every cell suddenly, painfully alive.

Everything stopped. Time crystallized around us. The room dimmed around her edges as if she pulled all the light toward her. She wore a cream sweater that hung off one shoulder, exposing skin I once knew by taste. Gold hoops caught the light when she moved, brushing her collarbone. Her locs—longer now—rippled down her collarbone, copper highlights woven through the dark strands. That slow, dangerous blink that always came before she spoke. The familiar tilt of her head that meant she was considering her words.

What could we even say to each other at this moment? The question bounced through my mind like ricocheting bullets.

Our eyes locked in electric recognition. Heat rushed to my face. My heart hammered against my chest, each beat painful and precise. My mouth turned desert-dry, tongue stuck to the roof. Run-or-stay impulses battled within me, neither winning, leaving me frozen at the threshold. Two years of distance—of calculated absences and declined invitations—evaporated in one second. Like they'd never existed at all.

BG's lips parted. A small intake of breath. That gesture I knew so well, that one that came just before she said something important. Something that would change everything.

"Ry—" The beginning of my name in her mouth.

I forced my feet forward before she could finish. My body brushed past hers, our shoulders connecting for the briefest moment. I offered only a slight nod as

I sidestepped her body and walked out, maintaining the deliberate posture I'd use when leaving a treatment room.

No dramatics. No words exchanged.

Just quiet devastation in how familiar it still felt. How right. How dangerous.

Back in my car, my hands gripped the wheel like a lifeline. My knuckles whitened under the strain. Breath rushed in and out too fast, as if I'd sprinted from Vine & Oak instead of walking with forced composure. The engine remained silent, but my heart raced wildly, each beat echoing in my ears.

Those eyes. Dark amber with flecks of gold near the pupils. The way they'd sliced through the crowded room, straight to me. Like she'd known exactly where I'd be standing. Like she'd been searching for me all along.

Her perfume lingered in my nose. Jasmine and something uniquely her—something I'd once found on my pillows, my clothes, my skin. The memory of how everything else disappeared when she entered the room pressed against my chest.

"Dammit." The word escaped between clenched teeth, fogging the cold air inside the car.

Two years of distance. Seven hundred and thirty-one fucking days of avoiding the same spaces. Of leaving parties early when friends mentioned she might show up later. Of changing coffee shops and running routes and favorite restaurants. And she still pulled like gravity.

My palm slammed against the wheel, the sharp crack echoing in the empty car. Pain bloomed across my hand. I welcomed the clarity. How could she still unravel me this way? One look and I was right back where I started. After everything—the betrayal, the midnight fights, the meticulous rebuilding of myself—I sat here exactly as before. Angry. Undone. Wanting.

The last admission burned most of all.

I jammed the key into the ignition. The engine roared to life, blasting cold air that matched the ice forming around my composure. Annoyance burned as I pulled from the lot—at her, at myself, at how familiar it all felt. At how easily I'd slipped back into her orbit.

"Not this time." My voice sounded strange in the empty car. "Not again."

I drove through the night as the snow picked up, thick flakes swirling through my headlight beams. Roads remained clear, and I didn't stop. Not at the red light on 125th. Not at the text notification that lit up my phone on the passenger seat. Not until the city was far behind me and the snow had buried everything familiar.

Cool Girls Don't Cry At Engagement Parties

BG

I CIRCLED THE BLOCK once, twice, three times for good measure.

Oops, I did it again. Late to another party. But honestly? This Friday traffic was out of bounds. Not my fault at all. And parking? Don't even get me started. I should've just sucked it up and hopped on the subway.

The digital clock on my dash blinked 7:28. Perfect. Just enough time to be fashionably late, but with no one actually getting annoyed. Deena would totally understand. She knows how these downtown streets get.

My thumb ran along the cracked seam of the steering wheel while I hummed along to the radio, some pop song I only half-knew the words to. Better than thinking about who might be inside. Not that I was thinking about that. Or

19

her. Nope.

"You could just turn around," I said to no one in particular, flipping down my mirror to check my lip gloss. "Go home, light some candles, journal about your feelings or whatever."

I snorted at my reflection. Yeah right. As if I ever actually journaled when I said I would.

7:34 now. I could text Deena: Almost there, girl! Had to take a work call! But that meant I'd actually have to go inside. See people. Maybe even see—

A car honked behind me, making me jump. Rude! Apparently circling the same block four times was suspicious behavior. Who knew?

"Fine, fine," I muttered, finally pulling into an open spot. "The universe has spoken."

I turned off the engine but stayed put, bouncing my leg to an imaginary beat. The parking meter glowed neon-green in the streetlight. I fished through my purse, coins jingling, definitely not stalling.

Cruz would be waiting, probably already three virgin drinks in, wondering where his self-proclaimed "party starter" was hiding. I'd have to bring extra BG energy to make up for being—I checked the time again—forty minutes late.

I grabbed my compact mirror. Quick check. Lip gloss? Needed a touch-up already. Something coconut-scented that I'd grabbed on impulse at the checkout counter last week.

"You look fine," I told myself. Then again, louder: "You look fine."

My Reiki Master said words are spells. So I said it like one.

My work phone buzzed. A client needing feedback on the social posts I'd designed yesterday. *Love the concept, but can we do the pink pop with more coral undertones?* I replied with a thumbs up emoji. Freelance graphic design paid the bills, but sometimes I wondered if I picked this career so I could do most of my work from home, in my pajamas, away from actual humans. Another thing I wouldn't be psychoanalyzing tonight.

I twisted in my gold hoops, the ones that caught the light just right. The ones that made me feel like I had my shit together, even when I absolutely didn't.

My phone buzzed. Cruz: *Where you at??* with eye emojis.

I texted back: *Just parked! Work call ran long. Be there in 5!*

I hadn't taken any work calls. Just spent twenty minutes orbiting the block like a satellite afraid to crash land. But no one needed to know that.

I dabbed jasmine oil on my wrists—my signature scent—and took a deep breath. The smell wrapped around me like a shield I could hide behind. Like I needed that. Which I didn't. Obviously.

I grabbed Deena's gift from the passenger seat. The wrapping paper was slightly crumpled in one corner where I'd nervously fidgeted with it. I smoothed it down, like I could smooth down the jitters fizzing through my body.

One more quick mirror check. Didn't dare look myself in the eye though. That was a conversation I wasn't ready to have.

"It's just a party," I said to myself, flipping a loc behind my shoulder. "Just friends. Just....people."

Just possibly Riley.

My stomach did a little flip at the thought, but I pushed it away. Tossed it right out with yesterday's problems. Ancient history. Water under the emotional bridge or whatever.

I stepped out of the car, the night air a slap of reality against my face. Locked the car. Unlocked it. Locked it again just to be sure. A classic BG move, as my friends would say. Overthinking the small things to avoid the big ones.

Music spilled out from the venue each time the door opened. Bass bumping, voices laughing. Life happening without me while I stood frozen on the sidewalk.

Becks, girl. Get it together. I straightened my shoulders like I was about to walk into a business meeting instead of my best friend's engagement party.

I walked toward the entrance, gift in hand, smile ready to deploy. Ready to be the BG everyone expected. Sunny, breezy, unbothered. Definitely not thinking about running into my ex. Definitely not checking my phone one last time for an excuse to bail.

Nope. I was good. I was great. I was—

—face to face with Riley as she headed for the door.

Time did that stupid slow thing it always does when I see her. Like someone hit pause on everything except my heartbeat, which decided to hold its own personal rave in my chest.

Our eyes locked. Recognition. Heat. Memory.

Her mouth opened slightly, that familiar gesture before a decision. My lips moved without permission from my brain.

"Ry—"

But she was already moving. Already slipping past me. Our shoulders brushed—just the whisper of contact—and the scent of her cologne was like hearing a forgotten favorite song for the first time in forever.

Sandalwood, leather, and something Riley.

Just a slight nod. Nothing more. No words exchanged.

Then she was gone, slipping past everything. Slipping past me.

I stood there, blinking at the empty space where she'd been, like maybe if I stared hard enough she'd reappear and we could try that whole interaction again. Maybe with actual words this time.

But nope. Just me, standing there like an idiot, gift clutched too tight against my chest.

"Well, that happened," I muttered, trying to laugh it off, but sounding more like I was choking on air.

Cruz touched my elbow, pulling me back to reality. Golden-brown skin warm against mine, his curls perfectly styled despite the January chill I brought into the space. "Everything okay?"

I snapped into performance mode instantly.

"Okay, outfit!" I said, eyes wide with exaggerated appreciation, gesturing at his electric blue blazer. My smile bright enough to blind us both to what just happened. "You weren't playing tonight, I see! And those sneakers? The coordination! I'm obsessed."

Cruz leaned in for air kisses, one cheek then the other, looking like a more muscular Bad Bunny in that blazer. That is, if Bad Bunny had a thing for electric blue and emotional rescue missions. "Girl, you know who just left," he whispered against my ear, conspiratorial and gentle.

I kept my voice light, floating above the deep place I didn't want to visit. "And not a moment too soon!"

"I know that's right, girl. Missed you, Becks."

"Missed you more! Now where's the bride to be? And more importantly, where's the champagne?"

I looped my arm through his, letting him lead me deeper into the party, away from the door where Riley had walked out. Away from thoughts I wasn't ready to have.

Time to be BG. Time to shine. Time to pretend that seeing Riley didn't just flip my whole world sideways.

I could do this. I was good at pretending. The best, actually.

"Let's find our girl," Cruz said, squeezing my arm. "She's been asking for her maid of honor."

I followed him into the noise and the light, leaving the quiet car and all its honesty behind.

Someone pressed a glass of champagne into my hand. The bubbles fizzed like my fake smile. All sparkle, zero substance.

"To the happy couple!" I lifted my glass, cheerful and bright. Completely normal. Totally fine.

Where had Riley gone? Not that I cared. Not that I was thinking about her walking past me like I was just another person, like we hadn't spent two years not breathing each other's air. Nope. Not thinking about that at all.

The party swirled around me in a kaleidoscope of faces and voices. I nodded at all the right moments. Laughed at all the right jokes. Performed the BG everyone expected—vivacious and carefree. Unbothered. Emphasis on that last part.

Meanwhile, my brain kept replaying those three seconds with Riley on a loop. Her eyes. That almost-maybe-something in them before she brushed past me. The scent of her cologne lingering after she'd gone.

Stop it. She's just your ex. One of many. *Ancient history.*

I downed my champagne too quickly and snagged another from a passing tray. Liquid courage, liquid distraction. Y'know, whatever works.

Cruz was magnetic as always, pulling people into his orbit, and I clung to him like he was the only stable thing in the room. I needed his energy. Needed to borrow some of his easy joy while mine felt stuck somewhere between my car and that doorway.

"Becks! We've been waiting for you!" Sakia waved from across the room.

"Where were you? We were worried!" Taj gave me that knowing look.

My answers flew out on autopilot. "Traffic was insane! Then a work emergency! You know how it is!" The excuses tumbled from my lips, rehearsed and polished like well-worn coins.

I saw her. She saw me. We didn't speak. It broke me all over again.

But I didn't say that. Obviously.

Instead, I flashed my megawatt smile—the one that never quite reached my eyes but was dazzling enough that most people didn't notice. I'd perfected it in college and had been riding that wave ever since.

My body moved through the party while my mind stayed stuck in the doorway. I hugged people I hadn't seen in months. Complimented outfits. Asked about jobs and partners and vacations.

"Sis, you look amazing!" I told someone whose name I couldn't remember.

"Yesss, earrings!" to someone else.

My mouth was on autopilot while my brain kept whispering *RileyRileyRiley* like a song I couldn't get out of my head.

I grabbed Deena's hand and pulled her to the dance floor when that Ne-Yo song came on. Our anthem. Her long dark hair whipped around as we moved, those big brown eyes sparkling with the same mischief they'd held back in our dorm room days. We used to scream the lyrics in her dorm room, hairbrushes as microphones. Back before Riley. Back when life was simpler.

"You still got those moves!" Deena shouted over the music.

I twirled dramatically, nearly sloshing champagne on my sweater. "Never lost 'em!"

From across the room, I caught Taj watching us with that huge smile that could light up a whole city block, her long locs swaying as she nodded to the beat. Even in her calm, collected way, I could see the pure joy radiating from her dark skin as she watched her bride-to-be lose herself in the music.

"Better not steal my woman for too long, BG!" Taj called out, that dimpled smile somehow getting even brighter. Maybe some day I might get her to drop her skincare routine, because she was going to be one of those women who could pass for 30 longer than was fair.

"Too late!" I called back, spinning Deena again. "She's mine for the next three minutes!"

The music thumped through me, drowning out thoughts. Almost. I danced until my feet hurt, until sweat beaded along my hairline, until I was dizzy enough that nothing else mattered.

The party was the perfect distraction: loud, lively, crowded. Just how I liked my social gatherings and my emotions. No room for quiet contemplation. No space for uncomfortable truths.

I threw my head back laughing at something Cruz said. Didn't even catch what it was. Just knew it was my cue to laugh. To be BG. To be the life of the party that everyone expected.

But my eyes kept drifting to the door. Stupid, traitorous eyes.

She's gone. She left. Again. Like she always does.

I pretended Riley hadn't knocked me off-center with her three-second appearance, but who was I kidding? My hands were moving too fast, my laugh too loud, my smile too wide. Classic BG overcompensation. I wondered if anyone noticed.

I let Deena lead me around, introducing me to colleagues I'd never remember, while I nodded and smiled on cue. Party puppet BG, strings pulled by the ghost of Riley's exit.

Laugh here. Smile now. Look interested. Don't let them see you're still bleeding.

I was so good at filling spaces. Rooms, conversations, awkward silences. I filled myself with noise and movement until there was no room left for the truth. Until I almost believed my own performance.

Almost.

The sugar rush from cupcake frosting was a sweet relief from the bitter taste Riley's exit had left. I licked buttercream from my thumb, wondering if sugar could erase the memory of her cologne. Of her eyes meeting mine before she walked away.

"Was that Riley I saw leaving earlier?"

The question hit harder than a slap. Some well-meaning friend who had no idea they'd just jabbed at an open wound.

"Oh!" My voice came out too high, too fast. Amateur hour. "I must have missed her."

The lie sat weirdly on my tongue, too big to swallow properly. I took another sip of champagne to wash it down.

My eyes darted to the door again. Habit? Punishment? Hope? I wasn't sure anymore. All I knew was that it hurt in a way that felt familiar. In a way that almost felt like home.

I tried to drown the ache with more champagne, more dancing. More empty chatter. Tried to convince myself it wasn't that bad. That I was over her. That seeing her hadn't reopened every wound I'd pretended had healed.

Was Riley here? Oh, I didn't see her.

The lie stung with the bubbles sliding down my throat, but I kept swallowing anyway. I'd gotten good at that. Swallowing hard truths with a smile.

Pretending they didn't taste like heartbreak.

Airplane Mode

Riley

TWO YEARS OF FORGETTING BG shattered in five seconds flat.

Snow fell overnight, and though it didn't stick, it coated my thoughts like a layer of static. Morning light crept into the townhouse through blinds I didn't close last night. I swung my legs out of bed and sat on the edge, taking in the stillness. Quick and clean. In, out, no damage. The words echoed through my mind with each slow, deliberate step toward the kitchen. Coffee, I thought. I needed coffee to clear BG's face from my head, the image of her at Velvet & Oak clinging to me like a stubborn knot of tension I couldn't release.

I yawned into my fist, dragging my feet over the hardwood floor. BG had been there. At the bar. I'd acted surprised, but not shocked, not like I hadn't expected to see her somewhere eventually. Her smile had cut right through the noise, but I played it cool, and kept it moving. It had to be that way. Even Tangi agreed.

The whole night replayed in my head, like a song you couldn't shake. Friends who came out of the woodwork. My circles were usually tight, but there we all were, taking up the corner booth, celebrating Taj and Deena's engagement. I wished I'd stayed home watching TV. If I had, maybe I wouldn't have seen her.

The townhouse felt too quiet, too off-center, as if everything had shifted three inches to the left overnight.

My fingers moved with precision, clean, like finding the right spot on a joint to press against. I let my hand hover under the water stream until it felt right, the ritual meditative. BG had shown up again, throwing everything out of order.

She did it without trying.

The last two years, I'd made plans. Sworn oaths. Said goodbye in my head and my heart. And yet, it happened again. Not just last night, either. There was a rhythm. I wasn't a dancer, but still. I felt the steps, moved to them. Every single time.

My chest tightened with an edge of panic. I forced my hands to keep moving, but they felt shaky. The machine dripped, the quiet surrounded me, pressing in. I couldn't breathe under it. I gripped the counter's edge, cold marble under my fingertips, hard and unforgiving. I focused on the pressure points where my hands met the stone, using the sensation to ground myself.

I made a decision. I wasn't going to do this. I'd cut it short. I put the coffee canister back in the cabinet. Turned the tap off. Even moved to shut the blinds so tight they'd leave the room dark.

Then I changed my mind. I grabbed the canister again, loaded the coffeemaker, and hit brew. My hands still shook as I positioned the mug under the stream, but I misjudged. Coffee dripped over the side of the mug, splattering onto the warming plate below. It sizzled on contact, filling the kitchen with the acrid smell of burning coffee. More spilled over the edge of the counter when I finally pushed the mug into place. I let it happen. The noise filled the room, too loud against the thick quiet, and I watched the drip-drip-drip until the mug was ready.

"Shit."

It looked like something I couldn't look away from. Like her. Like BG, in the doorway. I'd barely slept, and the hours had been as endless as the moment when she showed up at the bar. The same moment that now played itself out in every corner of the townhouse. I drank and watched and drank and waited for the silence to drown the memory.

But it wouldn't. It never did. BG had been there, breathing the same air, her eyes the same deep and steady amber. The memory was too big for the townhouse. It crowded everything, curled up on the couch with me, kept me awake, swallowed the coffee like it was breakfast. My mind took a sharp breath, took its own sweet time exhaling.

The image clung. I filled the mug to the brim with almond milk, like it might fill me with something else. I felt the spill-over run down my knuckles, hot and deliberate. I wasn't careful. I wanted to believe it was on purpose. That the noise was drowning out something other than me. It didn't.

The coffee. The shakes. The barely holding on. This time was supposed to be different, but last night proved nothing had changed, despite all the time and space I'd wedged between us.

Each thought landed in my hands, shook them hard, left me unsteady. I was a beginner, making the same old mistakes. As if time didn't change anything. As if I hadn't learned a thing.

I ran my thumb across my collarbone, back and forth, feeling the slight ridge where bone meets muscle, a familiar motion. It felt like an old tell. And maybe it was.

The phone chimed. My attention followed the sound, dragging itself away from memories of the night before. The dating app lit up with notifications. I opened it. Quick, precise, like the answer to a question I hadn't asked.

Several women had swiped right, their interest a casual challenge. I almost laughed, swiped back. Only one name stood out. Shaye. Her message was light, easy. Nothing too heavy or hard to hold.

Just finished episode 6 of that show you mentioned. I was supposed to go to bed three hours ago but here we are. You weren't kidding about the plot twists!

I replied with the same cool energy. Closed the app with the same effort. Knew better than to let myself think more of it than I should.

My fingers danced around the phone, an anxious tap-tap-tap, before putting it down. Its silence mocked me. Like it knew that, trapped in this house with my own thoughts, I'd be back.

I pulled eggs from the fridge, cracked them one-handed into a bowl, impressing myself. Beat them like they owed me money.

The townhouse held its breath, the morning moving slow and deliberate around me while I played chef. I poured the beaten eggs into a hot pan, watched the edges start to cook. My coffee was lukewarm by the time I remembered it. I picked up the mug and took a sip. Didn't feel a thing.

A quick blink, a thought unfinished. A connection that wasn't.

Another chime, another message, but I'd already closed the app. Wasn't about to open it again.

I turned my attention to the stove. Pushed the cooked edges of the eggs into the center with a soft spatula, swirled the pan just like that video said to let the uncooked egg run to the edges. I focused on the task, on the gentle butter sizzle, on anything but the device sitting on the counter. The names and faces would still be there, holding space, waiting for my attention. I let them. I wasn't pressed.

I added shredded cheese, seasoning salt and ranch seasoning to the eggs just the way I liked them. Real seasoning, not the plain salt and pepper Beckham always insisted on. The thought came unbidden, unwelcome.

I folded the egg onto itself, turned off the heat. Let the residual warmth melt the cheese.

While the eggs finished cooking, my hand betrayed me, reaching for the phone again. I swiped it up, made sure the app was closed. Checked again just to be sure. I gripped it firmly while telling myself I wasn't holding onto anything at all.

I slid the omelet onto a plate and carried everything to the table. Back to the same noise that crowded everything else. I shook my head and poured more coffee with a brand new pod. This time, meticulous. Like it mattered.

Scrubbed between my fingers before grabbing a clean cloth to wipe up the egg drips from the counter. Popped two slices of sourdough into the toaster and washed my hands under hot water.

I glanced at my phone, at the message I'd started typing to Shaye. *Maybe a coffee sometime?* The cursor blinked, patient, waiting. I hit send just as the toaster popped, the bread golden, crisp and perfect. She liked jazz, hiking, her texts had emojis. I could learn to want this. Probably.

Sounds like we have a lot in common, I added, setting the phone down. Like the rest of it was nothing. Like it didn't mean a thing.

The podcast came on with familiar language. Familiar, awful language.

I paused, fork halfway to my mouth, let it filter through the room like white noise. Listened in disbelief. *Emotional Detachment After Relationships End.*

My hand froze, omelet cooling on my fork. Years ago, I'd consumed episodes like this. Tried every method. Meditation, yoga, journals I'd filled to the margins about her, me and everything that went wrong between us.

I had to laugh at the irony. My chest caved in, breakfast forgotten, coffee cooling off again. I didn't need another fucking podcast telling me how the fuck to feel.

Heart on Airplane Mode: Emotional Detachment After Relationships End. The title might as well have been an accusation.

I knew what came next. Techniques I'd tried and failed at, miserably. Lists of things to do when your person one day decides she can't do this anymore and leaves.

Yoga, meditation, long baths, candles I'd burned down to the wick. Language that could've been my own, language that felt like betrayal now.

Books I'd read, unread, read again. Written by people who claimed to know what I was feeling. Told verbatim to the same people who'd let me cry on their shoulders, let me drink their wine until my words slurred together.

I know better than most how the body holds onto pain long after the original injury. How everything compensates around that one weak point, creating new patterns that become their own kind of normal. Which is why I turned off the podcast. Didn't need to hear it again.

The omelet sat on my plate, half-eaten and cold, melted cheese spilling out the edges. The mug was almost empty. My chest was as hollow as it had been the morning after she left.

Maybe more.

The memory came back like a bruise, and I traced the edges, testing how deep it went. It was my first birthday without her, and the silence had been deafening, worse than the cold outside. I remembered the package arriving, her handwriting on the card. Each letter neat and precise. Still here.

I felt the weight of the gift before I even opened it. She wanted us to try to be friends, she said. To linger at the periphery of my life, an observer, in and out like a secret she couldn't keep. I packed it back up, put it in the mail with words she needed to hear from me: I don't want anything from you. I held onto the hollow victory, let it stain me with a raw, uncertain shame. A feeling that stayed longer than she did.

When I saw the package on the doorstep, I should've known better. Should've left it unopened, let it sit there, let the rain get to it before I did. But I couldn't. It was the first thing that felt like her. Like she hadn't disappeared completely. Like she still meant it when she said forever.

I needed to believe in something, so I opened it.

When the paper came off, and it sat there, exposed, I hated her for knowing me so well. For being so goddamn BG about it. A record I'd mentioned once, casually. That time at the shop in Brooklyn, where we lingered for hours talking about music. I wanted to talk about it with her, spin it on the turntable she left behind. But that's not how we worked. That's not how it ended.

I thought she wanted it to be easy. She always wanted it to be easy.

I wanted it to be a mistake. The gift. The leaving. The world without her.

My fingers had worked fast, packing the record back up before I packed up myself. I didn't wait. Didn't think twice. I put it in the mail and wrote the note without stopping to breathe.

I tried to mean it.

Two days went by, and the silence grew. The snow fell, the chill settled.

Maybe she didn't get it. Maybe she didn't care.

BG. Always. She lingered like a slow, sad song. Probably Sade.

A chime startled me back to the present. It was Tangi, her name lighting up the screen, a reminder of what I'd tried to forget. I opened the message without thinking. Last night. The group photo. Beckham's smile hit like a shockwave, both warm and brutal. BG, in all her damnable glory. Her locs falling over bare shoulders, her smile like she knew. Everyone was there. Everyone but me.

I tapped the image away. One swipe brought up the group chat settings.

Mute notifications: 8 hours. 1 week. Forever.

I picked a week. Not rage-quitting. Not ready. Just...fucking tired.

I tossed my phone onto the couch. Left it there, lying in its own accusations, my mind unable to detach.

I told myself to breathe. That I had no fucks left to give for any of this. But the picture stayed in my head. Her shoulders were relaxed, head tilted just slightly, the way people stand when they're completely at ease in their skin.

My eyes landed on the magazines scattered across the coffee table. I straightened them without thinking, aligning the edges. The remote wasn't where it belonged. I moved it back to the charging dock. Took the weight off my shoulders and let it settle somewhere else. Somewhere like a couch, like a screen, like an unopened message.

I caught myself reaching for the dishrag and stopped. This was what I did when feelings got too big. Clean until I could think straight again. Absolutely not.

I tried to force myself to sit my ass down but couldn't even do that, the energy pushing and pulling me across the living room, drove me up one wall and down another. I kept my focus on anything that wasn't the photo. The woman with the dangerous smile. I made a circuit of the townhouse, restless, helpless, careless. The furniture stood its ground, waited for me to crash into it. I saw what was happening, saw the pattern before it played out. Hours of moping. Takeout. Netflix. More moping.

The idea hit first. Was on my feet before the other thought formed. Not today.

I left the blinds closed, dark as a cave. I would become a cave again if I stayed there.

My keys were on the table, right where I'd left them. They glared up at me, made their accusation.

I grabbed my jacket, wallet, phone. Anything that meant I wouldn't be back for a few hours.

Her face was burned into my mind, a slow and insistent brand. I took the stairs two at a time, ran to catch my breath.

It was the only thing I could do.

Party Crashing, Expert Level

BG

THE WORST PART ABOUT casual sex isn't the awkward goodbye. It's when your ex shows up uninvited right before you finish.

I bit down on my lip, a sharp catch of pain in a sea of almost nothingness. There I was, on top of Jai, her strap inside me, the rhythm mechanical. Jai's hands gripped my hips, her fingers digging in with a possessiveness that was almost endearing if I cared enough to notice. Her voice was a low murmur, trying to talk me through it, but like she was reading from a script. I wasn't really listening, anyway.

The room was hot, sticky with sweat and the scent of sex, like it was trying too hard to be a scene out of a movie. I felt every slide and shift of our bodies, and yeah, it felt good technically, but my mind was already hovering above it all, eyeing the exit.

Jai's hands moved up my back, pulling me into a warmth I didn't necessarily ask for. Her lips brushed my collarbone, and I had to give it to her—it was nice, in a "yeah, sure, why not" kind of way.

Then she did it. Her fingertips skimmed the back of my neck, right where my locs began. It was Riley's move, her way of catching my attention just before whispering something that would make me laugh or groan. I never let Jai wrap a palm fully around my throat. That was the kill move, and the only person who knew that brushed past me last week without speaking.

Apparently, my body didn't get the memo that Riley and I broke up two years ago. I got real hot all over. Jai's O-face looked like she was trying to solve a complex math problem, and suddenly closing my eyes seemed like the better option.

Riley's smile flashed again, uninvited, almost mocking in its clarity, and the tension inside me snapped. The sudden jolt snapped me back into my body, and I rode Jai faster, like I had something to prove. Jai gave as good as she got. Harder. Just the right amount of pressure, fucking *finally*. My orgasm hit like a shock, sudden and fierce, pulling a whine from my throat that didn't feel like mine. My thighs squeezed Jai in protest. The absurdity of it all landed like a punchline, sensation and memory colliding in a way that was almost funny if it wasn't so damn revealing.

Fuck!

"Damn, girl," Jai said, from somewhere below.

The world rushed back too loud. My chest heaved, fingers clenched tight on nothing, and I blinked fast. Jai's face slowly reappeared as the haze cleared, satisfaction fell over her features, but my stomach twisted with the mess of it, the crash of everything I couldn't avoid.

I was coming down, but I felt like I was still falling. Irritated with myself, I rolled off Jai.

I stared at the ceiling, breath shallow and ragged. The room felt too small, the air too heavy. Beside me, Jai was a pool of warmth, an anchor I didn't want. I shifted under the weight of her arm, but she only snuggled in closer.

Guilt lodged itself low in my gut. I couldn't push it out, couldn't will it away. My chest heaved like I'd been running. Everything was too much—the fan's soft hum, the stick of skin, the rush of blood pounding loud in my ears.

I rolled a little to the side, creating space. Jai murmured, unconcerned. Her leg tangled with mine, and she pulled me back against her. Trapped.

"Wow," she breathed, contentment dripping from the single word. She nuzzled into my neck. "That was...wow."

"Yeah," I said, distant. "Wow."

I really wanted to mean it. My brain latched onto the moment, tried to pry it open and examine the pieces. But all I could see was exactly what I was trying not to. There it was again, sharp and unrelenting, a flash of what I didn't want to admit. *Fuck.*

I hadn't just come thinking about my ex, right? I breathed in, deep. Let it out slow. Nope. Just a weird brain association thing. Nothing to panic about.

Jai tightened her hold, sighing. I counted the blades of the ceiling fan. Counted my own heartbeats. Utterly meaningless, I told myself. But the denial sat crooked. My mind circled back, and Riley's face was still there, more persistent than ever. Dammit. Why did Deena have to get married, anyway?

Apparently, I was so good at wanting people I couldn't keep and fucking the ones who couldn't keep *me*.

I slipped from the sheets delicately, my feet soft against the floor. Becks, the ghost. Becks, the afterthought.

I can take a hint, though. *Get lost.*

So I reached for my clothes, found them scattered and waiting, eager as I was.

I stretched my arms overhead. Freedom. This was the part I was good at. The quiet exit, the clean break. No expectations, no complications. I pulled on the long shirt, feeling a bit too naked for her eyes all of a sudden.

"Heading out?" Jai's voice was low, the early edges of sleep smoothing her words. No surprise in it, just quiet acknowledgment of our routine.

I turned to her with a smile. "You know me. Always moving. Can't sit still." The BG show, now playing its greatest hit: The Vanishing Act. Watch closely as she makes any chance at vulnerability disappear!

She opened one eye, a lazy grin spreading as she watched me. "See you around, then."

"Bet," I laughed, a little too loud. The echo of it felt fake, like canned applause on a sitcom no one's actually watching.

I ran my fingers along my locs, feeling the soft, tight coils against my fingertips. Each one its own little story, its own little world. My crown, my armor, my statement piece. Nothing awkward here. Nothing rushed. Her eyes drifted shut again, and I was already halfway to the door when she called out.

"Becks?"

"Yeah?"

"Plant or art piece? You never said."

Oops. Caught. "I think that huge fern's gonna eat the whole room." I grinned. "Like a plant-monster. Love it."

"Of course you do," Jai mumbled, the warmth of her voice curving around me as I stepped away.

I leaned against the wall, gathered up my jeans, my panties, my boots. Relief settled in, sweet and predictable. I'd always been good at this part, the easy departure, the clean getaway. Like a good party, it was best to leave before things got stale. I could already see myself on the street, the air biting cold, an Uber waiting.

The hallway stretched in front of me, empty and familiar. I was almost to the bathroom when I realized I'd left my other earring on the nightstand. Already, my mind was jumping to tomorrow, to the brunch I'd promised Sakia I'd be at, to the confirmation text I should have sent hours ago.

The bathroom was small, filled with us. Me and the other me. I shut the door, stared into the mirror. Touch-up time. Reality check. Who did I think I was?

I washed my hands, the water shockingly cold, tingling on my skin. Pre-war plumbing, ugh. My reflection was vague. Not vague. Definite, but unfamiliar. A person I couldn't quite pin down. I ran my fingers through my locs, fixed the strays. A swipe of gloss, pink and precise.

A quick splash of water on my face. Quick check of my eyes, a little red from the liner that kept running down from sweat. I blinked a few times, willing them clearer, brighter. Willing myself to be whatever version of me I needed to be. The water spiraled down the drain, and I was grateful for its distraction.

This was nothing. Just bodies doing what bodies do.

"Stop being weird about this," I told myself, my voice too loud for the small space. I smirked and tossed my locs to the side. I thought of going back for the earring, but that would've meant going back into Jai's bedroom. Oh well. Sacrificed for the cause.

Instead, I stared. Wondered. Tried to find myself in the mirror's sharpness. She stared back, skeptical. Was I so desperate to impress?

I was fine. I was great. Just another hookup. I tried on different versions of the truth, none of them fitting quite right.

The reflection arched an eyebrow. Sis knew better.

The apartment door was silent as I clicked it open, my pulse anything but. The hall was empty, ready to swallow me whole. I stepped forward, and then—her.

She was right there, close enough to touch. A woman I'd never seen, not once, never even thought about seeing, her hand holding a key that fit into the lock behind me. Her expression shifted slow-motion, like the earth was rotating too fast for her. Key, smile, shock. Understanding.

Anger.

My stomach dropped like spoiled fruit.

Oh, shit.

I froze, mouth open. Closed it quick, a quick suck of breath, my throat full of words I didn't know how to say. "I'm—I'm a friend." My voice, paper thin. I'm sure she could figure out which kind.

Right on cue, the woman's eyes narrowed, quiet fury, and the urge to explain knotted up inside me, heavy. But the air felt thick. My chest felt tight. The Uber waited.

And then I was moving. Too fast, but not fast enough. Just fast enough to hear Jai's voice behind me, and to duck whatever random flying object this lady could find. My heart pounded as I turned my back, my mind blank but racing. The woman yelled something about "community strap" but I didn't hear the rest. Thankfully, the elevator was sitting right at the door and welcomed me inside with a ding.

It's a shame. Cruz would hate missing out on the tea later, but it's kinda hard to spill it when you're in the ingredients, you know?

The elevator doors closed, and I caught my breath. My pulse slowed, beat heavy in my veins, matched the steady descent. Damn.

What were the odds? My stomach did a little flip as the floors counted down. A soft hum in my ears, like the distant echo of panic. I shook it off, tried to focus on the now, on the ride down, on what was coming next. The tang of cigarettes and piss in the air, some memory of another place, another time, tickled the edges of my thoughts.

My mind jumped from topic to topic, no commitment, no plan. A mess of frayed ends, nothing tied together. The near-miss fizzed in my body, a flash of adrenaline, the sweet sensation of escape. I was out, I told myself. Out and done.

Jai knew? Probably. Did it matter? Nope. Not even a little.

I don't know, maybe I should thank her? At least this way, I didn't have to make up some lazy-ass excuse about why I couldn't see her anymore, right?

As the elevator touched ground, I felt lighter somehow. Like I'd just dodged not just drama but a whole rom-dram plot I hadn't auditioned for. Another person mistaking my chaos for charm when really I was really just allergic to staying put. Riley learned that the hard way.

The lights flashed outside, harsh like an interrogation, but they were gone too quick to find answers. Thankfully, my driver pulled up right on time.

Release. Speed. Freedom. My head rested on the cool glass, and my breath came fast, keeping pace with the streak of buildings. Too much to process, or maybe too little. Was this how far I'd go to avoid anything sticky?

My chest thumped hard. The adrenaline lingered, sharp and sweet, a pulse beneath my skin, a refusal to settle. I closed my eyes, but it didn't stop the questions, the why and the how and the who did Jai think she was, playing like that? My lips pulled into a smile. The driver didn't notice. Or didn't care.

The evening felt crooked, and I couldn't decide if it meant something or nothing at all. The moments stacked up like the skyline in reverse. Riley in my head, the soon-to-be ex-girlfriend at the door. My boots off, my boots on, the beads of sweat drying quick. Me running like always.

Classic BG, serving escapist realness.

God, I was exhausting. Even to myself.

I let the release find me, fill my lungs, letting the outside lights calm whatever was churning inside me. Just a night, like any other. All my own. Just a series of moments and patterns and maybe home was the only thing that mattered.

The driver said something, but the music was too loud, the glass too thick. The leather seat held me snug and safe. I watched the city and tried not to think. The familiarity of nothingness, it felt like a hug. My mind went pleasantly numb while my body kept doing what it knew how to do. Stay moving, stay performing, stay two steps ahead.

Did I hear a buzz? Was that Jai? I checked my phone. Yep. Three texts already, trying to explain what didn't need to be explained. I ignored them, let them slide, let them slip. Let it all slip away. Not my problem.

I still had two hours before the client call, plenty of time to go home, shower, and put together the mood board for the skincare campaign. This was the nice thing about freelance life. I could have questionable hookups on a Friday evening and still make my deadlines. Creative director by day, emotional disaster by night.

My personal brand was nothing if not consistent.

The driver pulled up to my building, and I was out before he could tell me to have a good night. The sidewalk felt solid under my feet, a certainty I needed. My keys jingled in my hand, the familiar weight of home just an elevator ride away. No drama, no surprises, no girlfriends with keys showing up unannounced. Just BG, my sanctuary, and the promise of silence.

My apartment opened its arms to me, lit with a glow only I could see. Okay, maybe that was the street light. The smell of home lingered, a touch of sweetness that was nothing like the earlier hours.

I dropped my bag to the floor, kicked my boots into a corner. A relief so pure it almost hurt. My heart unclenched. My muscles uncoiled. I breathed deep, took in the scent of sage, a hint of vanilla from the diffuser in the main room. Comfort settled in like a guest that never left.

The outside world slipped away with each step. Books stacked high. Scents spiraled lazy. Everything exactly how I'd left it. I loved this space. I loved the aloneness.

The hibiscus tea in the fridge was still steeping, but I drank it anyway, letting it wash the night down. Down and away.

My reflection showed up in the window, quick and vague and barely there. I liked it that way. Too familiar to mean anything at all.

A hundred thoughts faded, gone before I could grab hold. BG on the run, always on the run, but never here. Not now. Not in the safety of this place.

I slipped out of my clothes at the bathroom door and cranked the water hot. Steam bloomed up, thick and warm, filling the empty spaces before I stepped inside.

The water was scalding, and I welcomed it. It did its work, rinsed the night from my skin, my heart. My thoughts were slow, sedated, surrendering to the gentle roar of nothingness.

Time stretched in that delicious way it only did here. The air hummed with comfort, a slow vibration, and I was the only one to hear it.

I put on an old tee and soft shorts, walked past the bed without looking too hard, and made my way to the couch. A heavy breath left my body. One last twinge of adrenaline, one final reminder.

I stretched, feeling my spine pop in that satisfying way until I relaxed into the cushions. Forwarded some Siberian Husky videos to Deena. Decompressed.

The couch had done its job—held me, comforted me, reminded me I was home. But the real sanctuary was waiting. I pushed myself up, padded across the floor, my slippered feet silent against the wood.

The bed waited. Cool, certain. A soft pull. I stood in the doorway, arms crossed, and let myself feel it. Didn't get in.

No one had ever stayed the night since Riley. Not once. Not even close. I didn't let them. Didn't want them to, either. Didn't need that kind of weight next to me. No one full of jokes and stories when all I needed was sleep.

The memory found me before I knew it was there. Her presence had been weighty and persistent in my head since we bumped shoulders at that damn party. Would have to start charging her rent, soon.

I blinked fast, tried to make it disappear.

My body, tight as a fist, remembering. Her breath, her arm heavy across my stomach, claiming me like I was something breakable and sacred. Her staying like it was easy. I hadn't known how to handle it. The heaviness. The stillness. The way her presence stretched, steady and constant, like time itself. Like everything I feared most.

Her breath slowing.

Mine matching.

Fuck.

She stayed. The certainty of it lodged under my skin. My pulse thudded thick, a memory within a memory.

What was Riley doing now?

I thought of Jai, of the chaos of other people. I thought of what it meant to be alone.

My eyes closed, but my mind didn't follow.

The thoughts floated around my head like summer gnats, impossible to ignore.

My choice, my pattern, my protection, right? But it wasn't as simple as I wanted it to be. As neat. Or as clean. Wasn't something I could sage away or journal out or mask with another new creative project that I'd abandon in two weeks.

Track star BG, on the run, always racing towards something, but the same old patterns held on. My own sweet mistakes. The ghosts of me, all the versions who chose wrong. I wish I was a time traveler who could undo them instead of being haunted by them.

My bed was empty.

But only because I needed it to be.

Not like I was waiting for her to slip back into it. Was I?

Swan Napkins

Riley

AMBUSHES COME IN MANY forms. Today, mine arrived via text message.

I lingered in the showroom's foyer, re-reading Taj's text, blinking.

The universe has a sick sense of humor and apparently, so do my friends.

Just take notes, don't let them stick me with those ugly swan napkins, and please don't fight Becks, she'd written. The words seemed blurry at first, my brain refusing to process what they meant. BG would be here. My fingers fumbled over the keys as I typed: *BG?! I thought I was meeting the vendor with Deena.* She didn't respond.

I stared at each letter until the sentence made sense in a way I wished it didn't. Don't fight Becks. I couldn't decide if it was shock or anger making me burn up. Probably both. I leaned against the wall, scanning the words over and over. Swan napkins, she'd said. Swan fucking napkins. A low hiss slipped out as I mentally cussed out Taj, the vendor, and every light fixture in the building.

BG. How the hell had she shown up again? The heat spread past my face, hitting the back of my neck and filling my chest. They were going to stick me with swan napkins and *her*. I should have bailed. Let her know what it felt like to be left holding the bag for once.

I pressed the cool wood of the door against my forehead. Anything to stop the world from spinning out of control. An hour at most, and I'd be done. In, out, no damage. *BG? Really, Taj?* I typed again. My thumb shook with adrenaline. *Is Deena not coming?* It wasn't a question, but I left it hanging like one, needing an answer I knew I'd never get. Just the sound of my pulse, quick and erratic in my ears, and the ghost of another voice telling me it didn't matter. Nothing personal, it's just how it was.

Taj and Deena were the *only* reason I was doing this. But they would definitely hear my mouth after this.

I released my grip on the phone, heard my knuckles pop. Like they'd been holding something for too long, then let go all at once.

BG was there, already seated at the table. My heart stuttered and skipped, stomach dropping as if I'd missed a step. I kept walking, not sure what I'd say, not caring if my smile looked like I was really just baring teeth.

She looked up, a flash of shock giving way to something more guarded, more aloof. It didn't fit her. She opened her mouth, but my voice beat hers to the punch, crisp and clinical, like I was introducing myself to a patient: "Riley Benson. Vendor meeting for the Joseph-Muhammad wedding. I hope I'm in the right place?"

Her locs were longer, fuller, spilling across her shoulders and down her back. Same amber eyes that used to meet mine across pillows.

She smiled, but it was wary. Not like before. Not like the smile that used to be my cue to relax. "Looks like you are," she said, steady as if she was expecting me all along. "Hello, Riley."

Hello. A five-letter minefield, ticking under my skin. I didn't respond. Didn't know how. Not without letting her hear how each syllable ripped through me.

My name in her voice. Dangerous. The way it had always been. Like she knew what it meant. Like she knew I'd do anything to hear it.

It wasn't fair. Not when I hadn't heard it for so long. Not when I still wanted to.

I exhaled slowly. I'd practiced for this moment. Prepared for it in my mind. But not here. Not now. It took everything I had to hold myself together.

My words were smooth, but my knees were about to give way. Everything in me moved in all directions. A thousand reactions, none of them safe. My bones were fragile and frantic, a cornered animal trying to decide which way to run.

I'd held myself tight for months, kept my feelings at bay, barely contained. Now it was all about to burst. Explode across the table in one long breath, leaving the walls and my heart painted the exact color of BG's lips.

I paused, taking my breath and a measure of space from her. "Taj told me I also need to sign a release for the booking. Here to do that and discuss details."

"Right," she nodded, calm and controlled as I couldn't quite feel. "Dee and Taj." She gestured at the open chair. Her pen moved to the edge of her notepad, tapping once, then stopping like she'd caught herself. "Join me?"

I almost laughed. It felt as strange and awkward as I did. Maybe as strange and awkward as she was. As awkward as everything had been since we broke up.

A marathon of misalignment. It would have been easier to go a hundred miles than the last ten feet to the table. She never made it easy.

I focused on each step. Not too fast, not too slow. As deliberate as I could, so she'd never know I wanted to run.

Maybe she'd think I had everything under control. Maybe she'd think she hadn't wrecked me.

My chair was too close to hers.

I reached for the back of it, trying not to let her see how hard I gripped the wood. Thought I might leave a dent. Thought she might hear me crack it, the way she always did.

This time, I wouldn't give her the chance.

The vendor—Layla according to the business card I'd clutched too tightly in my pocket—looked between us with an assessing glance. "You're in exactly the right place," she said, gesturing to the chair beside BG. "Please, have a seat."

My legs moved on autopilot, body remembering how to function while my mind went blank. The distance to her chair seemed impossible. Too long and too short at once. I settled into mine, keeping my spine straight, not leaning into the back. Poised for a quick exit.

BG stirred beside me, the sound of fabric against leather seats impossibly loud. Her scent hit me next. Different than I remembered, her signature scent mixed with something new I couldn't place. I breathed through my mouth to avoid it.

"Deena's client emergency turned into a nightmare," she explained. A flicker of nerves beneath her calm. Almost like vulnerability. Almost like we were still close enough to see the real things under the masks. I nodded stiffly. She hadn't changed that much after all. Still not the one to bail when someone needed her.

Present company excluded, of course.

She looked at me again, surprise still hiding behind those watchful eyes. "She asked me to cover since I know her vision."

"Awesome. Let's get started, shall we?" Layla's voice cut through the tension. "I understand you both are representing the brides-to-be?"

"Yes," I said, not looking at BG. "The couple has asked us to finalize the floral arrangements and general layout." I pulled my tablet from my bag, grateful for something to do with my hands. "I have their vision board here."

My fingers shook slightly as I navigated to the right file. I pressed them harder against the screen, willing them to steady. I could do this. I'd rebuilt spines that were more damaged than this.

"Great," Layla said, spreading photos across the polished table surface. "And Taj's preferences?"

There was a beat of silence. BG hesitated beside me.

"Taj is worried about allergies," she said finally. Her voice sent a current down my spine that I refused to acknowledge. "Nothing too heavily scented. And no lilies. Her mother hates them."

I nodded, not trusting myself to look at her directly. "And Deena wants color accents, but nothing too bright or traditional." I swiped through the vision board, keeping my eyes fixed on the screen. "More organic arrangements, seasonal blooms."

And then we were talking, discussing centerpieces and boutonnieres and altar decorations. Not to each other. Always through Layla, as if she were a translator for languages that once had no barrier between them.

"So, we're settled on the garden roses, anemones, and seasonal greenery," Layla summarized, looking between us. "With accents of ranunculus for the bridal bouquets."

"That sounds perfect," BG said, her voice softer than before. I risked a glance at her hands—they were fidgeting with a photo, turning it over and over. A habit I recognized from years ago. I clocked the tension low in my thoracic spine, automatic and useless. Immediately adjusted my posture out of habit. Didn't work.

"Wonderful." I was amazed it didn't come out strangled and rough.

Every question I posed found its mark with Layla. Fabric weights. Thread counts. Price points. BG listened attentively, occasionally interjecting with specific details about Deena's preferences.

As Layla spread out accent swatch cards for the navy-and-blush palette Taj and Deena had selected, I pointed to a faded pea green. "This would complement without overwhelming."

"Actually," BG suggested, her fingers hovering over a warmer copper tone, "I think this one might work better. Deena specifically wanted warmth to balance the coolness of the navy."

"The green would provide that warmth," I countered, my voice taking on that measured tone I used when explaining treatment options to skeptical patients. "Without overwhelming the other elements."

"Right, but—" BG's shoulders pulled back slightly, her chin lifting. "Deena's note couldn't be clearer." She flipped through pages, stopping when she found the right one. "Here." Her voice had shifted, become more careful, more controlled. Like she was defending her right to speak.

My jaw tightened, but she was right. The copper *would* work better. Dammit.

Layla turned to me. "Are we in agreement?"

I cleared my throat. "We're good here."

"Wonderful. Moving right along..." Layla spread swatch cards on the table. The colors were things I never could have thought about before: muted, soft, gentle as our past. The past I was trying not to remember. But she made me remember. Made me remember everything.

I kept my attention focused on the choices laid out on the table, like that was all that mattered. Like I hadn't lived this moment a hundred times before.

We reached for the copper swatch simultaneously. My fingers touched hers. Not gently. Like an accident. Like the kind of accident you have when you're still more careful than you need to be.

The contact lasted less than a second but jumped through me like electricity, familiar and foreign at the same time. Her skin still felt the same—warm and impossibly soft—but the ring she always wore on her middle finger was gone. I hadn't realized I'd memorized the feel of it until now, when its absence scraped against my senses like something vital missing.

I jerked back as if burned while BG froze mid-motion, her professional façade momentarily cracking open to reveal something raw beneath before we both recovered. Or maybe she was just too quick for me.

I should have been more careful. Should have known how it would feel. How much it would undo. The simple touch. The easy way we used to fit. The ease of knowing someone else's skin better than your own. It all exploded into the tiny space between us, a hundred thoughts and memories without a single word.

We weren't ready. We never were.

"Makes sense." My tone so neutral it could have frozen water.

I could have sworn I saw her wince, but it happened so fast that I almost missed it. Almost.

Layla smiled, flipping to a coordinating color strip. "You two really understand each other's style. Have you worked together before?"

I flinched. Not visibly. But inside, something folded. Before I could formulate a response that wouldn't reveal too much, BG leaned forward with that signature smile of hers—the one that never quite reached her eyes when she was uncomfortable.

"Oh, we've coordinated a thing or two in the past. Nothing wedding-related unless you count that disaster of a Halloween party where Riley vetoed all my decorating ideas." She laughed lightly, then smoothly redirected. "But speaking of these centerpieces, how much flexibility do we have with the height? The candles are pretty tall..."

The effortless deflection was so quintessentially BG, I could only shake my head. Two years and nothing had changed. She could still make the weightiest history sound like a charming anecdote. That Halloween party had been in our apartment. She'd wanted to hang fake cobwebs from every corner, and I'd argued they'd collect dust we'd never get rid of. We'd compromised with window decorations and door hangings, then spent the whole night stealing glances at each other across a room full of friends in ridiculous costumes, ready for them to leave.

Without warning, my body overruled me. Suddenly I could feel the wet heat of BG's mouth drawing my fingers deeper, the way she'd moaned around them as I pressed my tongue to the sensitive spot at the nape of her neck, my other hand wrapped around her throat, her witch costume that kept slipping off her shoulder all night long, now bunched around her waist.

By spring, she was finding reasons to work late. By summer, we were living like roommates.

Layla launched into an explanation about centerpiece dimensions, but my mind flashed elsewhere. To a velvet box and my reflection forming words that never left my lips. I blinked hard. Swatches. Not memories. My fingers whitened around my pen as if I could squeeze the thought away.

Instead, I found myself instinctively making a precise adjustment to the table's arrangement, aligning the centerpiece perfectly with the swatch samples. BG watched this small movement before breaking the quiet.

"You always did have an eye for balance," she said softly, the comment barely audible, almost like she didn't mean to say it aloud.

The air between us thickened. My throat closed around words I refused to let out.

"This isn't about us," I responded, with a firm, quieter finality, and closed the sample book in my hand like a seal slamming shut.

BG looked down at the sample books. "Never said it was," she said, softer now. Her jaw flexed, like there was more she wanted to say. There was exhaustion in her voice, a weariness I recognized because I felt it too—the effort of maintaining this separation, of pretending the past wasn't sitting between us like a fourth person at the table. Finally, she said, "I wasn't expecting to see you, either, you know. Can we just get through this and go home?"

Layla's eyebrows hit her hairline. She cleared her throat and suddenly became very interested in her pen, clicking it with the focus of someone pretending they hadn't just watched two people have an entire relationship conversation through fabric swatches.

My gaze slipped back to the table.

I didn't flinch, but my heart did. Maybe I heard it wrong. Maybe I heard it right, and I just wanted it to be wrong.

"Sure," I wanted to be cruel, but it was softer than I thought. Softer than I should have let it be. "That's the plan."

We went right back to where we'd started, formal and detached, acting like nothing had slipped. Like it hadn't been too much for us.

"Perfect!" Layla gathered the papers too quickly with an odd, nervous smile. "I'll send the finalized details to both of you and the happy couple by the end of the week. We'll need final approval on the fabric selections by the 15th, and then we'll be all set for production. The installation team will arrive three hours before the ceremony, but we'll coordinate all of that closer to the date."

We got up. I put on my coat. She looked at me like she wanted to say something more. She didn't. But I knew she would. Her lips parted slightly, her weight shifting forward then back, a hesitation I recognized from years of watching her gather courage.

I wasn't ready to hear it. Whatever words she was holding back—apology, explanation, small talk—would only open doors better left closed. I nodded a quick goodbye to Layla and walked out first, not waiting to see if BG would follow.

When I stepped outside, the January cold was a fist to the face. Brick as fuck. The temperature had dropped since I'd arrived, darkness bringing that special kind of New York winter chill that lifts every gap in your clothing to remind you it's there. My breath clouded as I hurried to my car, fingers already stinging despite my gloves.

The heater sputtered reluctantly to life as I sat shivering, waiting for warmth to fill the small space. Through the windshield, my breath still fogged up the car.

As I sat at a red light, I spotted her through the windshield. BG walking quickly along the sidewalk, shoulders hunched against the bitter cold, her breath making small clouds in the air. She was wearing her same favorite winter hat with the tassels on the side that I used to flick to make her laugh. Tiny snowflakes were beginning to catch in her locs. The wind pushed against her, making her tuck her chin deeper into her collar. Her cheeks were already reddening from the cold. She'd always been sensitive to it, always stealing my sweaters and complaining about the draft in our apartment. Six blocks to the subway in this? Even with proper winter gear, it would be brutal.

My hand moved toward the window control before I'd consciously decided to lower it. I knew how much she hated the cold, could still picture her huddled under three blankets on our couch, claiming hypothermia when I refused to turn the heat past seventy. It was muscle memory, the instinct to protect her from discomfort, overriding the last lick of good sense I had. It would be a ten-minute detour at most without traffic. The temperature was dropping by the minute, and even if she made it to the station, she'd still have to huddle with strangers in a tiny, cramped room leading to an outdoor platform.

Just basic human decency to offer her a ride. That's all this had to be.

Our eyes met through the windshield. For one electric second, I saw a flash of the BG I used to know. Vulnerable, unguarded, a question in her eyes.

My fingers hovered over the button. The professional, guarded part of me screamed to drive away and maintain the boundaries I'd spent two years building. But that other part, the part that remembered what it felt like to care, wouldn't let me.

The light turned green.

Fuck.

I started to drive, but found myself slowing down, pulling over to the curb just ahead of her. I lowered the passenger window.

"Come on, get in," I said. "It's freezing. I'll drop you at the subway."

BG stood there for a moment, snowflakes collecting on her shoulders, hesitation clear on her face.

"It's fine," I added, staring straight ahead. "Just get in."

Stupid Hearts

BG

I GOT IN. OF course I did.

Didn't say thank you. Didn't say anything. Just tugged the door shut and pretended like I hadn't been debating it with every freezing cell in my body. The heater was already on, too. Low and humming. So very Riley.

I pressed my gloves into my lap and stared straight ahead. My breath was shallow, fogging faintly near the glass, even though the heat was climbing. Or maybe that was just me.

Riley didn't look at me. Not even once.

You should say something.

Something casual. Something safe. Something that doesn't sound like a confession or a breakdown.

"Thanks," I said, finally.

She didn't answer.

Cool cool cool.

The silence between us was thick, like the fog on the windshield that the defroster hadn't quite cleared. I watched the wipers make lazy swipes across the glass, my pulse ticking away like some Doomsday clock.

That familiar knot twisted in my stomach. Riley's silence always did this to me. Turned me into a live wire, all crackling energy with nowhere to go. I'd rather she yell at me, cuss me out, anything but this quiet, I don't know, *processing* that made me feel like I was disappearing.

I could smell her. Same cologne. Stupid, warm scents that made you want to lean in even when you shouldn't. And I shouldn't. Especially not when she looked like this—tense jaw, both hands on the wheel like she was driving through a minefield.

We were maybe four minutes into a ten-minute ride. And I already wanted to jump out and roll.

She finally spoke. "You're still sensitive to the cold."

Something twisted in my chest at that word. Still. Like I was still hers to read, still hers to know. My head turned fast, and that was my first mistake, catching her profile like that. She wasn't looking at me, but her mouth had that familiar pull at the corner. That same damn Riley half-smirk she wore when she was saying something true and mean and not entirely unkind.

"Still?" I tried to laugh. It didn't come out right. "You make it sound like I haven't survived two whole winters without you being a whole prison guard about the thermostat."

Her mouth didn't twitch. Not even a little.

Right. Not a game anymore.

I turned toward the window, watching snowflakes dissolve against the glass.

Everything went high-definition slow-motion, like I was suddenly the main character in some indie film's pivotal moment, complete with an invisible director shouting 'and...hold that crushing wave of feelings. Action!'. Three seconds felt like an entire therapy session's worth of emotional processing, and I hadn't even made eye contact with her yet.

The truth was, I'd known she would be there. Deena had called this morning, frantic about a client emergency. *Please, BG, I can't lose this appointment slot. Riley will be there to help with the decisions, but I need someone who knows my vision.* I could have said no. Should have said no. But I'd agreed, telling myself it was just because Deena needed me, because I'd promised not to mess up this maid of honor thing.

Not because some part of me had been waiting for an excuse to see Riley again.

Thoughts set intentions, but what made them real were *words*. So I'd been real careful with mine lately, avoiding Riley's name like it might summon her. And here she was anyway, conjured by circumstance and my own inability to say no to our friends.

My fingers itched to fidget with something, anything. Skin felt too tight, like I was a size too big for myself suddenly. I tugged at the fringe of my scarf, winding it tight around my index finger until the tip cooled, then released it. Winding. Releasing. Like I could somehow compress all the words I wasn't saying.

The streets blurred past, Brooklyn storefronts decorated for Valentine's Day even though it was barely mid-January. Stupid hearts in windows. Stupid couples bundled together against the cold. Stupid me, sitting here pretending like my body wasn't hyperaware of every breath she took.

"You grew out your locs," she said suddenly, eyes still locked on the road. "You kept threatening to cut them."

My hand flew to my locs before I could stop myself. "Yeah. A year ago, I stopped freaking out about length and just let them go."

"It looks good." Clinical. Detached. Like she was complimenting a stranger's shoes on the subway.

"Thanks," I said, the word falling flat between us. I wanted to say more. Something about how she looked good too. How that scarf brought out the warmth in her eyes—or maybe I was just projecting warmth when there wasn't any left for me. Her eyes were dark as coffee grounds right now, almost black. Story of my life, seeing things that weren't there.

And *totally* not thinking about how the last time she'd given me a ride, we'd ended up making out in her car for twenty minutes, late to Sakia's shop opening.

Ugh. I could almost feel the ghost of us kissing in her parked car outside the shop. Her hands in my hair, my fingers tracing that sensitive spot below her ear that made her breath catch. The windows fogging up from our heat alone. Her whisper: "We're so late." Me laughing against her mouth. The way she'd looked at me after, all flushed skin and soft mouth, like I was the only person who'd ever existed. Like I was worth being late for. I kept my mouth shut instead.

We stopped at a red light, the car idling beneath us. Music played softly from her speakers. Something indie and melancholy that I didn't recognize. New. Something she'd discovered in the time we'd been apart. A tiny, stupid detail that shouldn't have hurt but did.

The silence stretched, tightening around my throat. I was drowning in all the things we weren't saying.

"So," I ventured, desperate to fill the void with something besides memory. "Exciting about Deena and Taj, huh?"

Her hands flexed on the wheel. "Yeah."

"The copper will look good," I added, immediately wishing I hadn't mentioned the wedding stuff. "With the flowers you picked."

Riley's jaw tightened. "We picked."

"Right." I nodded, over-eager. "We."

The car rolled forward as the light changed. Three more blocks to the station. I counted in my head, a silent countdown to escape. My heartbeat felt too loud, too obvious. Could she hear it? Did she remember how it used to sound against her ear?

"Did they—" I started, then stopped myself. "Never mind."

Riley glanced at me, just for a second. The first direct look since I'd gotten in her car. "Did they what?"

I swallowed hard. "Did they really need me? Or was this just...their way of forcing us to talk?"

Her eyes went back to the road. "Does it matter?"

Yes. No. Maybe. I didn't know. I just wanted her to keep talking, keep looking at me, even if it hurt.

"I guess not," I said, picking at a loose thread on my glove. "Just seems like something they'd do."

Her thumb tapped against the steering wheel once. "You said Deena said it was just a client emergency." A beat passed. "I don't believe her."

The corner of my mouth lifted. "Me neither."

We turned onto the street with the subway entrance. The end of the line. Riley pulled up to the curb, the car sliding to a smooth stop. My hand hovered over the door handle, but I couldn't make myself open it yet.

"I'm living in Bed-Stuy now," I blurted out, immediately cringing. Why had I said that? What exactly was she supposed to do with that information? I mean, in spite of the fact that I migrated from Kingsbridge to Bed Stuy. Her mail forwarding for me was probably still going to the wrong address.

Riley nodded, eyes forward. "Good for you."

"Yeah, it's closer to...everything." My voice trailed off. Closer to what? Our old neighborhood? The places we used to go? I couldn't finish the thought.

The heater hummed between us. Outside, snow was starting to stick to the sidewalk, a thin white dusting that would melt by morning. People huddled inside their coats hurried past, eager to escape the cold.

"Thank you," I tried again, meaning it this time. "For the ride. You didn't have to, but I appreciate it."

Riley's fingers tightened on the wheel and sighed. Wouldn't look at me. For a second, I thought she might say something real. Something that would crack open this careful distance between us. I held my breath.

"You're welcome," she said finally. Nothing more.

I nodded, throat tight, and pushed the door open. The blast of cold air was almost a relief after the suffocating warmth of the car. My boots crunched on the salt-covered sidewalk as I stepped out.

Before closing the door, I looked back at her. Riley's profile was lit by the dashboard lights, shadows playing across her face. Beautiful in that quiet, serious way she always had been. Steady as a heartbeat.

"See you at the wedding?" I asked, hating how hopeful I sounded. My voice sounded too soft, too open. I hated that. I hated how easy it still was to ask her for anything.

She didn't look at me. But I heard the hesitation in her breath, that tiny catch before she answered. "Yeah. See you."

I shut the door and watched her pull away, red taillights disappearing into the growing darkness. My breath rushed out like I'd been holding my breath underwater.

The subway station loomed ahead, a gaping mouth ready to swallow me into the belly of the city. I pulled my coat tighter and walked toward it, each step carrying me further from her warmth.

This was fine. I was fine. *Great, even.*

The wind cut through my layers, finding every gap, every vulnerability. I shivered, remembering the feel of her car's heater, the faint scent of her perfume that still clung to my clothes.

I paused at the top of the subway stairs, watching my breath cloud in front of me. When Deena called this morning, I couldn't say no. But, I don't know, maybe some weird, masochistic part of me had been wanting this chance. To see her again, to be in the same room with her, even if just for an hour.

Just to close a chapter, of course. Nothing more than that. Maybe for a bit of closure that wouldn't involve actual talking. Just to prove to myself that I was fine. And I was. Totally fine. Because seeing her lean over that table studying fabric swatches wasn't doing anything to me. That moment when our fingers brushed over the copper swatch? Didn't even register. So what if I could still pick her silhouette out of a crowded room? That's just...pattern recognition. Everyone has it.

"Not me having a whole breakdown in front of a subway," I said. Someone passing by the stairs turned around to shoot me side-eye for blocking the entrance.

Just having an existential crisis, nothing to see here.

The words vanished in the rush of warm, stale air from the train tunnel. I wiped at my eyes, telling myself it was just the cold making them water. Not the echo of Riley's voice saying my name like it still meant something. Not the memory of how easy it once was between us.

Not the truth I couldn't outrun: maybe I fucked up.

The subway platform was a special kind of purgatory. Overheated, smelling like body odor and stale air, with that persistent drip-drip-drip from a pipe somewhere overhead that matched the rhythm of my racing heart.

I found a spot against the tiled wall, pulled out my phone, and immediately put it back in my pocket. No. Absolutely not. No reception down here, anyway. And I was not going to dissect that car ride like some kind of emotional forensics expert. Riley had offered me a ride because it was cold and she was being nice when I didn't even deserve it. That's it. End of story. Nothing more to analyze.

The train announced itself with a rumble that vibrated through my bones. I stepped forward with the crowd, found an empty seat by the window, and watched Brooklyn blur past in streaks of brick and neon. My reflection stared back from the dark glass. Wide eyes, a tassle hat and flushed cheeks, looking like someone who'd just survived something significant and wasn't sure what to do about it.

See you at the wedding?

Yeah. See you.

Such simple words. Such complicated undertones. The way she'd hesitated before answering, like she was calculating something. The way my chest had performed a whole gymnastic floor routine when she'd finally responded.

Stop it, Becks. She was being polite. You were two people trapped in a car by weather and basic human decency. Nothing cosmic about it.

By the time I climbed the stairs to street level, the cold had sharpened into something that cut through my jacket and went straight to my bones. I walked the two blocks to my apartment quickly, head down, shoulders hunched, trying to outpace my own thoughts.

My building's lobby was mercifully warm, the radiator clanking out a familiar rhythm that meant home. I climbed a flight of stairs, muscle memory guiding me while my brain continued its endless loop of ESPN-level analysis and denial.

The apartment welcomed me with silence and the faint scent of the vanilla air freshener. I dropped my keys on the side table. Home. Safe space. No Riley Benson energy to complicate things.

I peeled off my layers methodically—jacket, scarf, boots—creating small piles of winter that I'd deal with later. The bathroom called to me with its promise of hot water and steam, a ritual cleansing to wash away whatever the hell it was that had just happened. Tucked my locs away into a shower-proof bonnet.

The shower was perfect. Scalding hot, pressure strong enough to massage the tension from my shoulders. I stood under the spray longer than needed, let it wash the evening down the drain along with the last traces of Riley's cologne that had somehow clung to my skin despite the brief contact.

Afterward, wrapped in my favorite purple oversized towel, I padded to the living room and lit my good candle. The expensive one I saved for special occasions or emotional emergencies. Coconut and citrus filled the air, immediately calming something restless inside me.

My tarot deck lived in the bottom drawer of my living room console, tucked away behind charging cables and old magazines like a secret I kept even from myself. I'd been reading cards for myself since college, using them less for divination and more for reflection, a way to externalize my internal chaos and look at it from different angles

After I read for Deena, and the cards read her for *filth* for having a crush on the shy stud her girlfriend used to date that turned out to be Taj, I had been banned from reading for her. But I still read for myself sometimes.

Tonight felt like a good night for cards.

I settled cross-legged on my couch, unwrapping the deck with the reverence I always felt for this ritual. The cards were worn soft from years of handling, edges slightly frayed, each one familiar as an old friend. I held them in my hands, feeling their weight, their warmth.

What do I need to know about tonight? I thought, shuffling slowly at first, then faster as my energy built. *What am I not seeing? What am I missing?*

The cards moved through my fingers with practiced ease, creating that soft whisper of paper against paper that always centered me. Shuffle, shuffle, shuffle—

A card shot out of the deck like it had been launched, spinning through the air before landing face-up on my couch cushion.

The Two of Cups.

I stared at it, my hands frozen mid-shuffle. The image stared back at me. Two figures facing each other, cups raised in offering. The winged, lion-headed caduceus of healing floating between them. Partnership. Stubborn love through devotion and work. Emotional connection. Reunion.

"Oh, come on," I muttered, scooping up the card and shoving it back into the deck. "Subtle much?"

If the Six of Cups was next, I was going to get up to throw the whole fucking deck away, for real.

I shuffled more aggressively, trying to distribute the card's energy throughout the deck. Sometimes cards just flew out because of how they were sitting, or because of static electricity, or because the universe had a twisted sense of humor. Sometimes they did the petty thing and reflected back exactly what you were thinking.

It didn't mean anything.

I took a deep breath, centered myself again, and focused on my intention. A simple three-card spread: past, present, future. Nothing fancy. Just a basic check-in with my psyche.

I dealt the cards face-down in a line, left to right. Paused. Flipped them over one by one.

Past: The Five of Cups. Grief, loss, focusing on what's been spilled rather than what remains. Yeah, that tracked. Two years of mourning what Riley and I had been, what we'd lost.

Present: The Star. Hope, renewal, guidance after a dark time. Interesting. I studied the image. A naked figure pouring water from two cups, one onto land and one into a pool, connecting the conscious and unconscious. Stars shining overhead, offering light in inky blackness.

Future: The Two of Cups.

"Motherfuck—"

The *same fucking card* that had jumped out of the deck five minutes ago.

I sat back, staring at the spread like it had insulted me and my mom. There it was again, smug in its certainty. Two figures facing each other. Partnership. Emotional union. The card that basically screamed "reunion" in tarot-speak.

"This is ridiculous," I said aloud, my voice echoing in the empty apartment. "Cards don't predict the future. They reflect internal states. They're therapeutic tools, not cosmic messaging systems."

But even as I said it, something cold and electric ran down my spine. Because the Two of Cups wasn't just about romantic reunion. It was about healing, about two people coming together as equals, about the kind of partnership that could only happen after both parties had done their individual work.

I stared at the Future card, willing it to make sense. The Two of Cups felt too simple, too easy. Too good to be true. What was I missing?

"Okay, universe, ancestors, whoever is up and being nosy this late," I muttered, shuffling the deck again. "What's the catch? What do I need to know about this supposed future?"

I pulled a single card and laid it across the Two of Cups.

The Hanged Man.

"Oh, come *on*." I tilted my head, studying the figure hanging upside down from a tree. One leg crossed over the other in some zen meditation pose, arms bound behind his back, but his face was totally serene. Like hanging upside down was his idea of a good time.

"Pisces," I said automatically, recognizing my own astrological symbol. The Hanged Man was ruled by Neptune, planet of dreams and illusions and emotional chaos. My planet. Naturally. But what the hell did that mean here?

I studied the card, trying to piece together the cosmic joke. Me, somehow tangled up in this future reunion. But how? The Hanged Man was about...what? Being stuck? Seeing things differently? Sacrificing something? Waiting around like an idiot?

The meaning kept slipping away from me like trying to hold water. Was I supposed to do something? Stop doing something? Was this about Riley, or about me, or about whatever mess we'd make together?

I couldn't grab it, like trying to remember a dream that dissolved the second you opened your eyes.

The cards just sat there, smug and mysterious, keeping their secrets.

I thought about Riley in that car. The distance she'd maintained that I had tried and failed to break with the gift she sent back. The way she'd offered help without conditions, without expectations. The woman who'd picked me up wasn't the same person I'd left two years ago. And maybe—maybe—I wasn't the same girl who'd run.

I thought about leaving Jai in her apartment. Who was I kidding? I was exactly that girl.

But what did these cards mean? That we were supposed to try again? That tonight's encounter was the universe's way of saying "second chance"? That two people who'd burned their relationship to the ground could somehow build something new from the ashes?

The candle flickered, casting dancing shadows across the cards. I reached for my phone before I could stop myself, scrolling to Riley's text thread. My thumb scrolled over her name, heart pounding with the possibility of—what? A text saying thanks again for the ride? A confession that sitting in her car had felt like coming home? A question about whether she felt it too, that pull that seemed to exist independent of logic or self-preservation?

I set the phone down without typing anything.

The cards sat there, patient in their certainty. Past grief, present hope, future connection. A narrative as clear as any story, if I chose to believe in such things.

But did I?

And more importantly, did I want to?

The Two of Cups caught the candlelight, the figures seeming to move in the flickering glow. Offering their cups to each other. Choosing connection despite the risk. Choosing love despite the possibility of loss.

I stared at the card until my eyes burned, willing it to change, to become something less loaded, less hopeful, less terrifying in its implications.

It remained stubbornly, impossibly optimistic.

I blew out the candle and went to bed with more questions than answers, the tropical scent following me into dreams where two figures stood facing each other on a beach, cups raised, choosing each other again and again and again.

Just Feel It

Riley

I WAS EARLY, WITH ten minutes to spare. Enough time to pick the perfect table in the corner with a clear view of the door. The Crow and Crumb surrounded me with the deep perfume of coffee and wood. A contrast to the brisk January air outside. I checked the positioning of my chair. Straightened my spine. Laced my fingers together on the tabletop. Waited.

The music overhead hummed at a low volume. Perfect. Warm air blew in through open windows, softening the room's sharp edges. My watch read two o'clock when I checked it. I scrolled through my dating app and saw her picture. Long hair and a dazzling smile that promised a lot.

I drew in the comforting smell of ground beans and butter. A hum of conversation surrounded me, low but constant. Just right. People sat on mismatched furniture—copper-topped tables, old leather chairs, worn and familiar like the ambiance they created. Vintage lamps threw muted light into cozy corners.

I scanned the other customers quickly. Registered two couples, one solo reader, a few regulars on laptops. That let me breathe a little easier. Behind the counter, baristas moved around each other with practiced precision. Espresso machines hissed. Porcelain met wood in familiar rhythms.

One barista caught my eye. Young woman, delicate locs tied back in a ponytail. My pulse quickened at that phantom reminder. A slight hitch in my regulated rhythms. She didn't notice me. Good.

I scrolled through Shaye's profile, flicking through our message thread on the app. No big expectations, I reminded myself. Just a first date. But still. This time, something about it felt different. The anticipation sat low in my gut when I thought of her—sharp, new, unclouded.

My phone vibrated against the tabletop. A text from Shaye.

Running 15 min late. Traffic from rehearsal. Sorry!

I tapped my reply. *No problem. Coffee's good here.*

The screen dimmed. I set the phone down, face-up. Fifteen minutes. The doubt crept in. That familiar worry that I'd be stood up. I'd seen it before: the apologetic text, then silence. Just another ghoster in a city full of them.

I pulled up the video she'd sent me last week—her band performing at some upscale lounge downtown. The Smith Band. The camera quality didn't do her justice, catching only glimpses of her behind the microphone. Blonde waves, curves and blood-red lips bathed in blue stage light.

It could be good for me. Someone like Shaye. A good fit. A safe match. The opposite of reckless.

The sky outside was a dull, wintry blue. A promise of snow to come, but not today. I allowed myself to compare it to other coffee dates, ones that felt awkward and off. Ones where I felt awkward and off. Dates since the breakup, each one uncomfortable and unsatisfying.

This felt different. There was potential in the air, potential in the woman who would walk through that door. If she walked through that door. I kept my eyes on my coffee, resisting the urge to check my watch. Emotional regulation through habit. Apparently, I missed my podcast host calling.

2:17. Still no Shaye. The thought of leaving crossed my mind, but something kept me anchored to the chair. Patient. Waiting. Another sip of coffee, black and hot. Quick and clean.

I saw her the second she walked through the door.

My heart did that strange flip as she stepped inside, and I didn't hesitate—I stood up, one hand raised in a small, contained wave. Her eyes found mine immediately, and what the video hadn't shown became instantly clear: Shaye was stunning. Her smile came easy, warm and knowing. Her skin was radiant under the afternoon light, each curve of her body wrapped in a mustard-yellow dress that made it hard to think.

She moved toward me with slow, graceful steps like she didn't care who watched. She saw me appreciating her. Her mouth curved into a deeper smile, red nails brushing her hair back.

"Riley," she said, my name sounding like music in her voice.

"Shaye. Glad you made it."

She gestured toward the pastry counter. "Mind if I grab something first? Rushed straight from rehearsal."

"Of course." I followed her to the display case, both of us standing side by side, studying the rows of caramel-drizzled confections.

"Those look amazing," she said, pointing to a row of chocolate croissants. Her arm brushed against mine, unintentional but electric.

"They're good. Especially with the sea salt on top." I kept my voice measured despite the unexpected warmth radiating from where our shoulders touched.

"You've tried everything here, haven't you?" Her eyes slid from the pastries to my face, teasing.

"Occupational hazard. I'm very, very...thorough." The words came out with more suggestion than I'd intended. I cleared my throat. "I'd definitely recommend the chocolate pistachio if you have a sweet tooth."

That earned me an eyebrow raised and a smirk. "Good to know."

After ordering, we returned to the table. She took the seat across from me. I knew when I was being sized up.

The conversation moved and flexed and expanded. Words didn't fail me the way I thought they might. She spoke about her music, what it was like to sing in front of strangers, and I couldn't help but admire her surety. I was the curious one now, asking too many questions, listening with more interest than I'd anticipated. Her story about a botched corporate gig caught me off-guard and made me laugh out loud.

Her presence was all I registered, like the whole place faded into nothing. She folded her hands on the table, watching me, and I had to hold my breath to remember how to breathe.

"I'm impressed," Shaye said. Her voice carried a playful melody. "You picked a good spot." She glanced around, a quick and measured scan. I watched the motion of her eyes, and there was something behind them. Something that surprised me.

"Seemed right," I said, keeping it even. Letting the coffee warm my voice before it gave me away. I caught the scent of her perfume, sweet and warm, like she'd just stepped out of a dream. It filled the space between us, and I found myself breathing it in deeper. Not something I could regulate. Not something I wanted to.

She sipped her iced coffee, and I leaned in. I didn't expect to. Her lips were gorgeous and full. "Just in case things heat up," she said, raising the cup. There was laughter behind her voice, teasing but also intent.

Mine stayed measured. "Let's see if they do." It felt bold. That wasn't what I expected. That wasn't what I came for. It excited me anyway.

She told me about her first time on stage, overcoming stage fright, her family's musical legacy, the unexpected path that led her here. I had no business feeling what I felt. Drawn in, curious, wanting more. The conversation expanded, my questions expanding with it.

"What about the name?" I asked. "Smith Band?"

"Just my last name," Shaye replied. "There were four of us, but then we kept adding." Her voice was like an alto sax, low and sultry. She described each member of her band, who played what. I nodded, I listened. My attention never wandered. My pulse did.

I noted how at ease I felt, how much easier than it should have been. We laughed over another story she told, some audition where everything went wrong, how the speakers exploded but they sang, anyway. A pleasant warmth spread through me. Maybe not butterflies exactly, more like the simple thrill of connecting with someone new. Clear. Uncomplicated. She made it easy. She made everything else fall away.

Time slipped past like it didn't know we were in it. We kept talking, kept exploring, kept finding places that were soft and unexpected. I got lost in Shaye's eyes again, in the openness and light that felt genuine.

My instincts said run.

My instincts said stay.

They couldn't agree, so I sat there. My head was full and fuzzy, light with the strange feeling of calm that I couldn't quite trust. Shaye talked about her songwriting process, her journey. I lost the thread and lost myself. Her hands moved like they were connected to the words.

"Like last summer, we were playing this corporate gig, and the crowd was so *dead*. So I shifted 'The Way You Look Tonight' down a half-step, slowed the tempo, and suddenly people were actually listening instead of just networking over drinks..."

I *was* drawn in, but not in the way I wanted to be. There was no pain in this, but there was no realness either. No heat. That realization came slow, and I was slower to accept it. It didn't strike like a lightning bolt. It seeped in, like the loose but tight fit of our words, our sentences, our interaction.

Then she said it.

"You're holding something back," her eyes holding mine with quiet certainty. "I can always tell when someone's performing." Her fingers tapped twice on the table, precise and deliberate.

The shock of her words hit like cold water. My shoulders pulled back automatically, spine straightening into that careful posture I knew too well. I set my coffee down carefully, buying myself three seconds to breathe.

I sucked in a breath and checked myself. Regulated. Realigned. Mechanical perfection was still perfection.

"We're all performing something," I said, voice steady despite the sudden dryness in my throat.

Shaye's smile didn't waver, but her eyes narrowed slightly. "Some are better at it than others."

I wasn't sure which category she'd placed me in.

The moment stretched between us, taut with unspoken assessment. I reached for my coffee, took a sip that had gone cold. This was exactly the kind of perceptiveness that both attracted and unsettled me. The same quality that had drawn me to BG—that ability to see through the surface to what lay beneath. But where BG had observed with chaotic intuition and blurted questions, Shaye did it with quiet, surgical precision. Chest engagement kicked in. Classic postural response to stress.

I pressed my fingertips into the paper cup, feeling the give of the material, the heat seeping through. Focus on the texture, the temperature—anything but the way Shaye was still watching me with those surgeon's eyes.

"There are people who show you everything right away," I said, feeling the truth of it vibrate. "And there are those who need to know it's safe first. Which one are you?" My question hung between us, a counter-assessment.

Shaye's lips curved into a half-smile. "I'm selective about what I reveal and when. But what I do show—" she tapped her fingers once more on the table "—is always authentic."

"You don't need to figure me out today," I said finally, attempting to redirect. "We've got time."

"Fair enough," she conceded, leaning back slightly. The intensity in her gaze softened, but didn't vanish completely.

We shifted to safer ground. Her upcoming gigs, my clinic schedule. The conversation found its rhythm again, comfortable but with a new undercurrent. She'd seen something in me, and I'd felt it. That was the problem.

Shaye laughed at another story, and I was with her. Not alone, not drifting. There was a strange charge between us, one that made it easy to say the right things. Everything about her drew me in. She told me about a disastrous gig at a wedding, how the bride sobbed because the groom was too drunk to say "I do," but they still paid in full. I laughed. For real. The sound surprised me, but she made it easy. Everything was too easy. "Sounds like a nightmare," I said, smiling back.

"A paycheck's a paycheck," she replied, grinning. Her nails were red and glossy. They matched the color of her lips. It shouldn't have fit. But it did. All of it. Shaye took another sip of her drink, and my eyes followed her mouth, the movement. My heart thudded, then stilled. Slow, then stopped. She reached across the table, fingers extended. Just barely touched my hand. Heat radiated through that tiny contact. Heat that she didn't have to say anything about.

I couldn't feel the surge of something new and wild. I could only feel safe, held, a predictable warmth that surrounded us both like a steady blanket. This was the comfort I thought I needed. This was the easy familiarity that seemed so impossible before.

"...Music," she continued, "is the easy part. All you have to do is feel it." Her face was so open, her presence so sure.

Just feel it.

The irony was a blade in the chest. Here was this beautiful woman telling me the easiest thing in the world, and I couldn't do it. I was floating somewhere on Mars, watching myself perform the motions of a date while feeling nothing that mattered. The awareness sat uncomfortable and heavy.

"Yeah," My own voice came out low and unsteady. Not a weakness, though. An opening. The barista with the locs passed by. The light hit them just right, just wrong, just enough to bring me back. Back to the awareness of where I was, who I was with, and what it all meant. I forced myself back into focus, drank more coffee. Cold this time. Needed that chill, too.

I felt suddenly exposed, needing to shift her focus. Mine too, if I was being honest. "So why did you swipe right on me?" I heard the edge in my voice too late.

Shaye's eyebrows lifted slightly, but her smile remained. "Your profile said you fix people for a living. I liked that you didn't call yourself a healer." She paused. "And you have nice hands."

Checking out my hands already?

Her confidence was attractive. It would have been more than enough before. But was it enough now? I let my eyes rest on her lips. On her knowing, gentle lips.

Shaye reached for my hand again, her touch light and easy. Her laughter filled the air. The heat from her palm was muted, warm. Not electric. Not painful. Her expression was a slow build, like she understood more than she should. I withdrew, and I wasn't sure it was intentional.

We left the coffee shop, and the January air was a wall of cold. But even that wasn't enough to wake me. It was a reminder. It was the clarity of open air and unexpected possibilities.

Shaye hugged me close, the heat of her body meeting the chill outside. There was restraint in that hug. There was the promise of closeness. My breath caught, and then I was moving, moving away.

"This was nice," Shaye said. She didn't sound convinced. Maybe she wanted to be. Maybe I did too.

I took her hand, squeezing it, allowing the moment to expand and collapse around us. "Yeah. Nice," I replied. She was everything I should've wanted. That's what made it worse.

"So, are we doing this again?" Shaye asked, her eyes warm and expectant. But direct.

"I'm the one who should be asking you," I said. I waited. I kept waiting. Needed to feel her out, so see if she could be brave enough for the both of us.

"I'd like to, yeah."

I hesitated for only a second, the doubt visible only to myself. "I'm free Thursday night. Are you free?"

The words came out more decisive than I felt, but that's who I needed to be. Someone who made choices instead of avoiding them.

"Thursday works." Shaye's smile widened. "Text me a place?"

"I know somewhere good in the Village." I squeezed her hand once before letting go. "I'll send you the details."

She looked happy. I looked composed. We said our goodbyes, and I turned toward my car, shoulders straight, stride even. The decision was made, even if I wasn't entirely sure it was mine.

The walk back to my car took forever and no time at all. My steps were deliberate, echoing the conversations I couldn't finish and the ones I needed to start.

Another disrespectfully cold wind whipped through the street, and I finally got to my car. The long and the short of it stayed with me. Progress. Not a straight line, but a line that bent back on itself. It should have made sense. It didn't. It should have felt different. It didn't.

My body was calm. My mind, the same. I sat behind the wheel, key in the ignition. The car didn't start, but something else did. An awareness of how close my past really was, how far it seemed until it wasn't. How far I had to go.

Her perfume still clung to my jacket. The memory of her smile still felt like something that should have mattered more.

Shaye was lovely. Our date was lovely.

I felt nothing that would keep me awake tonight, and it ate at me. I knew that would eat at me too.

When In Doubt, Mute the Group Chat

BG

SPIRITUALLY BYPASSING MY EMOTIONS was turning into an Olympic sport. Someone hand me my gold medal and a therapy voucher.

The essential oil diffuser in Sakia's studio was pumping out lavender like it was getting paid per puff. I closed my eyes as her fingers worked through my locs, each twist sending little lightning bolts of pain-not-pain across my scalp. Her hands moved with the same confident precision they had for over five years now—ever since she reopened the salon under her new name. Back when I was her only loyal client who'd followed her through the transition, and now I was her most featured face on Instagram.

"You're unnaturally quiet today," Sakia murmured, her voice blending with a Kendrick song humming from hidden speakers. "It's freaking me out a little."

I hadn't even wanted to come. Spent twenty minutes in my car drafting cancellation texts that started with "Sorry babe, can't make it" and spiraled into increasingly elaborate excuses involving fictional food poisoning and non-existent pipe bursts. But here I was anyway, letting Sakia's hands do their magic because apparently, I'd developed this annoying new habit of showing up for things instead of bailing.

Plus, we both needed the content. My followers ate up her styling videos, and her salon bookings always spiked after I tagged her in my stories. Win-win, even when my heart felt like a definite loss.

Growth? More like emotional masochism with better marketing.

"Just thinking," I replied, and the words came out softer than I'd intended. I caught my reflection in the mirror and did a double-take. Was that...actual peace on my face? The last time I'd looked this calm was probably pre-puberty. Before hormones. Before Riley. Before the cosmic joke of running into her at that vendor meeting two weeks ago.

God, that meeting. Walking in expecting some faceless wedding planner and instead finding Riley, her eyes widening like she'd seen a ghost. Both of us trapped in wedding napkin hell, making small talk about table arrangements like we hadn't once known every inch of each other's bodies. And then, because the universe loves drama, her offering me a ride to the train. Me actually getting in her car. The silence between us humming with everything we weren't saying.

"You're glowing a little," Sakia said, her fingers never stopping their precise movements. Her eyes caught mine in the mirror, one eyebrow arched with that psychic knowing she did so well. "Not hating the look." She paused to adjust the ring light mounted beside the mirror, the one I'd convinced her to invest in back when I was helping build her social media presence. "Head left a bit," she murmured. "The algorithm loves that angle on you."

"I'm not glowing," I protested, but even I could hear the lack of conviction in my voice. "It's just hot in here. Love you, girl, but your AC sucks."

My phone dinged with notifications. The content calendar I'd scheduled for a wellness brand was getting good engagement. My followers had jumped another thousand after that reel I posted about manifesting better friendships went viral. Ironic, considering my own friendship circle was currently giving me heartburn. The algorithm loved my chaos, even when it was artfully filtered and captioned with inspirational quotes. Being a social media manager and content creator meant I knew exactly how to package mess as authenticity. My greatest skill and my worst habit.

Cruz snorted from his perch on the spare styling chair. He'd been half-scrolling through his phone, half-eavesdropping, occasionally piping up with celebrity gossip nobody asked for. "Mm-hmm. And I'm just drinking this sparkling water because the bubbles are fascinating and not because I need something to do with my hands when everyone else is holding wine glasses." He tapped his fingers against the metal can.

I gave him a small nod, respecting the weight behind his comment.

"Don't you have somewhere to be?" I asked, raising an eyebrow. "Or are you just planning to ear hustle from that chair?"

Cruz clutched his chest like I'd stabbed him. "Betrayal! In my safe space! After I brought you both those vegan donuts nobody asked for!"

A laugh kicked up from somewhere inside me. Rusty, but real. When was the last time I'd laughed without thinking about it first? When was the last time anything had felt this...normal?

Cruz and Sakia bantered back and forth with the easy rhythm they'd perfected over the years. From Cruz's college boyfriend to his chosen sister, their transition from lovers to family had been smoother than Sakia's own transition years ago.

We became family to her and each other. That's what I loved about our little group. The way we all kept showing up for each other through every evolution, every change. Cruz's alcoholism, Sakia's transition, Tangi's single motherhood, Deena and Taj putting everyone through it. We've all taken turns being *the drama*. And every version of ourselves found acceptance around this weird little table we'd built.

"I'm doing better," I admitted, so quietly I wasn't sure Sakia would hear it over the music. She wound another curler around my loc, twisting it into place. "A tiny, microscopic bit. I think."

She nodded, her expression softening in the mirror. "I know."

"Don't you dare make it a thing," I warned, narrowing my eyes.

"Never," she replied, but the satisfaction in her smile was unmistakable.

I let my gaze drift back to my reflection. The woman looking back at me wasn't fixed. Nowhere close. But she wasn't drowning anymore either. And she had a kickass ponytail with curly locs spilling out everywhere to boot. For the first time in a good minute, my head was above water. I could breathe without each inhale feeling like fire.

I wasn't over Riley. That would take several lifetimes, another two cord-cutting sessions and possibly an exorcism. But I wasn't being consumed by her absence either. I wasn't using other women's bodies to try to forget hers. I wasn't filling every empty space with just enough noise to drown out my thoughts.

My spiritual advisor once told me that some souls recognize each other across lifetimes. Not soulmates, but twin flames, two halves of the same cosmic fire that find their way back to each other no matter how many worlds try to keep them apart. I didn't know what to do with that information, since we weren't together anymore and reunion looked like showing up to Riley's door with a

PowerPoint presentation titled 'Why I Deserve Another Chance.'

It wasn't much.

But it was something.

"And we're done," Sakia declared, stepping back to admire her handiwork. She held up a mirror to show me the back. Sun-bleached tips added natural highlights. "Perfect edges, if I do say so myself." She peeled off her gloves and reached for her phone, holding it up. "Quick story before you move? My followers have been DMing me for a tutorial on your protective style for weeks."

"Food," Cruz announced, already standing. "We need food immediately. My treat."

"*You* buying?" I raised an eyebrow, running my fingers lightly over my freshly twisted locs. "That's a first."

"Don't get used to it," he warned, but the smile didn't leave his face. "Consider it payment for letting me crash your hair therapy."

Sakia checked her watch. "I have time before my next client. Fusion Junction?"

"Is there anywhere else?" I stood, feeling oddly light despite the added weight on my head. Maybe it wasn't just the hair that felt settled into place.

"I'm starving," Cruz announced, stretching his arms dramatically over his head.

"And if I don't get one of Trang's bulgogi tacos in the next fifteen minutes, I might actually evaporate."

Sakia rolled her eyes and smiled but said nothing.

"You sure you have time?" I asked her, knowing her schedule was usually packed tighter than a subway car at rush hour.

"My two o'clock called to push back thirty minutes," she said, tucking her keys from her bag. "Besides, I need food that isn't eaten standing up for once."

I checked my angles in the mirror while Sakia cleaned up and Cruz went on about this week's crush. The DJ from the party. Sakia locked up her salon, flipping the sign to "BACK AT 2PM" as we stepped out into the Brooklyn afternoon. The sun hit different in Bed-Stuy—warmer somehow, like it was personally invested in the neighborhood.

Three blocks later, we pushed through the door of Fusion Junction, the corner café that had somehow become our unofficial meeting spot over the past year. The place was a culinary identity crisis in the best possible way—Cuban-Vietnamese-Korean mashups that shouldn't work but absolutely did. The mismatched chairs, potted herbs on every table, and salt shakers shaped like tiny animals gave it a chaotic coziness that matched my current mental state.

Not completely falling apart, but definitely not color-coordinated either.

We slid into our usual spot by the window. Cruz always took the chair facing the door, Sakia preferred the bench seat for her back, and I took whatever was left. The server, Mai, nodded at us without bothering with menus. She knew our orders by heart: Cruz's bulgogi tacos, Sakia's lemongrass chicken banh mi, and my Cuban rice bowl with extra plantain.

"So," Cruz said, drumming his fingers on the table while we waited, "are we going to talk about your hair emergency last week, or are we pretending that didn't happen?"

"We're definitely pretending that didn't happen," I replied, fiddling with the tiny succulent centerpiece. "Temporary insanity. Never to be discussed again."

What I didn't say: that at 2 AM, after three hours of scrolling through Riley's cousin's girlfriend's Instagram (rock bottom has sub-basements, apparently), I'd convinced myself that dyeing my locs purple would somehow solve all my problems. Thankfully, Sakia had talked me down from that particular ledge.

"Smart choice," Sakia murmured, taking a sip of her water. "Purple isn't your color, anyway."

"The disrespect," I gasped, but there was no heat behind it.

The weird thing was, I actually felt...okay. Not great, not even good necessarily, but not like I was constantly trying to outrun my own thoughts either. Something felt different. Lighter. Like maybe there was a door somewhere that wasn't completely sealed shut after all.

Mai arrived with our food, and we fell into our rhythm: Cruz stealing a piece of Sakia's pickled daikon, me grabbing one of his tacos in retaliation, Sakia pretending to be annoyed while secretly enjoying the chaos. Normal. It felt startlingly, blessedly normal.

My phone buzzed against the table, and I glanced down to see a group text from Dee and Taj flash across the screen: *Rehearsal Dinner Checklist!!!* with a row of flower and heart emojis. Gag.

I flipped my phone face-down without opening it. "Those two should be lucky I don't block them after the honeymoon."

Cruz snorted mid-bite. "Girl, don't tempt me. I already muted that thread."

"That emoji overdose was," Sakia paused, searching for the right amount of shade, "a bit violent, yeah."

I pushed my plantains around my bowl, gathering courage for what I wanted to say next. "I forgot to tell y'all. They knew Riley would be there," I said finally, the words coming out quieter than intended. "At the vendor meeting."

Sakia popped a carrot into her mouth. "Wait, that's how you saw her?"

I nodded, keeping my eyes on my food. "Deena begged me to sub for her because she got held up with a client. Ry—" I caught myself before the nickname slipped out completely. Old habits. Didn't have the right to use that anymore. "Riley was expecting Deena and got me instead."

"That's foul," Cruz said, his expression darkening. "They just threw you into it?"

"Mmhmm," I hummed, taking a bite to buy myself time. "We sat across from each other talking about floral arrangements and napkins like we weren't two people with history grenades in our laps."

Sakia's hand settled briefly on my wrist, a silent gesture of support. "How'd it end?" she asked softly.

I shrugged, aiming for casual and probably missing by miles. "She offered me a ride to the train. I got in."

A short silence fell over the table as they both processed this. Then Cruz's face split into a grin, clearly trying to lighten the mood. "So you're telling me the two of you, alone, in a car, and no one died?"

The corner of my mouth lifted. "I behaved. Mostly. I at least saved the mental breakdown for the ride back home. You would've been proud!"

Something shifted inside me when I said it—a flutter of something. Not hope exactly, but not despair either. The door between us had been closed for so long, but for a brief moment in that car, it had felt like maybe there was still a small crack of light underneath it.

I didn't dare say this out loud. Didn't dare acknowledge it, even to myself. But the feeling stuck around anyway, buzzing under my skin like I'd had too much caffeine.

Across the table, Sakia's eyes met mine. She didn't say anything, didn't ask the obvious follow-up questions, but I could tell she noticed. She always did. She just nodded once, the movement so slight I almost missed it, and returned to her sandwich.

The conversation ebbed into a comfortable silence, just the sounds of forks against plates and ice shifting in glasses. Sunlight sliced through the windows, turning Cruz's La Croix can into a disco ball on our table. I traced my finger through a puddle of condensation, drawing nothing in particular.

I felt...not good exactly, but not like I needed to jump out of my own skin either. Like maybe I could exist in the same universe as memories of Riley without immediately needing an escape hatch. Progress, I guess. The bar was in hell at this point.

"That's why you seem different today," Sakia observed quietly, her eyes doing that X-ray thing they did when she was trying to read beyond my bullshit.

I shrugged, poking at my food. "Just tired of being tired, you know?"

Cruz nodded like this was deep wisdom and not the spiritual Instagram caption it actually was. He took a long sip of his drink, then set it down with purpose, like he was about to drop knowledge.

"The universe is healing. Hallelujah," he announced dramatically. "Riley's been looking less, I don't know, stabby lately too."

My chopsticks froze midair. "What?"

"Yeah, ran into her at Tangi's birthday thing. She actually smiled when someone mentioned the wedding." He gestured vaguely with his taco. "Seems like maybe you're both finally in a better place, you know? Moving on and stuff. Didn't she start seeing that singer? What's her name, Shaye?"

The words hit me and my brain just...stalled, piling on top of each other. Riley. Seeing. Singer. Shaye.

My face went completely still. Not the fake blankness of regaining composure, but the absolute stillness of system failure. Like when your laptop freezes and you can almost hear the spinning wheel of death whirring inside it.

"She's seeing someone?" The words tasted like ash in my mouth. I swear, my entire spirit left the chat.

Cruz's expression shifted from casual to oh-shit in record time. "Wait—I thought you knew."

Sakia's eyes went wide, her hand shooting out to grip his wrist in warning, but it was too late. The damage was done.

I stared down at my plate, suddenly fascinated by the arrangement of my food. The soft, almost-calm feeling that had been following me around all day went poof, like it had never existed. In its place, the familiar cold settled back into my chest—the sensation of doors slamming shut, one after another, all the way down a long hallway.

Of course Riley had moved on. Of course she was kissing someone new, laughing with someone new, while I was over here constructing entire fantasy reconciliations based on a ten-minute car ride and some wedding napkin samples.

Not me taking crumbs and turning them into a whole feast.

Pathetic didn't begin to cover it.

My spiritual advisor always said the universe gives you exactly what you need to see, when you're ready to see it. Apparently, I'd been pulling Death and Wheel of Fortune cards for months. All that transformation and change bullshit. But somehow my deck conveniently forgot to show me the Tower first. You know, the card that means everything you thought was stable is about to come crashing the fuck down?

Classic cosmic oversight. Or maybe I'd just been shuffling wrong this whole time. Me and the cards were going to have a nice, long, one-way conversation about all the ways in which they failed me.

"I'm gonna go," I said, pushing my plate away and standing up in one fluid motion. My voice came out weirdly even, like it belonged to someone else entirely.

"Becks, I'm sorry," Cruz started, guilt splashed across his face. "I didn't—"

"It's fine." I was already gathering my things, movements quick and efficient from a lifetime of strategic exits. The old BG, sliding back into place like a perfectly fitted mask. "Totally fine. Just remembered I have a content shoot."

The lie rolled off my tongue, smooth as honey. A performance so natural even I almost believed it.

Sakia just stared at me, saying nothing, which told me everything about how badly I was hiding my reaction. When Sakia went quiet, things were dire. She'd always been the one who understood transformation, who recognized when someone was wearing a fake face. Before her transition, she'd spent years perfecting that same skill, pretending to be fine when she wasn't. Now she could easily clock anyone, including me.

"I'll text you later," I added, another lie I had no intention of following through on. I was damn near out the door, skin electric with the need to be anywhere but here.

The mask stayed firmly in place until I hit the sidewalk. Then the real work began. Holding it together long enough to get out of sight.

The cold hit me like a slap. February in Brooklyn. It was always that special kind of cold that seeps through layers, finds the gaps between scarf and collar, between glove and sleeve. Perfect weather for a complete emotional breakdown.

I walked fast, head down, hands shoved deep in my pockets. No destination in mind except *away*. Away from Sakia's concerned eyes. Away from Cruz's guilt-stricken face. Away from the image now seared into my brain of Riley with someone else.

Riley with Shaye. Even their names sounded good together. Probably made disgustingly cute couple hashtags. (Hashtag PerfectlyTuned) Probably had inside jokes already. Probably didn't have two years of wreckage between them.

My scalp throbbed where Sakia had twisted too tight, a dull ache that matched the one spreading through my chest. The sidewalk blurred beneath my feet. I refused to acknowledge the heat behind my eyes. Not tears. Just the cold. Just the wind.

Three blocks passed in a blur. Four. Five. I stopped keeping count, just kept moving. My phone buzzed in my pocket—once, twice, three times. Cruz apologizing, no doubt. Sakia checking in. I didn't look.

At the corner of Malcolm X and Greene, I paused at a red light, suddenly aware I was heading in the exact opposite direction of my apartment. I could turn around. Should turn around. Instead, I pulled out my phone.

The group chat from Deena and Taj sat unread at the top of my screen.

I stared at it, thumb hovering over the delete button. But I couldn't bring myself to do it. Not because I cared about napkin choices or centerpieces, but because deleting it felt like one more thing I'd be giving up. One more connection to a life that included Riley, even if only peripherally.

Pathetic.

I scrolled down instead, past the unread messages from Cruz that were already piling up (probably all variations of "OMG I'M SORRY" and "CALL ME"), straight to a thread I hadn't opened in months. My thumb hovered over it like it might actually burn me. Digital self-harm, thy name is BG.

It wasn't even a real conversation, just digital ghosts. Memory lane's greatest hits, curated by yours truly.

I stopped on a photo she'd sent me two birthdays ago, before everything imploded—the two of us at that little beer garden in Fort Greene with the string lights and vintage juke box. The one where they played nothing but 80s music and served those ridiculous giant pretzels I couldn't stop eating.

Her arm draped around my shoulders, my smile wider than I'd let myself smile in public these days. My face practically glowing, like I was lit from within instead of just tipsy on overpriced craft beer. Her caption: Birthday girl and her favorite human.

The light changed. I put my phone away without deleting anything. Some masochistic part of me wanted to keep it all, even if just to remind myself why moving on was necessary. Self-flagellation via Instagram. My spiritual advisor would have a field day with this one.

Before that, nothing but archives of better days. Inside jokes about her patients who couldn't say "subluxation" without mangling it. Late-night confessions about our families whispered into each other's necks.

Plans we never got to keep. That weekend trip to Montreal, the cooking class we signed up for, the playlist we were going to make for road trips. All of it preserved in digital amber like little time capsules of what could have been.

I stopped on the last photo from before everything fell apart. Riley half-asleep on my couch, hair wild, smile lazy, looking at the camera like she trusted the person behind it completely. Like she loved them. Like she thought I'd stay.

God, past-BG, you really messed this up, didn't you?

I walked the rest of the way home in a fog, noticing nothing, feeling everything. My body pushing on while my emotions had a full five-act Greek tragedy inside my chest.

The key stuck in my door lock as it always did when the temperature dropped, but I barely registered the familiar frustration. Didn't even do my usual jiggle-and-curse routine.

Inside, I tossed my keys on the table with a clatter that echoed through the empty apartment, kicked off my boots like they'd personally offended me, and sat on the couch without turning on a single light.

Just me and my feelings and the darkness. Name a more iconic trio. I'll wait.

Typing Dots

Riley

Second dates should feel like possibilities, not obligations. This one was neither.

The comedy club's doors swung shut behind us, sealing away the warmth and laughter as we stepped into the Harlem night. February air bit through my jacket, sharp and clean. Shaye pulled her coat tighter, her professional smile never wavering despite the sudden cold. Streetlights caught in her blonde hair, creating a soft halo effect that should have moved me. It didn't.

"That was fun," she said, her voice melodic and precise. Her laugh still echoed in my ears. "I don't think I've laughed that hard in months."

I nodded, scanning the street. "The second comedian was a plum fool." My breath clouded between us, dissipating into nothing. Traffic hummed three blocks over, the distant pulse of the city at night.

Shaye stepped closer, her perfume filling the space between us. Something expensive and sweet with spicy notes I couldn't identify. Nothing like the simple jasmine oil that still lingered in my memory like a stubborn ghost. She touched my arm lightly. "You're quiet tonight."

"Just processing," I replied, the lie smooth and automatic. I was processing, but not the comedy show. I was processing why I felt absolutely nothing as this gorgeous, successful woman stood before me, clearly interested. Why dinner had felt like an interview: her descriptions of her upcoming tour, the precise way she cut her food into equal portions, how she never once interrupted me. Everything calculated for maximum effect.

Everything I should want.

My car waited at the curb. I unlocked it with a beep that felt too loud in the quiet street. The headlights cut through light fog rolling in. "I'll drive you home."

"Such a gentlewoman," Shaye said, sliding into the passenger seat. Her movements were fluid, graceful. The streetlight caught the elegant line of her neck as she settled in, and for a brief moment, I wondered what it would be like to place a kiss there. Whether her skin would be warm or cool to the touch. Whether she'd sigh or hold her breath if my lips pressed against that perfect curve.

I circled to the driver's side, giving myself five more seconds in the cold to recalibrate. To remind myself that moving forward meant exactly this. new people, new patterns, new possibilities. The attraction was there, undeniable and physical. So why did it feel like working a stubborn knot?

I settled behind the wheel, the leather cold against my palms. The engine purred to life, heat beginning to flow through the vents.

Shaye reached down, fingers searching for the seat adjustment. "You must know some tall people."

My stomach tightened instantly, hands gripping the wheel until my knuckles whitened. Three weeks ago. BG in this same seat, her scent lingering long after she left the car. The memory came, unwelcome. Her longer locs, her intentional distance, the burning point of contact when our fingers had accidentally brushed over fabric swatches.

I gulped. "Sorry about that. Last passenger was...different."

"No problem," Shaye said lightly, settling back once she'd adjusted the seat. "So what'd you think of that bit about New York apartments?"

"Accurate." My responses shortened, each word measured and controlled.

Shaye laughed softly as she folded her scarf across her lap. "Reminds me of my first place when I moved here. Six-hundred square feet in Hell's Kitchen that cost more than my parents' mortgage payment. I could touch both walls of the bathroom at the same time."

"Two grand for a place you can't even put a king-sized bed in is a ripoff," I replied, the words absent. My mind cataloged the sensations around me. Temperature dropping outside, the radio playing something weird and instrumental that neither of us had chosen, the strange silence settling between us.

Not comfortable. Not uncomfortable. Just...there. Like placid water with nothing beneath the surface.

My fingers felt cold despite the heat now blowing steadily from the vents. I flexed them against the wheel, feeling the slight resistance, the necessary tension to maintain control. Shaye talked about the show, about some inside joke from the second comedian that I'd missed while lost in thought. I nodded at appropriate intervals, made the right sounds of agreement.

"Take the next left," she directed, pointing toward a tree-lined street of renovated brownstones. Expensive. Established. Perfect.

I signaled, turned, kept my eyes fixed on the road rather than on her profile illuminated by passing streetlights. Everything about this evening was correct. Dinner at a well-reviewed restaurant, tickets to a sold-out show, engaging conversation with a woman dudes would throw hands over, who laughed at my stupid, dry observations.

But it also felt like moving through quicksand.

I bit down as we approached her building. We pulled to the curb, shifted into park. The engine hummed, waiting for what came next—the expected end-of-date ritual that suddenly felt like trying to read sheet music in the dark.

She turned to say something else about the show, probably, but stopped mid-sentence. The way she looked at me changed. Slower, heavier, somehow, and I wasn't sure what I'd done to cause it.

"What?"

"You have really beautiful eyes," she said softly. "I've been wanting to tell you that all night."

The compliment threw me off my game, genuine and unguarded. Before I could overthink it, she leaned closer, and I found myself meeting her halfway. When our lips touched, it wasn't the careful, polite contact I'd expected. It was warm and sure and tasted faintly of the wine we'd shared. My hands found her waist instinctively, and she made a small sound against my mouth that flushed heat straight through me.

When we broke apart, I was breathing harder than I should have been.

"Okay," she said, slightly breathless herself. "That was...*not* what I expected when I agreed to this date."

"Good not-expected or bad not-expected?"

"Very good not-expected." Her thumb traced along my jawline, and I leaned into the touch before I could stop myself.

"Good," I said, and meant it completely.

Shaye's expression softened with a slow blink. The dim streetlight caught the curve of her lips as she smiled. "I had a nice time tonight." Her fingers found mine where they rested on the gear shift, warm and deliberate. "Would you—would you like to come up for a drink?"

The invitation hung between us, simple and clear. Her thumb traced across my knuckles, and warmth spread up my arm. No games, no uncertainty. And God, I had needs that had gone unfulfilled for too long. When was the last time I'd found pleasure from somewhere other than a toy?

This was just an honest question from someone who knew what she wanted. Someone whose touch was making my pulse quicken in ways I'd forgotten were possible. My mouth went dry. Everything in me should have said yes.

"I—" The word started to form. Yes. Such a small word. Three letters that would change everything.

My hand moved toward the door handle. Actually moved. My fingers brushed the cool metal, and for a split second I could see it all: walking up to her apartment, the soft click of her door closing behind us, me putting down the drink to pull her into my lap. Decision settling into certainty.

Six seconds of silence stretched between us. I counted each one, watching Shaye's body language shift. Fingers tapping once against her thigh, head tilting slightly, lips parting then closing. The moment extended too long, becoming its own presence in the small confines of my car.

"Yes," I said finally, my voice barely above a whisper.

Shaye's eyes brightened. She reached for her purse strap, gathering herself to get out.

But my hand was still frozen on the door handle. Still touching the button but not pushing. Something deep in me was pulling in the opposite direction, like a muscle in spasm.

The silence stretched. Ten seconds. Fifteen. My fingers didn't move. The door stayed closed. My throat did that annoying lock-up thing it does when I'm trying not to lie.

Something twisted in my chest, sudden and inexplicable. Here I was, about to go upstairs with someone who'd kissed me like she meant it, who wanted me, who was everything I should want. But it felt wrong, and I couldn't even explain why.

"Actually—" The word cracked on exit. "I can't."

My body had betrayed me before my mind could intervene. A subtle tensing, shoulders drawing up, breath catching. Small tells, barely perceptible, but Shaye missed nothing. Her expression shifted, retreating somewhere I couldn't follow. I clocked it.

"I'm not saying no," I said quickly, damage control kicking in. "I'm just—"

"Not quite there yet?" Shaye finished, her voice gentle but probing. She settled back into her seat, purse still in her lap.

The perceptiveness in her tone made me rub the back of my neck. I couldn't tell if she saw through me completely or was just reading my hesitation.

"Something like that," I admitted, my hands finding the wheel again, needing something solid to grip.

The confusion on her face was devastating. "Did I...did I misread what just happened? Because that kiss felt pretty mutual."

"No, you didn't misread anything." I ran a hand through my hair, searching for words. "You're amazing, Shaye. That's not the issue."

"Then what is?" Her voice was gentle but direct.

I stared at the steering wheel, trying to find an explanation that made sense. "I told you I can be guarded. Sometimes that means I need to take things slower than...than what just happened between us."

"Slower than a kiss goodnight?" There was amusement in her voice now, not hurt.

"Slower than going upstairs after a kiss like that." I met her eyes. "Because that wasn't just a goodnight kiss, and we both know it."

She tilted her head, considering. "No, it wasn't." A pause. "So what are you saying? That you want to pretend it didn't happen?"

"I'm saying I need to process it. Figure out where my head is before we..." I gestured vaguely toward her building. "Before we potentially complicate things."

"Yeah." Shaye was quiet for a moment, studying my face. "Okay. I can respect that. But Riley? Don't overthink this to death. Sometimes good chemistry is just good chemistry."

"Is that what this is?"

"You tell me." Shaye nodded, a brief smile that didn't quite reach her eyes. Then she leaned in, placing a soft kiss on my lips. I registered every aspect of the contact with clinical detachment. Light pressure, 2.5 seconds duration, warm but not hot, slightly sweet from her lip gloss. "Call me when you figure it out."

Relief flooded through me, followed immediately by guilt. I kept my face neutral, features arranged in the expression of mild disappointment I'd perfected in clinic when delivering less-than-ideal news. "Next time would be great."

She smiled again, but this time it felt like watching a curtain fall. "Would it be?"

The question caught me off guard. Direct. Challenging.

"Yes," I said, but even I could hear the uncertainty threading through the word.

"Good night, Riley."

"Good night, Shaye. Text me when you're inside safely."

She slipped out of the car gracefully, the cold rushing in to fill the space she'd vacated. I watched her walk to her door, wave without turning back.

I sat there for a long moment after she disappeared inside, my hand still resting on the door handle. Still feeling the ghost of that almost-decision, the after effects of what I'd nearly done.

And wondering why the hell I'd pulled back.

Taj would roast the hell out of me, call me a scary ass. And I'd deserve it.

Only when she disappeared into the building did I exhale, shoulders dropping, jaw unclenching. My forehead touched the steering wheel for just a moment, the contact cool and grounding. Then I straightened, shifted into drive, and pulled away from the curb, The mess of dirty February slush and salt splashed against my car. Not quite rock hard, not wet, either.

The universe had jokes. All of them at my expense.

Thursday night traffic moved with unusual fluidity, streets emptier than typical for just after ten. I followed the familiar route home on autopilot, mind categorizing and analyzing every moment of the evening, searching for the malfunction. The dinner where conversation flowed easily but predictably. The show where Shaye laughed freely while I recognized humor without feeling it. The invitation that should have thrilled me but left me cold.

What the hell was wrong with me?

Tangi's phone rang through the car speakers, the display lighting up with her name when she answered.

"You had better be calling from Shaye's bathroom and not driving home already." Tangi's voice filled the car, equal parts exasperation and concern.

"I'm driving," I confirmed, signaling for a lane change. "Date's over."

"Riley. It's barely ten o'clock. On a Thursday night. After a second date with a woman who looks like *that* and sings like that and clearly thinks you hung the moon. What happened?"

I adjusted the heat down a notch, suddenly too warm. "Nothing happened. It was fine. We had dinner, saw the show, I drove her home. Normal date stuff."

"Mm-hmm." The skepticism in those two syllables was palpable. "And?"

"And nothing. She invited me up, I declined, we said goodnight. End of story."

A dramatic sigh filled the speakers. "Why do you hate happiness?"

"I don't hate happiness," I protested, a defensive edge creeping into my voice. "I'm just taking it slow."

"Taking it slow is postponing sex until the third date. This is a funeral procession."

I focused on the road, watching headlights approach and fade in my peripheral vision. "It didn't feel right."

"Did she disrespect you? Say something offensive? Have terrible breath?"

"No, nothing like that. She was perfect."

"Perfect," Tangi repeated. "Perfect is bad now?"

"I didn't say that." My knuckles tightened around the steering wheel. "It just felt..." I searched for the right word, mouth slightly open, the heat of the car drying my lips. "Calculated. Like we were following a script written by someone else."

Tangi was quiet for a moment. "Okay, so maybe Shaye isn't the one. But you have to at least try, Riley. You can't measure every woman against—"

"*Don't.*" The word came out sharper than I intended. I softened my tone. "This isn't about her."

"Everything with you is about her," Tangi said, gentler now. "Has been for two years. And seeing her at that vendor meeting didn't help, did it?"

My stomach clenched at the mention. Three weeks, and still the memory of BG in my passenger seat remained sharper, more vivid than tonight's actual date. "I told you I don't want to talk about that."

"Yeah, well, sometimes what we want isn't what we need." A pause. "You know Taj is having us all over for Cruz's birthday dinner next week, right? The whole crew. Including her."

My chest tightened. "I have a thing."

"You don't even know what day it is."

"I have multiple things. Very busy."

Tangi's laugh was both fond and exasperated. "You can't avoid her forever, Riley.

Not with this wedding happening."

The light ahead turned yellow. I slowed to a stop, watching it change to red, feeling the gentle pressure of the brake beneath my foot. Control. Precision. Everything in its proper place, everything following the correct sequence. Yellow, red, green. Stop, wait, go.

Why couldn't my heart follow the same rules?

"I know," I said finally. "Just not yet."

"When, then?" Tangi pushed. "Because from where I'm sitting, you're stuck. Not moving forward, not going back. Just...idling."

The light turned green. I pressed the gas, the car moving forward into the intersection. "I'm handling it."

"Are you, though?" Her voice softened. "Riley, my day one, my ride or die. Love you like we're blood. But you're a whole mess. You're dating women you don't care about, working too much, and avoiding half your friends because they might mention your ex. That's not handling it. That's barely surviving."

I swallowed, focusing on the physical sensation of my throat working, the steady rhythm of my breathing. In, out. Controlled. Measured. "I'm fine."

"You're not," Tangi said simply. "And that's okay. But can you at least admit it to yourself?"

The truth of Tangi's words caught in my throat. "I'm trying."

"I know you are." Her voice softened. "But trying doesn't mean torturing yourself. You can't put your heart on airplane mode indefinitely."

Did everyone listen to that podcast? "I'm not—"

"You are," she interrupted. "And I get it. I do. But life's happening whether you engage with it or not."

I turned onto my street, the familiar row of brownstones coming into view. "What do you want me to do, Tangi? About everything?"

"I want you to come to dinner next week. I want you to try. Actually try, not this half-step dance you've been doing."

The car slid into my usual parking spot. I killed the engine but stayed seated, streetlights casting long shadows across the dashboard. "And if she's there?"

"Then you'll deal with it. Like an adult." I could hear the shrug in her voice. "You were lovers, now you're not. It happens. The world doesn't end."

Except it had. Two years ago, my world had imploded, leaving behind this hollow substitute. A life of self-imposed distances and measured emotions. Clinical. Safe.

"Tuesday at eight," Tangi continued. "Taj is making Escovitch fish. You damn near tried to run off with the platter last time."

"Fine," I conceded, too tired to argue further. "I'll be there. But tell Taj I want my own to-go platter."

"Your greedy ass." Her tone lightened. "And Ry? It's okay if you're not over her. But it's not okay to stop living because of it."

We said our goodnights, and I finally exited the car, winter air cutting straight through me. Inside, my townhouse greeted me with empty silence. I flipped on lights as I moved through the rooms, creating islands of warmth that never quite reached my core.

The routine unfolded automatically: keys on the hook, coat on the rack, shoes by the door. Each movement precise and mindless. I turned the shower to exactly 103 degrees, the temperature where the water felt hot without scalding. Steam filled the bathroom as I stripped off the day's clothes, tossing them on the bathroom carpet.

Under the water, I closed my eyes, letting it sluice over my shoulders, working out knots of tension that had formed during the date. My muscles loosened, but my mind remained locked. I mapped the familiar contours of my shower routine: shampoo, rinse, conditioner, body wash, rinse again. Every motion efficient even here in this private space.

I dried off methodically, wrapping my hair in a second towel. My face in the bathroom mirror looked tired, eyes shadowed. I washed away the last traces of makeup, brushed my teeth, applied moisturizer with mechanical efficiency. Sleep clothes came last. Soft pajama bottoms and an old T-shirt that felt gentle against my skin, a sensation registered but not fully experienced.

The house was warm, thermostat set at exactly 72 degrees, but didn't feel comforting. Everything in its place, nothing out of alignment. Perfect and hollow.

I sat on the edge of my bed, phone heavy in my hand. Before I could think better of it, I opened my thread with BG. Stared at the thread longer than made sense. The last message between us—something transactional about a book might as well have been from strangers. But we weren't strangers. Not really. Just something slightly worse.

I didn't want anything big. Just a crack in the wall.

My fingers moved before my brain could stop them.

Hope you're doing well. Delete.

Thinking about you. Delete.

How are things? Delete.

Finally, I just typed what I was actually thinking: *Had a date tonight. Kept thinking about you instead. Hope you're hap—*

I hit delete before I could finish *that* thought.

Hope vendor day didn't kill you. Good luck with everything.

I hit send. Not because I expected a reply, but because I needed to stop pretending I didn't care if one came. Watched the screen as if it might explode in my hands. The read receipt appeared. Then typing bubbles. One. Two.

The bubbles appeared and disappeared several times. Four, five, six times. I watched them like they held the secrets of the universe, willing something—anything—to come through. Each time they vanished, I felt a little more pathetic for staring at my phone like a teenager.

Finally, I set the phone down, face-down on the nightstand. My throat felt tight, like I'd swallowed something hard. I pulled my weighted blanket around my shoulders, but it didn't help. The warmth didn't penetrate. My body registered the increased pressure, the added heat, but comfort remained elusive.

I lay back against the pillows, staring at the ceiling. I'd driven home from a date with a beautiful woman to an empty bed in an empty house where nothing was out of place and nothing felt right. Two years of distance, and for what? So I could feel nothing about everyone but her?

Maybe she'd typed "I miss you" and deleted it. Maybe she'd typed my name and couldn't figure out what came after. Maybe she'd typed nothing at all, just stared at my message the way I was staring at the ceiling.

Tangi was right. I had put my heart on airplane mode. Disconnected from everything that might disturb my peace. And what did I have to show for it?

A text message sent into the void, typing bubbles that disappeared, and this persistent, relentless ache that I couldn't adjust away.

Not Exactly Hiding, But...

BG

Escovitch sauce dripped onto my fingers as I transferred the fish to the serving platter. The vinegar sting found a tiny paper cut I didn't know I had. I sucked in a breath through my teeth but kept going. Pain was something to focus on. Something real. Something not-Riley.

"More sauce, BG?" Taj asked, hovering beside me with the pot, steam rising between us like a fragile barrier.

"Sure," I said, voice bright enough to power a small city. "Drown it. You know Riley likes it extra saucy."

The words left my mouth before I could catch them. Seriously, brain? This is what we're doing now? Taj shot me a quick look that I pretended not to notice. I arranged another piece of fish, careful not to break it apart. So careful. Like the whole universe might implode if I pressed too hard. Like my sanity was directly connected to this fish's structural integrity.

Behind me, Deena arranged the plantains in a spiral pattern, her movements precise and nervous. The silence between us had weight. A month since the vendor meeting. A month of me saying "it's fine" when it was about as fine as a flaming dumpster. A month of them knowing exactly what they'd done.

"Becks," Deena said finally, her voice soft enough that only I could hear. "I'm sorry about the vendor thing. We should have told you."

I didn't turn around. My fingers kept working, arranging, fixing things that didn't need fixing. "Mmhmm." The universal sound *of I hear you but I'm not over it yet but I don't want to actually fight about it.*

"We thought—I don't know what we thought," she continued, guilt threading through her words. "Maybe that seeing each other would help somehow?"

I laughed, just once. Not bitter, not quite. Empty, maybe. "Help what exactly?"

Cruz's laughter exploded from the living room, followed by a chorus of responses. Someone made a joke about his age—probably Tangi. The warmth of it all should have pulled me in, but instead, I pressed my palms against the cool counter, anchoring myself to the kitchen. Earth to BG, kitchen to BG, fish to fingers, anything to stay present.

More laughter from the living room. Cruz doing his impression of someone. Probably his boss. The contrast between their joy and whatever was happening in this kitchen felt like two different planets. Jupiter and, like, whatever sad planet astronomers just discovered that's made entirely of tears and regret.

"You're both just so..." Deena trailed off, almost daring herself to finish the sentence.

"Broken?" I supplied, finally turning to face her. "Pathetic? Still hung up? Writing sad poetry in the Notes app at 3 AM?"

"Sad," she finished, eyes meeting mine. "You're both just so sad."

Something sharp and defensive rose up, but I swallowed it back down like a bitter pill without water. Instead, I put on my most dazzling smile. The one that always did the heavy lifting when my heart couldn't. The one I perfected in theater class and have been using ever since for every emotional emergency.

"Well, don't worry about my sad little heart tonight," I said, patting her arm. "I told myself this would happen eventually and she couldn't stay single forever. But knowing isn't the same as being ready." Understatement of the millennium, but whatever. I was coping. Kind of. In my own special BG way.

Deena's face softened with sympathy, and somehow that was worse than judgment. I turned back to the fish. Scooping more veg onto the fish. Taking it off. I needed something to do that didn't involve my fists pounding the counter.

"Is she bringing her?" I asked, the question barely audible over the sizzle of the batch of plantains Taj was frying.

A hesitation. "Yes. But they're not staying long. They have another thing after."

Of course they did. Riley and her perfect new life with her perfect new girlfriend who probably never ran from hard conversations or slept with other people to avoid feeling things.

I nodded as if this information didn't feel like swallowing broken glass. "Good to know."

The doorbell rang, and my whole body went still. My fingers froze mid-motion, a piece of fish suspended above the platter.

But it wasn't her. Not yet. Just Sakia arriving with dessert, her voice mixing with the others in greeting.

I exhaled slowly, hating how my heart was racing, hating how my body still reacted to even the possibility of Riley. Two years. Two years should be enough

123

time to get over someone.

For normal people, maybe. Not for me, apparently.

Taj squeezed my shoulder as she passed, a silent acknowledgment of what was coming. What we all knew was coming. I leaned into her touch for just a moment before straightening up.

"Just so you know," I said to both of them, my voice steadier than I felt, "I'm not mad at you guys anymore. Not really. But next time you decide to play matchmaker or whatever that was, maybe ask first?"

Their relief was palpable. Deena hugged me from behind, her chin resting on my shoulder.

"No more ambushes. Wedding vendor or otherwise. We've just had...a lot going on," she added, and something in her voice caught—not guilt, exactly. Something closer to exhaustion. Or maybe nerves. "Anyway, we handled it wrong. I know that."

I turned halfway, catching her profile. Her eyes were locked on the plantains like they held the answer to world peace. I filed it away as one more mystery I didn't have the time or the energy to solve tonight.

I nodded, allowing myself one moment of genuine softness before the performance began. Because that's what tonight would be—a performance. BG the unbothered. BG the over-it. BG the totally fine with seeing *the ex* with someone new.

The greatest role of my career, and the hardest audience I'd ever face was about to walk through that door.

I wiped my hands on a dish towel and stepped into the living room, remote in hand. The TV needed changing because Cruz had somehow landed on one of those cooking competition shows where everyone's yelling at each other while chefs race around a kitchen and try not to crash into each other. Not exactly birthday dinner vibes. More like "anxiety with side of garnish" vibes.

"Let me just..." I waved the remote vaguely, scrolling through the Music Choice channels. Something with a beat, but not too much. Background music. The kind that fills silence without demanding attention. Kind of like me tonight. Present but not demanding emotional labor from anyone. Look at me growing.

The knock came soft at first, then a little firmer. I froze mid-channel flip, my thumb hovering over the button like it was suspended in invisible jelly.

"Hey! Come in, come in!" Taj's voice from the entryway, bright and welcoming.

Then Riley's voice. Low, smooth, controlled. "Sorry we're late. Traffic was ridiculous."

And then another voice. Melodic. Confident. "Happy birthday, Cruz! These are for you." A pause. The rustle of gift bag paper. "Hope it's okay we stopped by. Riley's told me so much about everyone."

The way she said Riley's name. Like she'd been practicing it. Getting the cadence right. Like it belonged in her mouth.

My jaw clenched so hard I could practically hear my lower teeth screaming. I kept my back to the door, pretending intense focus on finding the reggaeton station. My pulse raced, a thundering in my ears that almost drowned out the introductions happening behind me. Heartbeat by Usain Bolt, srsly.

The vinegar from the fish clung to my skin despite the thorough hand-washing. Sharp, acidic. It filled my nostrils but couldn't cut through the wave of nausea rising from somewhere deep in my gut. I jabbed the button on the remote with more force than necessary. The plastic made a sad little cracking sound. RIP remote, another casualty of my emotional damage.

"And this is BG," Taj was saying, her voice pitched slightly higher than normal. Warning in her tone.

Riley and her were standing in the doorway now. I felt their presence without turning. My shoulders locked up, back going rigid like someone had replaced it with a steel rod overnight. Still facing the TV, I kept scrolling through music channels, pretending I hadn't heard.

What's that? Did someone say something? La la la, I can't hear you over the sound of me dissociating!

I took a breath. Reset my face. Swallowed the acid rising in my throat. My esophagus was probably developing trust issues at this point.

"Hi!" I might've jabbed the remote again with too much force. Maybe.

Riley brought her. Actually brought her. Here, where everyone would see them. Where I would see them. Where we'd all have to play the world's most uncomfortable game of "pretend everything's normal."

A twisted feeling kicked up. Something between hurt and a bitter kind of admiration. Riley wasn't hiding this one away. Not like she used to hide me when things got complicated. Well, look at you, growing and healing and bringing your new girlfriend to social functions. Gold star, Dr. Benson!

Before I could turn around, Taj appeared at my side, voice low enough that only I could hear.

"There's extra plantain in it for you if you help me in the kitchen?"

The lifeline. Thrown out just in time. My spiritual advisor would call this divine intervention. I call it Taj knowing exactly how close I am to a public meltdown.

I met her eyes, saw the guilt there, the silent apology. For a second, I considered telling her off, too. Making her feel just how badly this hurt. But pride wouldn't let me. And honestly? I was grateful for the escape route. My therapist would call this "healthy boundary setting." Ha. As if anything about me is healthy right now.

"You had me at plantain," I said, handing her the remote with a casual flourish that took every ounce of my acting skills. Where's my Oscar? My Tony? My "didn't break down in front of ex" participation trophy?

As we retreated to the kitchen, I heard Riley introducing Shaye to everyone else. Animated voices. Laughter. The easy way she slipped into our circle. Into the space that used to be mine.

In the kitchen, I busied myself monitoring the bammy, looking for the right moment to pull it out of the coconut milk. Another was ready to come out of the oil. My hands shook slightly, betraying me like the little traitors they were. I tucked them close to my body, hoping Taj wouldn't notice.

"It's just the heat from the kitchen," I muttered, more to myself than to her. Lying to myself. A skill I've perfected.

Taj didn't say anything, just handed me another tray to cover. The sympathy in her eyes was almost worse than if she'd called me out.

"The fish smells amazing," I said, desperate to fill the silence with something, anything other than what we both knew was happening.

"You don't have to do this, you know," Taj said quietly. "Stay in here all night."

I smoothed the foil with more force than necessary. "Do what? Help my friend on her fiancée's best friend's birthday? I'm being useful." My voice came out light, easy, like I wasn't hiding in a kitchen while my ex paraded her new girlfriend around.

Taj's hand covered my wrist, stopping the nervous folding. "Becks. I appreciate the help, but you're a guest."

I looked up, met her eyes, and for a second, let the mask slip. Let her see how much this was costing me.

"I know," I whispered. "But I need a minute, okay?"

She nodded, squeezed my hand once, then let go. "Take all the minutes you need. I'll run interference as long as I can."

"Taj, my hero. My emotional bouncer." I said, the sarcasm not quite hiding the genuine gratitude. "Extra plantain better not be a lie, though."

Taj's laugh was soft, relieved. "Have I ever lied about plantain?"

"No, but you lied about a vendor meeting," I said.

She hesitated, her hand still on my wrist, thumb brushing once like she was weighing something. Then: "There's been some stuff behind the scenes. Big stuff."

I opened my mouth to ask, but something in her face made me stop. Not sadness exactly. Just...full. Like she was carrying more than the room could hold.

"Tell me later?" I said.

"Later," she agreed, already pulling away. "Tonight's not the night."

Tonight was about surviving the next hour with minimal emotional damage.

I heard Riley's voice again, floating in from the living room. The easy charm she used in social settings. The fake laugh she held for colleagues.

I popped another piece out of the milk, feeling, the cool wet texture against my fingertips. Anything to ground myself in the moment. Anything to not think about what came next.

Because what came next was inevitable. Eventually, I'd have to leave this kitchen. Eventually, I'd have to say hello. Eventually, I'd have to look Riley in the eyes and pretend I was totally, completely fine with her moving on.

My hands continued their work, but my mind was already rehearsing the lines I'd need to say, the smile I'd need to wear, when that moment finally arrived.

I was flipping the last piece of bammy when I heard footsteps approaching the kitchen. Not Taj's quick, light steps. These were measured. Deliberate. I knew that walk before I even looked up. Could probably pick Riley's footsteps out of a crowded subway station blindfolded. Is that sad? That's probably sad. I rubbed my fingers quickly on a dishcloth as if to rub the sadness away.

"Cruz said my plate's in here?" Riley's voice, hesitant but calm.

I kept my eyes on the platter, making minute adjustments that weren't necessary. "Almost ready. Just finishing up." Just staging this fish like it's about to be photographed for a fancy food magazine instead of eaten by my ex and her date because I'm *definitely* not stalling.

"It smells amazing." A different voice—warm, melodic. Her. *Shaye.*

I heard Deena call from somewhere in the apartment, "Taj! Can you help me with this real quick?" And just like that, my buffer disappeared. The betrayal was swift and complete. Et tu, Taj? Et tu?

"Beckham," Riley said, her voice so painfully neutral it hurt. "This is Shaye."

Not BG. Not even Becks. Beckham. *Ouch.*

I turned slowly, plastering on my good-guest smile. The one I used at networking events and awkward family reunions. Not too happy, not too dim. Just right. Just fake enough. Performance BG, reporting for duty!

Shaye was even more stunning up close. Because of course she was. Golden waves of hair cascaded over her shoulders, and her smile was easy, confident. She wore a burgundy dress that hugged every curve perfectly, and her eyes—deep brown, keen with interest—studied me with a kind of friendly curiosity that made me want to crawl out of my skin and possibly the state.

I waved my hands around, making sure they didn't shake. "My hands are full of cassava, sorry. But, hi. Nice to finally meet you." Wow, I sound almost normal. Someone give me an Emmy.

Her hands fluttered for a moment until she folded them in front of her. "No, I understand. It's nice to meet you, too! I've heard so much about you."

I doubted that very much, but I nodded anyway. My eyes flickered briefly to Riley, who stood slightly behind Shaye, her expression unreadable. The eye contact lasted half a second before I looked away. Emotional hit and run.

"You've got good taste in fish," I said, gesturing to the platter. The words came out too bright, too friendly, like someone turned my personality up to eleven. "Taj saves this recipe for special occasions. Riley loves it, though. Extra scotch bonnet." Did I just tell her about Riley's fish preferences? Am I actually losing it?

Stop talking, Becks.

I motioned to Riley's fish platter at the same time Riley reached to pull back the foil, our fingers brushing for the briefest moment. The contact shot an electric jolt up my arm that I refused to acknowledge. Riley's eyes searched my face, looking for what, exactly? Hurt? Anger? Whatever it was, I wasn't giving it to

130

her.

"How'd you two meet?" I asked Shaye, deliberately not looking at Riley now. Keeping my focus on the safer target.

Riley shifted her weight, a tiny tell I recognized from years of knowing her. Discomfort. Good.

"On the app," Shaye began, her voice animated. "She mentioned seeing every episode of NCIS and she was fine as frog hair, so I couldn't resist saying hi—"

"Shaye's a singer," Riley interjected, the interruption slightly too quick. "With her own band."

I nodded, arranging my face into an expression of polite interest. "That's amazing. What kind of music?"

Before Shaye could answer, Taj reappeared in the doorway. "Shaye! I completely forgot to offer you a drink. What can I get you?"

Shaye turned toward Taj with a grateful smile. "I'd love a glass of wine, if you have it."

"Red or white?"

"White, please."

Taj gestured toward the living room. "Come with me, I'll show you our options."

Shaye touched Riley's arm lightly. "I'll be right back," she said, then turned to me. "It was really nice to meet you, Beckham."

As they left, her perfume lingered. Nothing like the essential oils I wore. Nothing like me at all. Maybe that was the point.

And like that, we were alone in the kitchen. Riley and me. The familiar stranger who knew all my secrets.

The kitchen fell silent after Shaye left. Just the soft hum of the refrigerator and distant laughter from the living room. I busied myself with cleaning my hands. Rearranging the already-perfect bammy platter, buying time. Delaying the inevitable. Classic BG avoidance technique #47.

Riley stood motionless across the counter, watching me work. The distance between us felt both vast and suffocating at the same time. Two feet of counter space. Two years of silence. Approximately five million unspoken words.

Her gaze pressed against my skin like a physical touch, leaving goosebumps. We're talking nerves lit up like a billboard, here. Like gravity had suddenly doubled, tripled.

I looked away to wipe invisible crumbs from the counter. Adjusted a serving spoon that didn't need adjusting. The seconds stretched, turned elastic and strange. Time doing that weird thing it does when you're trapped in emotional quicksand.

Riley's eyes dropped to the counter, tracing the marble veining like she was studying for a test. Riley shifted her weight, that tiny adjustment she made when she was bracing herself.

"Beckham—"

"The plantains turned out good," I cut in, not ready for whatever she was about to say. My voice did a weird thing. Too high. Too brittle. Like someone doing a bad impression of me. "Deena was worried they wouldn't."

Riley nodded, accepting the deflection. "They look perfect."

Another silence. Heavier this time. So heavy it pressed on my lungs, making each breath a conscious effort.

I looked up finally, allowing myself to really see her for the first time since she'd walked in. Her hair was different—shorter on the sides, the curls on top more defined. The kind of effortless style that actually took plenty of effort. She wore a deep blue button-down that brought out the warmth of her skin.

Her eyes that used to look at me like I was everything? Now they looked guarded. Like I was a potentially dangerous animal she wasn't sure would bite.

She looked good. Healthy. Rested in a way she hadn't when we were together. When I was putting her through the emotional wringer of my inability to commit, to be honest, to stay. When I was being peak BG—chaotic, intense, running when things got too real.

The realization landed like a stone in my stomach. No, not a stone. A whole damn boulder.

"She seems nice." The words tumbled out before I could stop them. "Shaye."

Riley rubbed the back of her neck, another tell I'd picked up. Like watching a documentary about a place you used to live. "She is."

I nodded, my fingers tracing the edge of the counter. "Her voice is amazing." I'd only heard a few words, but I could tell. Of course Riley would find someone with talent. With stability. With everything I lacked. With a whole musical family instead of my chaos.

"She's in a jazz band," Riley offered, almost apologetic. "They're pretty good."

"I bet." Two syllables carrying all my inadequacies.

The silence returned, stretched taut between us. So many words left unsaid they practically vibrated in the air. I could hear Shaye laughing in the other room, the sound musical and free. I wondered if she knew about me. About us. About how spectacularly I'd ruined the best thing I'd ever had.

I met Riley's eyes again, steadier this time. I'd rehearsed this moment in my head a dozen times since I'd heard about them. Rehearsed what I'd say, how I'd say it. The only way to survive it.

"She's good for you."

I said it lightly. Not with bitterness. Just even. Like an observation about the temperature. A simple truth.

Inside, something tore. A final ripping away of hope I hadn't even admitted I was still holding onto. It wasn't a blessing. It was a release—and it killed me.

Riley's expression flickered, something complicated passing across her features too quickly to read. Her lips parted slightly, like she was about to respond.

I didn't wait. Couldn't wait. I knew better than to look for hope in her answer.

I turned away, picking up the tray of bammy. "I should get these out there before the people revolt."

"Becks—"

And then I was moving, slipping past her, escaping the crushing weight of everything we weren't saying.

I played my part. Laughed at Cruz's jokes. Complimented Deena's plantains. Asked Sakia about her latest clients. All while running orbits around Riley and Shaye, never getting too close, never staying too far.

The performance was flawless. So many roles, I had managed to earn an EGOT in one night.

I was rinsing my hands in the kitchen when I heard Riley's voice.

"We should get going. Early day tomorrow."

I glanced up through the kitchen doorway, my hands still scrubbing away. Riley and Shaye stood by the front door, collecting their coats. Cruz was giving them each a hug, thanking them for coming. The casual farewell of friends who would see each other again soon.

I stayed where I was, watching from a distance. Not hovering. Lingering.

Riley reached for Shaye's coat, holding it open for her. A small, intimate gesture. As Shaye slipped her arms into the sleeves, Riley's hand grazed the small of her back, light and familiar.

Shaye didn't lean into the touch. Didn't acknowledge it at all.

The distance between them was subtle but unmistakable. Like two people playing the roles of a couple without quite believing in the script.

Shaye's smile remained in place as she buttoned her coat, but her eyes scanned Riley's face a little too carefully. Searching. There was an edge to Riley's voice as she made their excuses—the same professional tone she'd used at the vendor meeting. Polite. Controlled. Remote.

She was pulling away. But not from Shaye. From me. And she wasn't even looking back.

As they stepped out, I caught a final glimpse of them. That gap of space between their bodies. The stiffness in Riley's shoulders was sharp as a starched crease.

135

The questioning glance Shaye threw her way.

Then the door closed, and they were gone.

I stayed in the kitchen a little too long after that. Stole a few extra pieces of plantain, as was my given right. Wiped counters that were already clean.

Laughter rumbled from the living room where everyone else had gathered for dessert. Banana pudding. Blech.

It sounded distant, as if coming from another world entirely. I didn't join them. Couldn't join them. Not when every cell in my body was busy holding myself together.

Instead, I stared at my reflection in the dark window above the sink. The familiar stranger looking back at me. Party BG had left the building, leaving only the real me behind. The me that no one else got to see.

I let her go once. I told myself it was love. But this felt like grief. And I was still pretending she's the one who left. Still telling myself I did the right thing, because it meant she finally found someone right, someone better. Or, would. Someone who wasn't me. No amount of waving burning sage around like emotional Febreze would change that.

Still lying even when there's no one left to lie to but myself.

Not Exactly Leaving, But...

Riley

THE PARTY NOISE FADED like a tide going out.

Shaye walked beside me, our steps falling out of sync on the winter-slick pavement. Not even our footfalls matched tonight. The gap between us stretched wider than the six inches separating our shoulders.

I unlocked the car with a click, the beep cutting through the midnight stillness. Shaye slid into the passenger seat gracefully, settling in without brushing against the center console. The door closed with a soft thud that seemed too final.

My fingers flexed against the wheel. One, two, three points of pressure. The leather cool and smooth against my skin. I adjusted the temperature dial, clicked it twice to the right, a ritual to gather my thoughts. She folded her scarf into her lap.

"Cruz really seemed to enjoy himself," I said, reversing out of the parking spot, my voice deliberately light. Casual. Nothing to see here. "Especially after he found out Tangi made those stuffed mushrooms he kept going back for."

Shaye smiled—a small, polite curve of her lips that didn't reach her eyes. "He's sweet," she said, her fingers tracing her seat belt. Nothing more.

I tried again. "The food was good. Taj and Dee always goes overboard for these things." My words hung in the air, waiting for a response that barely came.

"Mmm." A noncommittal hum. Her gaze fixed on the passing streetlights, each one illuminating her profile in brief flashes before returning her to shadow.

The silence filled the car like water, rising inch by inch. I reached for the stereo, turning on something low and instrumental—jazz without words—then adjusted the volume until it was just loud enough to fill the space between us without demanding attention. The notes slid around us, a buffer against the quiet.

I drove with precision, taking turns at exactly the right angle, stopping at the perfect distance from each light. My hands steering while my mind raced ahead. The route to her apartment was familiar now, each landmark a checkpoint in a journey I'd memorized.

It wasn't a bad night. It couldn't have been. Everyone was kind. Shaye was fine. My friends were welcoming. So why did it feel like I couldn't breathe in that kitchen? Why did the air turn solid in my lungs every time BG's laugh echoed from the kitchen?

I hadn't expected her to stay. BG never stayed at gatherings these days, especially not ones I attended. She'd show up, make her presence known, then find a reason to slip away. But tonight, she'd lingered. Planted herself at the counter with Sakia, laughing too loud, gesturing with her hands the way she did when she was performing casual for an audience. I'd caught myself watching her movements from across the room, the way her shoulders tensed slightly when I entered a space, the deliberate way she kept her back to me.

Precise calibration of distance. Something we'd both become experts at.

"The light's green," Shaye said quietly, pulling me back to the present.

I eased forward, my foot finding the gas pedal with mechanical familiarity. The car moved smoothly into the intersection as if nothing had stuttered. As if my mind hadn't been elsewhere.

My diaphragm caught mid-breath, like my body didn't trust what came next. Noticed the way my chest expanded against the constraint of my seatbelt. It was little too tight for comfort.

A few blocks into the drive, the music shifted to something with piano, soft notes that punctuated the quiet rather than filling it. I adjusted the heat again, clicking it one notch higher. Outside, streetlights created rhythmic patterns across the dashboard. One, two, three. Dark, light, dark.

"Your friends were really welcoming," Shaye said finally, her voice breaking through the careful silence we'd constructed. She paused, fingernails scratching against her thigh. "Especially the ones who stayed in the kitchen all night."

My shoulders tensed slightly, a small adjustment only I could feel. I kept my eyes on the road, maintaining the exact speed limit.

"BG's...private," I said, the name feeling strange in my mouth. Too casual. Too familiar. "She doesn't really do groups."

My explanation sounded hollow even to me. BG loved groups. Thrived in them. Commanded attention in rooms full of strangers with that magnetic energy that pulled everyone into her orbit. It was one of the first things I'd noticed about her. How easily she filled spaces with her presence.

Shaye turned slightly in her seat, angling toward me. Her gaze felt a physical weight against my profile.

"She also didn't look at you all night." Her voice was calm but pointed. Not accusatory, just observant. As if she were simply noting the weather.

The truth of it hit like a blunt impact. My grip tightened on the wheel, knuckles whitening under the pressure. BG hadn't looked at me once. Not when I entered rooms. Not when I spoke. Not when I laughed at Tangi's stories. She'd done everything but physically leave to avoid acknowledging my existence.

And I had noticed. Every moment of it.

I swallowed, feeling the contraction of muscles in my throat. "It's complicated."

"Most things worth talking about are," Shaye replied, her voice softening slightly.

The silence that followed felt heavier than before. I watched the traffic light ahead change from green to yellow, slowing the car with precise timing before it turned red.

"I should have told you more," I admitted, keeping my eyes fixed on the intersection. "About BG. About...everything." The words felt strange in my mouth, like speaking a language I'd grown rusty with.

Shaye's gaze remained thoughtful, her expression difficult to read in the low light. "It was an interesting night," she said finally. Her tone was careful, measured in a way that reminded me of my own tendency to choose words precisely.

"I'm sorry if it was uncomfortable." The apology came out more stiffly than I intended.

"You don't need to apologize." She turned slightly toward me. "Just...I don't know, help me understand the room I was in tonight."

The light changed. I pressed the gas pedal with careful pressure, easing the car forward.

"The way people watched you two," she continued, her voice gentle. "Even when you were across the room from each other. It felt like everyone was holding their breath."

My fingers tightened around the steering wheel, knuckles pale against the dark leather. I could feel myself pulling back, the familiar urge to protect myself from exposure.

"I brought you." It came out more intensely than I'd planned. I modulated my tone, bringing it back under control. "I don't take that lightly. If I didn't want you there—if this didn't matter—I wouldn't have."

Shaye didn't argue. She looked down at her hands for a moment, then back up at the road ahead.

"I know," she said finally, her voice softening. "That's what makes this harder. Because I like you."

"I like you too," I said, the words feeling both true and insufficient at the same time. My hands adjusted on the wheel, finding the precise ten-and-two position. "That's why you were there tonight."

I paused, searching for the best words while focusing on the road with deliberate attention. A streetlight illuminated the interior of the car for a brief moment, highlighting the tension in Shaye's posture.

"I'm not—" I stopped, recalibrated. "I want this to work. I'm trying."

The admission cost me something, left me feeling exposed in a way I hadn't planned for. My jaw worked overtime, contracting with the effort of containing everything else I wasn't ready to say.

Instead, I focused on driving. Turn signal. Mirror check. Smooth left turn. Little touches to ground myself when emotions threatened to pull me out of alignment.

"She's important to you," Shaye observed simply. Not a question, not an accusation. Just a quiet statement of what she'd witnessed.

I nodded, a single controlled movement. "We have history."

"I can see that." Her voice held no judgment, just a gentle understanding that somehow felt worse than anger would have. "You know, I think I finally understand what you meant that day about needing to feel safe before revealing yourself." She paused, her breath fogging slightly in the cool car. "To truly understand you, I'd have to know her too, wouldn't I?"

My breath caught, a small hitch that betrayed more than I wanted. The car suddenly felt too small.

"You perform connection really well, but you don't actually let people in. The moment things get messy, you retreat into this...professional version of yourself. It's like dating a very polite wall."

"I—" My voice failed. I swallowed, tried again. Heat inched up my neck as I focused on the road with almost painful intensity.

Her observation landed with surgical precision, finding the exact center of something I hadn't fully acknowledged. But I didn't want it to be the end of the conversation. Or us.

My fingers flexed once on the wheel before returning to their proper position. I could sense her watching me, patient in her silence.

"There's truth in that," I finally said, the admission costing me something. "Maybe I do retreat when things get complicated. But I'm trying not to do that with you." I risked a quick glance in her direction. "Being here, having this conversation—that's me trying to stay present instead of running."

The admission hung between us, both a concession and a promise. Not denying the complication of BG, but not surrendering to it either.

We turned onto her street, rows of brownstones pressed together in the darkness. The familiarity of the route grounded me. Something concrete I could hold onto while everything else seemed to be shifting beneath my feet.

Instead of focusing on driving, I found my attention divided between the road and the weight of what remained unsaid between us. We pulled up to Shaye's brownstone, the streetlight casting long shadows across the steps leading to her door. I shifted into park, the car settling into stillness that matched the tension in the air.

I lingered, engine idling. Waiting. For what, I wasn't entirely sure.

Shaye unbuckled her seatbelt, the click sharp in the quiet car. She gathered her purse, movements deliberate and unhurried. I watched her hands, the way they moved with precision, trying to read intention in their path.

"Thank you for tonight," she said, turning toward me. Her voice was genuine, warm despite everything. "Really."

She leaned over—not across the center console like she usually would, but just enough to place a gentle kiss on my cheek. Brief. Chaste. The kind of kiss that closed a door rather than opened one.

I nodded, throat suddenly tight. "Of course."

No invitation upstairs. No suggestion of continuing the night. Just the quiet finality of a goodbye that felt heavier than usual.

I watched as she stepped out of the car, her figure illuminated briefly in the dome light before disappearing into shadow. She didn't look back as she climbed the steps to her building, keys already in hand.

The door closed behind her with a definitive click that carried even through the sealed car windows. I sat there, hands still on the wheel, not immediately pulling away. The engine hummed beneath me, a steady vibration I felt through my palms.

One minute passed. Two. I finally shifted into drive, easing away from the curb.

The drive home felt longer than usual, each traffic light an opportunity to think thoughts I'd been avoiding. Each stop sign a moment to breathe through the tension in my shoulders. I avoided my own reflection in the rearview mirror.

At home, I moved through my nighttime rituals, one after another. Clothes in the hamper. Face washed. Teeth brushed. Blinds closed with a definitive snap. The routine was comforting in its predictability, each movement exactly where it should be.

In bed, I reached for my phone. The screen's glow illuminated my face in the darkness. My finger hovered over the messaging app before tapping it open.

I scrolled to Shaye's name, but for just a second—just one stupid second—I hovered over BG's contact instead. Her name sat there like a dare I wasn't brave enough to take. Scrolled back to Shaye's contact, instead.

Thanks for tonight. You looked incredible, by the way. See you tomorrow.

I hit send before I could talk myself out of it, then set the phone on my night-stand. Face up. Volume on. The room settled into darkness around me, but sleep remained elusive, my mind replaying moments from the evening in high definition.

BG's laugh from the kitchen. The way she'd angled her body away whenever I entered a room. The way Shaye had carefully folded her scarf in the car, that precise little ritual she did every time, smoothing it, then folding it exactly in thirds. I'd never told her how endearing it was to find someone who liked order as much as I did. The careful distance she had maintained on the drive home.

My phone lit up. Nearly an hour had passed. I reached for it too quickly, the eagerness betraying something I wasn't ready to examine.

Thank you. Sleep well.

No emojis. No x. Just clean punctuation. The message sat on my screen, stark in its simplicity. I read it three times, looking for meaning in the spaces between the words.

The message felt smaller the longer I stared at it.

My finger paused over the keyboard. What would I even say? What could I possibly type that wouldn't unravel everything I'd spent two years carefully containing?

I closed the thread without typing anything, set my phone down, and turned over in bed. The sheets were cool against my skin. I counted my breaths. In for four. Hold for seven. Out for eight. A rhythm to force my body toward sleep when my mind refused to quiet.

It almost worked. Almost.

We're Not Doing This, Babes (We're Absolutely Doing This)

BG

I was late. Again.

But this time not because I was circling the block like a vulture eyeing roadkill. Look at me with my emotional growth, practically the poster child for therapy success. Progress?

Twenty minutes past the start time wasn't even that late by BG standards. The real reason for tonight's tardiness? I'd spent forty-five excruciating minutes perfecting my eyeliner wing, debating whether my pink pantsuit was trying too hard or not trying hard enough for Deena's bachelorette. Not to mention the half-day I spent making sure every detail in the space was perfect. Even tested a few lemon pepper fresh wings out of the kitchen for spice level.

Was I dressed for a corporate takeover or an Elle Woods cosplay? The jury was out. Hopefully gagging somewhere.

The fabric caught the glow of street lamps as I hovered outside Velvet & Amber, tugging my leather jacket tighter against the early March chill. My gold hoops swung against my cheeks, practically the only part of me not developing frost-bite.

"Okay, game plan." I muttered, digging through my clutch with increasingly frantic energy. I pulled the tiny bottle of jasmine oil out, my fingers immediately calming at the familiar shape. I dabbed it on my wrists, then a little behind my ears, at the base of my throat. The scent wrapped around me like an invisible cloak, my personal armor before walking into any room where I might need to perform.

Not that tonight was a performance. God, listen to me. This was for Deena. My best friend. The woman who'd seen me ugly-cry into a pint of ice cream while watching dog rescue videos at 3 AM and somehow still wanted me as her maid of honor.

"Just be a person," I whispered, my breath forming little clouds that disappeared instantly. "A normal, functioning adult person who doesn't make everything about her ex."

Since Cruz's birthday dinner—since seeing Riley with her—I'd been trying something new. Something my therapist called "emotional sobriety" but I called "not being a complete disaster for five consecutive minutes." No desperate hookups with women whose names I deliberately forgot by morning. No 2 AM deep-dives into Riley's cousin's Instagram, scrolling back 157 weeks to pictures where my arm might be just visible at the edge of a frame.

Instead, I'd been doing the unthinkable: feeling my feelings. Sitting with them like unwelcome house guests who refused to leave. It was uncomfortable as hell, but maybe I was getting better at it. Close enough to functional, anyway. Close enough to pass as human in low lighting.

And tonight wasn't about me or my growth or my broken heart. Tonight was about Deena—the countdown to her forever starting right here, right now, with overpriced cocktails and embarrassing games someone had probably ordered off Etsy. I adjusted my suit jacket, pinned my locs into curls, and stepped fully into the light—BG the Supportive Friend, reporting for duty.

"BG!" Deena squealed, rushing toward me with a glass of champagne sloshing dangerously in one hand. She threw her arms around me, the impact nearly sending liquid gold down my back. "You made it!"

"Missed you more!" I exclaimed, matching her energy and then raising it fifteen percent. Our old greeting ritual, perfected over years. I handed her the gift bag with an exaggerated wink. "Hide this one from your mom. Unless you want her to learn things about her future son-in-law that can't be unlearned."

The lounge was transformed—plush velvet booths circled an intimate dance floor, string lights dripping from exposed brick walls like someone had melted constellations against the backdrop. A tower of champagne glasses stood half-constructed on a central table, precarious in a way that felt metaphorical for my entire emotional state.

"Girl, look at this place!" I gestured widely, my voice lifting to that slightly higher register I used when I wanted to seem enthusiastic instead of terrified. "You've outdone yourself! You know I'm obsessed with these lights!"

Sakia caught my eye from across the room and raised her hand in greeting, busy arranging what looked like a photo backdrop with "Deena's Last Rodeo" spelled out in gold balloons.

"BG, help me convince my sister that we don't need an itinerary for a bachelorette party," Deena said, pulling me toward a woman I almost didn't recognize—same eyes as Deena but with a focused intensity that made me think of a kindergarten teacher who took no shit on the playground.

Wait—little Nia? Last time I'd seen her, she was a shy teenager hiding behind her textbooks whenever I crashed at Deena's parents' place during college breaks. Now she was grown, clutching a clipboard with her expression hovering between celebration and stress.

"The champagne toast is in twenty minutes, followed by gifts, then games. We're behind schedule already." She checked her Apple Watch with military precision.

"Time is just a construct, sis!" Deena laughed, already delightfully tipsy.

"Look at you, all grown up and organized," I said to Nia. "Last time I saw you, you were rocking braces and giving Deena attitude about borrowing her clothes."

Nia's professional demeanor cracked slightly. "And you were teaching me how to forge my mom's signature for permission slips."

"Life skills!" I defended, grinning wide enough that my cheeks immediately started protesting. "It's good to see you again. Those earrings are absolutely killing me!"

From across the room, I felt someone approaching with purpose. A woman with a bold red lip and confidence that radiated like heat appeared at my side, her gaze direct and unabashed as it traveled from my face down to my gold-tipped boots and back again.

"Oh my god, you're actually BG!" she exclaimed, eyes narrowed with recognition. "I follow your content—that series you did on manifesting with color psychology? Changed my life. I'm Yara." She extended her hand with a lingering touch that definitely wasn't professional. "Deena's told me so much about you, but she didn't mention how beautiful you look in person."

I accepted the compliment, though something about her directness made me blink. "Nice to meet you, Yara," I replied, slipping into the slightly more polished version of myself I used when someone was clearly interested. "Any friend of Deena's..."

"Yara was my roommate at NYU," Deena explained, giving me a look that screamed she's into you with the subtlety of a neon billboard.

"What can I say?" Yara leaned in slightly, her perfume expensive and intoxicating. "I have excellent taste." The way she looked at me made it clear she wasn't talking about social media content.

Great. Nothing like being hunted at a bachelorette party. Though I couldn't deny the little flutter of validation, that familiar itch to be wanted.

Just like that, I slipped into full BG mode. Taking over DJ duties from Deena's Spotify playlist, finding the perfect mix that had everyone nodding along within minutes. I pulled my phone from my pocket, made a show of silencing it and placing it face down on the table.

"I'm all yours tonight, ladies!" I announced, raising my glass in a toast. "To Deena—the most beautiful bride-to-be in Brooklyn. May your marriage be as perfect as your eyebrows!"

The champagne fizzed down my throat, bright and sharp, bubbles popping against my tongue. I was good at this. Being the BG everyone expected. Vibrant. Present. Holding the attention of the room like it was something I'd purchased and intended to keep.

An hour in, and the party had found its rhythm. I leaned against the bar, watching Deena open gifts with theatrical gasps and giggles, her happiness so genuine it made me ache with something between joy and envy. That unfiltered quality she had, the ability to feel things without immediately calculating how they looked to others.

My fingernails tapped against my glass, a nervous little percussion section only I could hear. I'd lost count of how many drinks I'd had. Enough that the edges of everything felt slightly softer, but not so many that I'd lost the hypervigilance that kept me constantly scanning the room.

"Tell us more about the final wedding details," Kayla prompted, passing around fresh drinks.

Deena launched into an animated description of the venue's floral arrangements. "And the rehearsal dinner is basically handled. Taj's uncle is catering, and Riley's putting together the playlist. She knows exactly what music my parents will tolerate while still being actually listenable."

The mention of Riley's name struck like a physical thing. A tiny pebble thrown at a window. Not enough to break the glass, but enough to make me flinch, a full-body response I tried to disguise by reaching for my drink. Too fast. Liquid sloshed over the rim, catching on my fingers. Cold and sticky.

"Riley has good taste in music," I said, the words out before I could stop them. My voice sounded normal to my own ears. Totes unbothered. "Remember that playlist she made for your birthday road trip? The one with those Jadakiss guest verses? Genius."

Girl, stop talking about that woman.

Deena's eyes flicked to mine, a momentary pause. A silent check-in. I gave her my brightest smile, the one I'd pulled out for moments exactly like this.

"You know what we need?" I said, pushing away from the bar with exaggerated enthusiasm. "Shots! Real ones, not those baby sips of champagne. Let's get this party properly started!" I flagged down the bartender, ordering a round of top-shelf tequila before anyone could object.

"None for me," Deena said, placing her hand over her glass. "Just seltzer with lime tonight."

I squinted at her, a moment of confusion flashing across my face. Deena never turned down tequila at celebrations. She caught my look and gave a small, almost imperceptible shake of her head. I didn't press it, filing the information away for later.

When the shots arrived, I raised mine high. "To Deena—who deserves every bit of happiness coming her way." I felt the words catch slightly, too sincere for comfort. A crack in the performance. "To finding your person and keeping them. To love that stays."

Did I just say that? About love that stays? Jesus, the irony was thick enough to spread on toast.

"To love!" the group echoed, glasses clinking while Deena raised her sparkling water with a smile.

The tequila burned a clean path down my throat, washing away Riley's name. I set the empty glass down, the sound sharp against the bar top.

My phone buzzed against the table where I'd left it. I didn't reach for it. Didn't even look directly at it. Growth, right?

"So," Yara's voice slid into my awareness, suddenly much closer than before. "Deena tells me you're some kind of creative genius."

Her eyes were the color of good bourbon, warm and intoxicating. The kind that promised a night of forgetting, of uncomplicated pleasure.

"Deena exaggerates," I replied, leaning slightly against the bar to create some space between us. "I just make pretty things on the internet for brands with too much money. Visual clickbait for corporate overlords trying to seem relatable."

"Don't believe her modesty," Deena called out, overhearing. "BG's an actual artist. You should see her personal work—the stuff she doesn't post."

Yara's eyebrow lifted, interest piqued. "Now that sounds intriguing."

"Less intriguing, more half-finished canvases collecting dust in my apartment," I deflected, though I felt a small pulse of pleasure at the interest. "My living room's basically a graveyard for abandoned creative projects. There's a half-finished sculpture of a woman that looks like she's melting. Very horror movie chic. Probably scares my neighbors when they look through the window."

My phone buzzed again. I kept my eyes on Yara, refusing to be distracted. Look at me, being present! My therapist would be so proud. Or concerned that I might be having a manic episode, hard to say.

"I'd love to see them sometime," Yara's voice dropped slightly, turning the innocent comment into something that sounded very much like an invitation.

"Maybe someday," I replied, noncommittal but not unkind. The flirtation was familiar territory, comfortable ground. "Only if you're very lucky and I'm very drunk."

Yara smiled, sensing the opening. She leaned in slightly. "I've always had a thing for artists. They see the world differently."

Once, I would have leaned right back. Would have fallen into the easy exchange of attraction. But tonight, it felt like my body was rejecting the script.

Instead, I picked up my refilled champagne flute. "To seeing the world differently, then."

Our glasses clinked, and Yara's eyes held mine a moment too long. The game was on, whether I wanted to play or not.

"Okay, okay!" Nia clapped her hands, gathering everyone's attention. "Game time, people!"

We arranged ourselves in a loose circle. Nia unveiled a glossy black box with "TRUTH OR DARE: BACHELORETTE EDITION" stamped in gold lettering.

"Nothing too scandalous," Deena warned, glancing at her sister. "Mom would literally appear in a puff of smoke if she knew we were playing anything inappropriate."

"Relax," Nia said, pulling out a stack of cards. "It's PG-13. Mostly."

The first few rounds were tame—innocent questions about first kisses and celebrity crushes, with occasional dares that involved chugging drinks or sending ridiculous texts to exes (which I smoothly avoided by offering to take a shot instead).

"I am not choosing between Aldis Hodge and Michael B. Jordan," Kayla said, cheeks flushed. "It's called 'Why Choose' for a reason. Look it up!"

"Preach!" I raised my glass in solidarity. "That's like asking if I prefer oxygen or water, hello! Both are necessary for survival, thank you very much." This earned a round of laughter, as I'd known it would. I was on a roll tonight, serving exactly the right amount of BG that everyone expected.

I was doing great, honestly. Keeping it light, making everything into a joke, deflecting on expert level. Classic BG. The center of attention without revealing anything real.

Deena had just finished demonstrating her surprisingly impressive twerking skills when Nia pulled the next card and looked directly at me. Her expression shifted to something that made my stomach drop.

"BG," she read, "What is your biggest relationship regret?"

The laughter quieted, everyone leaning forward with gleeful anticipation. I reached for my drink, buying a second to compose my thoughts, to prepare the performative answer they were expecting.

"Ooooh, I want to hear this," Deena said, her eyes sparkling with mischief.

But something shifted in me, a tiny crack in the façade I'd maintained all night. Maybe it was the way Deena was looking at me. Maybe it was the champagne. Or maybe I was just tired of wearing the mask.

"My biggest relationship regret," I repeated, rolling the words around like I was tasting something unfamiliar. "Thinking that loving someone loudly was the same as loving them well."

The words hung in the air, too honest for the frivolous game we were playing. Whole room's energy titled with the subtle realization that I'd gone off-script, or maybe that was just me. Who knows?

I quickly recovered, adding with a deliberate lightness, "Also, letting my ex organize my spice rack. Two years later and I still can't find the cumin without having an existential crisis. Like, who puts cinnamon next to cumin? A psychopath, that's who."

That earned the laugh I was looking for, breaking the momentary tension. Yara touched my arm, her fingers lingering. "Their loss," she said, as if it were that simple.

"Damn, that's deep though," Deena said, her expression softening. "I was expecting you to say something about that guy who wore socks during sex."

"Oh, that's still in the top five," I replied, grateful for the lifeline back to safer territory. "Along with anyone who referred to themselves as an 'entrepreneur' in their dating profile."

The conversation shifted, but I caught Sakia watching me from across the circle. Her eyes held a quiet understanding that made me look away first. She'd heard what I hadn't actually said. The regret behind the regret.

I loved Riley loudly—with grand gestures and passionate declarations—but I never loved her in a way that felt safe to me. Not in the quiet, consistent ways that mattered. I'd run when things got too real, then sabotaged because they got too good.

That first night she turned those eyes on me, I had made her chase me because I was too scared to stay put long enough to be caught.

Never braced myself for the day she stopped chasing.

"Enough about my tragic love life!" I announced, voice pitched just a little too high. "We're here to celebrate Deena finding someone who actually puts the toilet paper on the holder the right way!"

But something had shifted, a small truth escaping into the night that couldn't be recaptured.

Two hours in, and the bass of the music had shifted to something deeper, more insistent. The shots had done their work. Deena was dancing to Uncle Luke with abandon, and Yara's eyes kept finding mine across the space, a silent question I wasn't answering.

My skin felt electric, too sensitive inside my clothes. The room was spinning just enough that I had to concentrate on appearing sober.

"Bathroom break," I announced to no one in particular, grabbing my clutch and slipping away from the group. The truth was, I needed air. Space. A moment without eyes on me.

The bathroom was ridiculous in the best way. All art déco fixtures and mood lighting, with a velvet bench before a vanity that made everyone look like they belonged in a magazine spread.

"Okay, what the actual hell was that?" I whispered to myself, bracing my hands on the cool marble of the sink. Loving someone loudly isn't loving them well? What, are we auditioning for a greeting card company?

The mirror reflected someone both intimately familiar and strangely foreign. My makeup was still flawless, gold hoops catching the light as they swayed with my movement. But there was something different in my eyes. Something less frantic, maybe. The desperate edge that had been there since Riley—since we ended—had softened into something more like resignation. Or acceptance. Or maybe just exhaustion.

Should've been home vibing out with a charcuterie board, a dry red, and Kate Bush instead. But here we were.

Two years. Two years of pretending I was fine, of hookups that left me emptier than before, of avoiding places where I might run into her. Two years of constructing a version of myself that could survive in a world where Riley Benson was no longer mine.

What was my grand reward for all that effort? A growing social media following who thought I had my shit together. A perfectly curated feed full of aesthetic coffee placements and manifestation techniques I only half-believed in.

Before I could punk out, I pulled out my phone. The last thread with Riley sat untouched for months. Some perfunctory exchange about returning some book she'd left at my place, followed by the text from last week. My half-typed answer, abandoned.

I erased the lie, fingers hovering over the keyboard, heart racing like I was about to jump off a cliff.

I saw you with her. You looked happy.

I stared at the words, then kept typing, my fingers moving almost without my permission.

I want that for you. I just didn't think it would hurt this much when it happened.

My thumb hovered just over the send button, the blue arrow suddenly the most terrifying thing in the world. What was I doing? What could this possibly accomplish except dragging us both back into the mess we'd finally started to climb out of?

Two years of near-misses, of choreographed avoidance, of mutual friends running interference. Two years of healing, slowly and painfully. And I was about to undo all of it with one drunk text from a bathroom at a bachelorette party?

"Classic BG," I muttered, watching my own reflection as I considered pressing send. That scared look creeping back into my eyes, the slight wobble in my jaw I refused to let have the floor. This wasn't growth. This was the same old pattern, just with fancier packaging and better lighting.

But maybe that's what I needed. Maybe the clean break wasn't working. Maybe we needed one more messy moment to finally let go. One more truth between us before I could finally stop scanning rooms for her silhouette.

A flash of memory hit me. Riley's hands cradling my face outside that dive bar in Bushwick, rain soaking us both. Her eyes locked with mine, a smile playing at the corner of her mouth. "Worth the wait," she'd murmured, just before her lips found mine. The certainty in her voice had made my knees weak, like she'd just unlocked something I'd kept hidden even from myself.

When we broke apart, I kept my forehead pressed to hers, both of us breathing hard. "Took you long enough," I managed, trying for teasing but landing somewhere closer to wonder.

"I was being careful," she admitted, and the way her voice went soft on those words made me melt a little. Okay, a lot. Truth is, I was gone the moment she joked about not color-coordinating her study notes to save face in front of me. A whole tall glass of fine with that handsome face, those eyes, perfect teeth, and had the nerve to be smart. Had me down bad from jump, even if I didn't want to admit it at the time.

"Careful's overrated," I had said, and kissed her again because I could, because she was finally letting me, because three months of crushing hard had built up like pressure in my chest and now it could finally find release.

I blinked how right we had felt in that moment.

And then I pressed send.

The whoosh of the message leaving my phone made everything inside me freeze, and instantly, I knew I'd made a mistake. Shit. Shit, shit, *shit*. My cheeks burned as I stared at what I'd done.

"What the fuck, Becks? What the actual fuck?" I whispered.

I couldn't bear to watch for her response. Couldn't stand to see those three dots appear, knowing Riley was on the other end, reading my vulnerability, formulating a reply. What would she even say? "Thanks for the update on your emotional state, but I'm very happy with Shaye now"? Or worse, nothing at all?

With shaking fingers, I switched the phone to airplane mode—a childish panic move, but effective. Whatever Riley might say in response would have to wait until I was ready to see it. Which might be never. Or at least until I was sober enough to handle it without a complete meltdown in this fancy bathroom.

I shoved the phone in my pocket, heart punching hard against my chest like it was trying to escape my chest altogether. What had I expected? That she'd confess she was miserable with Shaye? That she'd been waiting for me to reach out? That two years would just dissolve because I had a moment of champagne-fueled honesty?

I grabbed my lip gloss from my clutch, the expensive one with the subtle gold shimmer that made me feel put-together even when I wasn't. Applied it carefully, focusing on the simple ritual to ground myself. The familiar scent of vanilla, the slight stickiness against my lips.

Then I looked myself in the eyes again and practiced my smile. Not the dazzling, room-commanding one I'd worn all night. Something quieter. Something that acknowledged what I'd just done without surrendering to the panic.

Great job, Becks. Really nailing this growth thing.

I gathered my things, tugged the hem of my suit, checked my hair one last time. Then I stepped back out into the noise and light of the party. Back to Deena's celebration. Back to pretending I hadn't let my feelings borrow my phone and send that goddamn text.

My phone stayed in airplane mode in my clutch. Whatever Riley's response might be—or worse, her silence—I couldn't face it tonight. Tonight was for Deena. Tonight was for proving I could still function in the world.

Tomorrow would be soon enough to deal with the consequences of my midnight confession. Or maybe next week. Or never.

Never was looking pretty good right about now.

And the Academy Award for Most Spectacular Relapse goes to Beckham Grace Adams, for her groundbreaking performance in *Drunk Texts from the Bathroom.*

Thirty Seconds

Riley

THE WEDDING INDUSTRY DESIGNED rehearsals to eliminate surprises.

They missed a few.

I arrived at the rehearsal thirty minutes early, parking behind the converted warehouse where Dee and Taj would exchange vows tomorrow. Late afternoon sun washed the brick façade in honey-gold light. Spring finally trying to show up after ghosting us all winter.

This was the last of my duties this week: Help Taj with the sound system. Stand where they tell me to stand. Smile when appropriate. One more day of keeping my composure, then I'd be free from the exhausting vigilance of being in the same room as BG.

Inside, transformation was underway: exposed brick walls softened by gauzy fabric, industrial beams wrapped in lights, copper accents gleaming against coral arrangements. Taj waved me over to help fine-tune the speaker placement—a welcome distraction that occupied fifteen minutes of technical problem-solving before the coordinator approached.

"Dr. Benson? Perfect timing." She extended her hand. "Vanessa Kim, day-of coordinator. I need to go over the processional with you." She swiped through her iPad. "You'll be walking with Sakia, and Beckham Grace is with Cruz." She showed me my position on the diagram.

"Great," I said, studying the layout. Perfect arrangement. Maximum distance from BG throughout the ceremony.

Sakia entered, her smile widening as she spotted me. "There's my walking buddy," she said. "Ready for our runway moment tomorrow?"

Before I could respond, movement by the entrance caught my attention. BG stepped through the doorway in emerald pants and a silk blouse. Her eyes scanned the room before landing on me. Something flickered across her face before she shifted into easy grace and bright energy.

She moved through the space dispensing hugs and kisses to everyone she passed. Her laughter carried across the room as she embraced Deena.

"You okay?" Sakia asked quietly.

"Fine," I replied automatically. "Just been a long week."

Across the room, BG approached Cruz, her smile never faltering. "Looks like you're stuck with me," she said, loud enough to carry. Her laugh sounded perfectly genuine unless you knew her *before*—knew the slight strain around her eyes.

The rehearsal began in earnest, with Vanessa herding everyone into position. For the next hour, I occupied the same physical space as BG without direct interaction. A choreography of avoidance that required constant awareness of her location.

"No, no," Vanessa called out, halting our procession rehearsal. She consulted her iPad with a frown. "This is per the final instructions from Deena. She wants to mix things up for the recessional." She looked up. "After the ceremony, the couple exits first, followed by the parents, then the wedding party pairs need to be arm-in-arm."

She pointed to me, then to BG. "For balance in the photos, we'll have Dr. Benson with Beckham Grace, then Cruz with Sakia."

My mouth went dry. "I thought—"

"Just for the recessional," Vanessa clarified, already moving on. "Different from the processional pairings. Deena wants variety in the album."

I tried to catch Deena's eyes from across the room, but she made herself busy smoothing out her dress.

"Places, everyone!" Vanessa clapped her hands. "From the top of the recessional."

I moved woodenly to BG's side. She didn't look directly at me as she offered her arm.

"Hey, Ry," she murmured, the old nickname slipping out.

When my fingers brushed against her bare forearm, her breath caught audibly. Her skin was warm beneath my touch, jasmine oil clinging to her pulse points. I focused on breathing normally as we waited for our cue.

"And...go!" Vanessa directed.

The newly minted Muhammads went first, radiant with excitement. Then the parents. Then us. My fingers tightened involuntarily around BG's arm as we stepped forward, our strides automatically syncing from years of walking side by side. The muscle memory was instant and overwhelming. Our bodies still knew exactly how to move together.

Her pulse thrummed beneath my fingertips. Or maybe it was my own.

The moment we reached the end of our marked path, I dropped her arm as if burned, flexing my fingers to shake off the lingering warmth. I caught Sakia's eyes as she approached with Cruz, her expression soft with understanding. She squeezed my shoulder once as she passed—an acknowledgment requiring no response.

When Vanessa finally released us to the rehearsal dinner, I exhaled for what felt like the first time in an hour. Twenty-four more hours. That's all I had to survive. Then we could go back to not being in each other's space all the time. Back to pretending the other didn't exist except in the stories our friends were too cautious to tell. Back to normal.

Except normal had never felt so hollow.

I pushed the thought away. One more day. I could handle one more day.

The hotel room door shut behind me, and I slumped against it, the blank mask falling away. For several seconds, I breathed, eyes closed, letting the air conditioning hit my flushed skin.

Thirty seconds. That's all it had been—thirty seconds of BG's arm linked with mine. What was thirty seconds when we had years behind us? Apparently everything. That's what I'd forgotten. How BG's intensity could collapse time, make a moment feel infinite and devastating all at once.

The nerves in my hand were still firing like they hadn't gotten the message: we weren't doing this anymore.

I pushed away from the door and headed straight for the shower, twisting the knob with force. While waiting for the water to heat, I methodically folded my clothes despite the tremor in my hands. Control what you can control. I'd repeated that through two years of rebuilding myself.

The shower's heat enveloped me, but my mind replayed the rehearsal on loop: BG's skin against mine, our steps automatically synchronizing, her casual "Hey, Ry" as if two years of mutual avoidance could be dismissed so easily.

I adjusted the temperature dial until it stung my skin. The physical discomfort gave me something else to focus on. Something present.

Fifteen minutes later, I emerged wrapped in the hotel's robe, skin pink from the heat. The rehearsal dinner would start soon. I needed to armor myself with whatever passed for poise. One more night, then the wedding, then I could return to my life where BG was just a name I no longer mentioned.

My phone lay face-down on the nightstand. I picked it up, checking the time.

The message notification sat there like a splinter under my skin—BG's text from the night of Deena's bachelorette party. I'd read it a dozen times, but never responded.

My jaw clenched as I read it for the sixteenth time. The audacity of BG to play the victim after everything.

I opened my Notes app, scrolling through the graveyard of draft responses I'd written and deleted:

"You don't get to feel hurt about me moving on."

"Did you mean it? That you want me to be happy?"

"What did you expect after what you did?"

"Miss you."

"Two years is a long time to suddenly care about my happiness."

"We're not doing this, Beckham."

I let my thumb hover over the last one. The simplest. The truest. We weren't doing this. Reopening old wounds wouldn't help either of us.

A text yanked me back to the present. Tangi: *Where are you hiding? Dinner in 20 and Deena's freaking about the seating chart.*

I set the phone down, moving to the closet where I'd hung my dinner outfit—tailored black slacks and a slim-cut button-down with subtle copper threading. Nothing flashy. Just elegant enough for the occasion.

My fingers moved through the familiar motions: moisturizer applied with precise strokes, a quick pass of the trimmer to neaten my short fade. I ran styling product through my tight curls, ensuring everything lay perfectly without looking deliberate. I added my grandfather's watch and the silver cuff Deena had given me years ago.

Each step was a ritual. With every layer, I became more Dr. Riley Benson and less the woman who had once loved BG with a rawness that still frightened me.

When fully dressed, I checked my reflection. Only I could see the hairline fractures in my composed façade.

I slipped my phone into my pocket and left the room. The elevator carried me down to the parking garage. One more moment of privacy before facing the night ahead.

Sliding into the driver's seat, I gripped the steering wheel until my palms burned.

The dinner was just blocks away. I could do this. I would do this. For Taj and Deena. For our friendship. For my own pride.

I started the engine but didn't drive. Instead, I focused on the cool leather beneath my fingertips, the motor's hum, the muted sounds of other cars.

Twenty-four more hours. Then I could put this—put her—behind me once and for all.

If only I could convince my racing heart to believe it.

I arrived at the restaurant precisely on time. 7:00 PM, not a minute earlier or later. Early would risk solo encounters; late would draw unwanted attention. The private dining room glowed with amber light, walls adorned with vintage botanical prints that seemed to breathe against the exposed brick. The tables formed a lazy U-shape, with Taj and Dee positioned at the center like royalty holding court.

My eyes automatically scanned the room, cataloging positions, identifying the safest path. BG was already seated on the far side, deep in conversation with Cruz. Perfect. I'd take the empty seat at the opposite end, maintaining maximum distance while still fulfilling my obligations as a friend.

"Dr. B!" she called, gesturing emphatically. Her tailored suit fit perfectly across her broad shoulders, the burgundy color bringing out the warmth in her complexion. "You're here by Tangi and Sakia."

She pointed to the vacant seat diagonal from where BG sat—close enough that I'd be able to hear her laugh, smell her perfume, catch every familiar gesture from the corner of my eye.

"I thought I'd sit down there," I began, nodding toward my intended sanctuary.

"No way," Taj insisted. "We need our core crew together. My mom's already asked me three times if you're bringing a date. I need you close to run interference."

The genuine plea in her eyes made refusal impossible. "Fine," I conceded, "but you owe me."

"Always," she agreed, squeezing my shoulder before returning to Deena's side.

I approached my assigned seat with the neutrality of a diplomat entering contested territory. Tangi was already there, glass of red wine in hand.

"Look who finally showed up," she said, embracing me tightly. "You're doing amazing, honey. So proud of you," she whispered.

The sincere encouragement threatened to crack something inside me. I pulled back quickly, settling into my chair.

"How's the wine?" I asked, deflecting.

"Necessary," Tangi replied, taking another sip. "Unlike you, I don't have the superpower of turning feelings into stomach ulcers."

I reached for the water pitcher, pouring myself a glass, letting the simple action ground me. "I don't know what you're talking about."

Across the table, BG laughed at something Cruz said, the sound oddly muted compared to her usual boisterous self. She wore a royal blue wrap dress, gold accents at her ears and throat. She raised her glass—sparkling water with lime, not her usual cocktail—and took a delicate sip.

I noted the choice with mild surprise. BG had always been the first to order something colorful and potent at social gatherings.

"Sure you don't," Tangi muttered, rolling her eyes.

Three years next month," Cruz was saying, pride evident in his voice. "Best decision I ever made."

"That's amazing," BG replied, her smile genuine. "Seriously, I'm impressed as hell."

Her nails were shorter than she used to wear them, painted a subtle shade that complemented her outfit rather than the bold colors she'd once favored.

Tiny changes. Evidence of her life going on without me.

"That color on you, Becks," Tangi remarked, raising her glass slightly. "Unfair to the rest of us."

BG's laugh was smooth. "Just something I had in the back of my closet."

"It's stunning," Tangi continued, ignoring my warning glance. She tilted her head toward me. "Don't you think, Ry?"

BG tried to turn her face away before it turned red. Too late.

Before I could respond, Nia saved me by announcing it was time for appetizers. The moment passed, but Tangi's half-smile made it clear she wasn't done making trouble.

Throughout the first course, I maintained focus on the conversations around me, contributing appropriately without drawing attention. I commented on the catering choices, asked Deena's father about his garden, discussed an upcoming medical conference with the guy Sakia was seeing. All while acutely aware of BG's presence across the table.

Halfway through the main course, Tangi clinked her glass with her fork, silencing the room. She was visibly tipsy now, cheeks flushed, eyes half-lidded. She told stories about her and Taj getting into shenanigans as kids and managed to include a story their mom wagged her finger about.

She was doing the same thing. Being pleasant, engaged, present without being conspicuous. Our eyes never met directly, though I felt her awareness of me in the way she angled her body slightly away, her typically animated gestures now restrained.

"I'd like to make a toast," she announced, rising unsteadily. "To Deena and my big sis, Taj, who found each other and were smart enough to hold on." She raised her glass higher. "And to finding your person, even when you're both too stubborn to admit it."

Sakia coughed loudly, covering the awkward silence. "To Deena and Taj," she echoed firmly, redirecting attention to the couple.

"To Deena and Taj," everyone repeated, glasses raised.

I took a long sip of water, focusing on the cool liquid against my throat rather than the flush creeping up my neck. Across the table, BG studied her water glass with intense concentration, running her finger around the rim as if trying to coax music from it.

When I looked up, I found Taj watching me with sympathetic eyes. She leaned over to whisper something to Tangi, who sighed and handed her car keys. Taj promptly passed them to me with a meaningful look.

"She's staying at your hotel," she murmured. "Maybe after dessert?"

I nodded, grateful for the excuse to leave early. "Not a problem."

As the plates were cleared, Deena announced it was time for toasts from the wedding party. BG stood first, smoothing her dress with fluttery hands. I told myself I wouldn't watch her. I'd study my water glass, my napkin, anything else.

I failed immediately.

"Dee and Taj," BG began, her voice carrying that familiar warmth that always drew people in. "You two have taught me what real partnership looks like."

I meant to look away. Planned to. But something in her tone held me captive. She'd always been beautiful, but tonight there was something about her. I couldn't look away.

"Love isn't just the grand gestures," she continued, her smile widening. "It's showing up, day after day. It's choosing each other when the shine wears off and the real work begins. Like when Taj leaves her protein shaker in the sink for the fifth time that week, or when Deena rearranges the bookshelf by color instead of author and then can't find anything for a month."

Laughter rippled around the table and BG pointed at them both. Taj protested good-naturedly while Deena threw her napkin across the table with a "That was ONE time!"

BG's eyes stayed carefully away from mine as she spoke of commitment, of forgiveness, of building something that lasts.That intensity in her voice, even now. Even talking about someone else's relationship. BG never did anything halfway. Not love, not loss, not hope. Not us.

"What I admire most about you two," she said, her glass catching the light, "is how you fight—which sounds weird, I know. But you fight fair. You fight to understand, not to win. You taught me that conflict isn't the end of something.

Sometimes it's just the beginning of something better."

Her voice caught on those last words, the slight tremor unmistakable. She paused, hand briefly over her heart before continuing. "To Deena and Taj. Y'all make love look easy even when we all know it isn't. May your biggest fights always end with both of you forgetting what you were mad about in the first place."

Cheers and laughter erupted as everyone raised their glasses. I lifted mine automatically, my gaze still fixed on her face, catching the moment of vulnerability before her radiant smile returned.

Only then did I realize I'd forgotten to breathe.

The dessert course passed in a blur of chocolate mousse and coffee. Tangi grew progressively louder, telling increasingly embarrassing work stories with Deena until Taj caught my eye. I took the raised eyebrow to mean *get my sister out of here.*

"I should get her back to the hotel before she starts telling more childhood stories," I announced, standing and gathering my clutch. "T, come on. Time to go."

"I'm not even drunk," she protested unconvincingly, even as she allowed me to help her up.

I made my goodbyes, making deliberate eye contact with everyone—Deena, Taj, Sakia, Cruz, the parents—everyone except BG. I couldn't risk meeting those eyes. They said too much.

As I guided Tangi toward the exit, I noticed BG watching me intently. She half-rose from her seat, her expression shifting to something more vulnerable than she'd allowed all night. A look I recognized from years ago—the one that meant she had something important to say. Something that might crack the careful walls we'd both constructed.

Our eyes met for two pounding heartbeats. I couldn't move. Her gaze held me, heavier than gravity itself. She took a step toward me, and panic surged through my system.

Breaking eye contact, I turned to Tangi and spoke too loudly about getting her home safely. One look back showed BG staring at her hands the way she used to after our arguments. The sight hit me with a flush of sharp, unwelcome guilt.

I'd shut her down before she could say anything that might break me. Taj caught the interaction, her knowing look following me as I practically rushed Tangi toward the door.

BG's gaze burned into my back as we left, her unspoken words pressing tension into my shoulders. The text she'd sent. The conversation she clearly wanted to have. All of it threatened to unravel the distance.

I couldn't do it. Not tonight. Not after those thirty seconds of contact at the rehearsal. Or that fucking speech. One more conversation might break me.

Outside, the night air was cool against my flushed skin. Tangi leaned against me as we walked to my car, though I suspected she was far more sober than she appeared.

Once inside the car, she confirmed my suspicion by sitting upright and fastening her seatbelt with perfect coordination. Apparently, sometime during the evening, she had sobered up.

"You're still so angry with her," she said quietly. Not a question.

My hands tightened on the wheel until my knuckles turned white. "Wouldn't you be?"

Tangi studied me for a long moment. "Yeah," she admitted finally. "I probably would be."

The words hung between us, honest and raw. My left hand flexed involuntarily against the wheel, and for a split second, I almost felt the phantom weight of that ring box I'd once carried everywhere for two weeks. The ring with the amber stone that matched BG's eyes. The ring that still sat in the back of my sock drawer, too painful to look at but impossible to discard. The future I'd planned and lost in the span of a single night.

The drive to the hotel was silent. I pulled up to the entrance. Tangi lingered, hand on the door handle.

She didn't look at me when she said it. "Be careful tomorrow, Ry."

"Will do. Night, T."

After dropping her off, I sat in my car, engine idling, BG's message open once more. The words glowed on the screen, demanding a response I wasn't prepared to give.

I finally typed: *I can't do this right now.* Simple. True. Not a permanent door closing, but not an opening either.

My chest hurt from holding everything in. I started at the 'send' button.

But even that felt like too much.

I deleted the message.

The quiet closed in, too dense to breathe through. What would happen after tomorrow? I carried the question with me, alongside the memory of the toast, the catch in her breath when our arms linked, the glimpse of something raw and honest beneath her performance.

Tomorrow, I'd wear the cuff Deena gave me and the smile I'd perfected over two years. I'd pose for pictures. Laugh in the right places. Pretend the ache beneath my ribs was just the price of standing too straight for too long.

I'd pretend I didn't still know the exact shade of amber in her eyes, too.

My phone buzzed against the console. Taj's name lit up the screen.

I answered after a moment of hesitation. "Hey."

"Just checking you got in okay," Taj said, casual but probing.

"Still in the car, actually." I glanced at the dashboard clock. Twenty minutes had passed since I'd dropped off Tangi.

"Sitting in your car in the dark? Very normal, totally healthy behavior." The teasing in her voice didn't quite mask the concern.

I shifted, uncomfortably aware of how pathetic this must seem. "Shouldn't you be getting your beauty sleep? Big day tomorrow."

"Deflection noted and denied," Taj replied. I could practically hear her eyebrow rising. "I've got plenty of time for sleep. Right now I'm more interested in why my best friend is having an existential crisis in a parked car."

"I'm not having a—"

"*Riley.*"

I traced the steering wheel with my thumb, focusing on the sensation of leather beneath my fingertips. Grounding myself in something in the flesh when everything emotional felt dangerously unstable.

"I don't know what I'm doing, Taj." The words escaped real quiet, like I was measuring each syllable for safety.

"With BG?"

"With any of it." I adjusted the rearview mirror unnecessarily, avoiding my own reflection. "She texted me. After Deena's bachelorette. Said she saw me with Shaye and that..." I swallowed hard, the words sticking in my throat. "That she wanted me to be happy but didn't realize it would hurt so much."

"And you haven't responded." Not a question.

"What am I supposed to say? 'Thanks, I'll file it with the other two years of silence'?" The bitterness in my voice surprised even me.

"You could try honesty." Taj's tone remained steady, a counterbalance to my rising tension. "Novel concept, I know."

"The night before your wedding isn't the time for this conversation." Another deflection, desperate this time.

"Perfect time, actually. Consider it my last act as a free woman. Solving your love life before I dedicate myself to my own."

I let out a short laugh that felt more like a pressure release than actual humor. "Pretty sure Deena would object to that characterization."

"Deena would agree with me, and you know it." A pause. "Riley. Just say it. Out loud. To someone. Even if it's just me."

My throat tightened. The car was suddenly too small, too close, too everything. "Say what?"

"Whatever you're sitting in your car at night avoiding saying."

The pressure in my chest built until I couldn't contain it anymore. "I still love her." The words rushed out, leaving me breathless and exposed. "I never stopped. Even when I hated her, even when I convinced myself I was over her, even when I was trying to get with Shaye—who, like, deserved *way* better than being a placeholder—I was still..." My voice broke. "I was still waiting for BG. Still comparing everyone to her."

Something wet hit my hand. I touched my cheek, surprised.

The truth expanded in the small space, pressing against my bones with the precise discomfort of a joint finally popping back into alignment.

"I know," Taj said softly.

"What?"

"We all knew, Ry. Y'all are pulling a Jordan. Different number on the jersey but same player who can't stay retired."

I leaned my head against the cool window, feeling oddly lightened by having the words out in the open. The glass cooled the flush on my face. "So what now? I just...text her back? After this long? After everything?"

"That's up to you," Taj replied. "But it matters that you finally said it out loud. That's a start."

I exhaled slowly. "Some start. Two years too late."

"Maybe. Or maybe exactly on time." Taj's voice carried a certainty I couldn't feel. "You both needed to grow separately before you could grow together again."

"When did you get so wise?"

"Imminent marriage. Comes with automatic wisdom download. Very efficient."

I smiled despite everything, grateful for her ability to lift the heaviness even momentarily. "You should get some sleep. I've monopolized the bride-to-be enough for one night."

"You good to drive home?" The concern was back in her voice.

"Yeah. I'm good." And for the first time in weeks, I almost meant it.

"Dr. B?" Taj's voice stopped me just as I was about to end the call.

"Yeah?"

"Whatever you decide, we've got you. All of us. No matter what."

The simplicity and sincerity of it made my eyes sting unexpectedly. "I know. Thank you." A pause. "Love you, T."

"Love you too. Now go home and stop being dramatic in parking lots. That's Cruz's job."

The laugh that escaped me felt real, clean, unburdened. I wiped my face with the back of my hand. "Yes, ma'am. See you tomorrow."

I ended the call and started the engine. The knot in my stomach had loosened. Not gone, but different. Less like pain, more like awareness. I adjusted the rearview mirror and caught my own eyes. Tired as fuck, red-rimmed, but somehow clearer than they'd been in months. Checked my side mirror, adjusted my seat, and pulled away from the curb. Simple mechanics to ground myself when everything else felt uncertain. The small rituals of control that kept me moving forward when feelings tried to pull me under.

Maybe that was enough for now.

One more day.

So, You've Been Emotionally Eviscerated at Your Best Friend's Wedding: A Guide

BG

WEDDINGS, THE GREAT COSMIC joke of the universe.

Spend thousands of dollars so everyone can watch two people promise not to hook up with other people anymore. And here I was, trying not to hyperventilate in shapewear that could double as a torture device while Deena—my ride or die, the bride, the woman I would literally take a bullet for—floated around the warehouse space like some kind of otherworldly being.

The ceremony had been perfect because, duh, of course it was. Taj and Deena had transformed this Brooklyn warehouse into something magical. Exposed brick walls adorned with trailing greenery, thousands of twinkling lights hanging from industrial beams, and those copper accents I'd helped pick out actually working exactly like I'd said they would. Not that I was keeping score or anything.

"BG, can you help with this?" Deena called, gesturing at the back of her dress where some intricate button had come undone. Her gown was a masterpiece—vintage-inspired with modern details, practically engineered to make everyone cry when she walked down the aisle. It worked. Even I—keeper of the emotional fortress—felt that telltale burn behind my eyes when Taj's voice cracked during her vows.

I rushed over, my maid-of-honor blush-colored dress swishing around my ankles. "Got you, babe," I said, my fingers working quickly to secure the tiny pearl button. "Can't have you falling out of this dress before the reception. Though it would definitely make for a memorable wedding album."

Deena laughed, the sound light and easy. No more pre-wedding jitters, no cold feet—just pure, uncomplicated joy radiating from her like she'd swallowed the sun. "You've been my rock through all of this," she said, squeezing my hand.

I winked, brushing off the weird twinge. "That's what they pay me the big bucks for. Well, that and my exceptional taste in bachelorette party decorations."

The cocktail hour was in full swing now, guests mingling in the reception space while the wedding party prepared for photos. The bartenders hopped around the bar making the wedding signature drink, the Hudson Sunset, whatever that was. The DJ kicked things off with that godawful Jagged Edge remix that shouldn't be a wedding song but is. March in Brooklyn was taking a rare merciful turn—unseasonably warm, with a golden sunset painting everything in golden-colored light that made everyone look like they were extras in an episode of *Insecure*.

I scanned the space automatically, a habit I couldn't seem to break. The search was always the same—looking for one specific silhouette among the crowd. And there she was, standing near the bar in her tailored suit, the deep navy setting off her warm brown skin in a way that made my stomach do that stupid little flip it always did.

Riley.

She was nodding at something Taj's uncle was saying, that polite smile firmly in place. The one that didn't reach her eyes. I knew that smile intimately—had cataloged its variations like some kind of weird emotional botanist. Nobody else would catch that micro-twitch at the corner of her mouth, but I could practically hear her internal countdown to escape.

"Family photos first, then wedding party!" The photographer clapped his hands, gathering Deena's parents and siblings, then Taj's extensive family. I hung back, checking my lipstick in my compact mirror, focusing intently on my reflection rather than the woman standing fifteen feet away who still hadn't looked in my direction.

"Maid of honor and best man, please!" The photographer gestured.

My heart did a pathetic little stutter-step. I moved forward at the same moment Riley did, both of us executing the careful dance we'd perfected over the past few months—maintaining precise distance, avoiding direct eye contact, keeping our smiles fixed in place. Nobody else would notice the deliberate calculations in our movements, the invisible force field we maintained.

"Let's have you on either side of the happy couple," the photographer directed, motioning for Riley to stand beside Taj and me beside Deena.

I stood close to Deena, my smile wide and fake. For a brief, disorienting moment, I caught Riley's scent. That same cologne that used to cling to my sheets. *Shit.*

"Perfect! Now everyone look this way and smile!"

I did what I was told, the performance automatic. Stand up straight. Angle slightly to the right. Chin down just a touch. Smile with your eyes. All those years of theater finally paying off in one perfectly composed wedding photo where no one would ever know I was falling apart inside.

After the fourth configuration of family members, the photographer announced, "Now let's get the full wedding party up on the rooftop garden! The light is flawless right now."

Everyone began migrating toward the stairs. I hung back, pretending to adjust my bracelet, needing a moment to recalibrate. In two minutes, I'd be standing beside Riley on that rooftop, surrounded by flowers and sunset and romance, like some cosmic joke designed specifically to torment me.

"BG."

Tangi's voice, low and serious, appeared at my elbow. I looked up to find her watching me with that look that always made me feel like she could see right through my bullshit.

"What's up, gorgeous?" I replied, voice weird, a little too high. "Ready for your closeup? That dress is criminal, by the way. Like, actually illegal in several states."

She didn't smile. Just took my elbow gently and steered me slightly away from the migrating wedding party, toward a quiet corner beside an enormous potted fern.

"I saw the text," she said simply.

The words landed like a stone dropping into still water, sending ripples of panic through my chest. I blinked, mind racing to catch up. "What text?"

Tangi gave me a look that said she didn't have time for my shit. "The one you sent Riley. After Deena's bachelorette."

My stomach lurched. That text. The one I'd sent at 1 AM from the bathroom of that fancy lounge, tipsy on champagne and emotional exhaustion. The one I'd immediately regretted. The one I'd put my phone on airplane mode to avoid seeing the response to.

The one I never checked because I was too much of a coward.

"Oh," I said, small and hollow. "*That* text."

"Yeah," Tangi nodded, her expression gentle but uncompromising. "Look, I'm not here to lecture you. You're both adults. But I need to say something before we go up there."

I swallowed, throat suddenly dry. "I'm listening."

Tangi's eyes held mine, steady and serious. "If it's just to make yourself feel better, don't."

The simplicity of it knocked the air from my lungs. No accusations, no judgment—just the quiet, devastating truth of what I'd been doing. Using my pain as permission to disrupt Riley's life. Again.

"I'm not—" I started, then stopped, the lie dying on my lips. Because wasn't that exactly what I'd been doing? Sending that text hadn't been about giving Riley closure or even about honest communication. It had been about easing my own

185

guilt, making myself feel better about seeing her move on.

Tangi squeezed my arm gently. "She read it, BG. And it messed her all the way up. Just...be careful with her heart. She's been through enough."

I *put* her through enough. Unsaid, but heard.

The guilt was a hot, suffocating wave. I'd been so caught up in my own pain that I hadn't considered how my midnight confession might affect Riley. Hadn't considered that my selfish need for release might reopen wounds she was trying to heal.

"I wasn't thinking," I admitted, the confession barely audible over the party noise.

"I know," Tangi said, and there was no condemnation in her voice, just understanding. "But now you are. So make better choices."

Before I could respond, the photographer's voice called out, "Can we have the wedding party, again? We're losing the light!"

Tangi held my gaze for one more moment. "She deserves peace, Becks. Even if that means peace without you in it."

The words were a sucker punch to the soul. Peace without me in it. The concept was so foreign it almost didn't compute, like trying to imagine a color I'd never seen before. Could Riley ever be at peace without me? More terrifying: could I ever be at peace without her?

The question opened up something hollow and vast inside me, a black hole where my bravado used to be. Peace without Riley. Like trying to breathe underwater. Like missing a limb. Like losing gravity.

Two years of pretending had gotten me nowhere close to peace. Two years of sketchy hookups and midnight runs and avoiding places where memories lived. Two years of giving "over it" so convincingly I almost believed it myself. And still, one whiff of her cologne and I was gone—caught in her orbit, terrified and electrified and so goddamn alive it hurt.

What would peace even look like? A life where I didn't scan every room for her silhouette? Where I didn't mentally catalog which streets, coffee shops, and subway stops to avoid? Where her name didn't feel like a tiny grenade in my chest every time someone said it?

The thought alone made me want to run—fast and far, anywhere but here, facing this truth that felt too big to hold. Because if peace without Riley was possible, what did that say about everything I'd been feeling? And if it wasn't possible, if this ache was permanent, what the hell was I supposed to do with *that*?

"Earth to Becks?" Tangi's voice pulled me back from the abyss.

I nodded, not trusting my voice. Not when it might betray how utterly terrified I was by the question echoing in my head like a scream in an empty room.

"Good." She rubbed my arm, her expression softening slightly. "Now put on your best smile, sweetie. These pictures are forever."

I watched her walk toward the stairs, my mind spinning like I'd gone from zero to drunk in five seconds flat. Peace without Riley? That concept made about as much sense as skinny jeans on a cat. Both technically possible, but deeply unnatural.

I took a deep breath, pinched my cheeks for some color, and plastered on my "everything's totally fine" smile—the one I'd nailed through years of awkward family dinners and surprise performance reviews. Then I followed Tangi up to the rooftop, where Riley was already in position with the rest of the wedding party, looking like a goddamn vision in that navy suit.

I floated through the rest of the photo session like some kind of emotional zombie in an expensive dress. Smile, pose, pretend I'm not low-key dying inside. By the time we hit the reception, I was three champagnes deep and almost convinced myself I was handling things like a grown-ass adult.

Spoiler alert: I wasn't.

This time, when our eyes met across the garden, I didn't look away like I usually did. I gave her a small nod—nothing dramatic, just a tiny acknowledgment that yeah, this sucked, and yeah, I knew it was mostly my fault. No grand gestures. No desperate attempts to fix what I'd broken.

Maybe that was what actual growth looked like. Not fixing everything, but at least not making the mess bigger.

I was halfway through my second Hudson Sunset when the first notes hit.

My body recognized it before my mind did—a memory that traveled from my ears straight to my gut. That rich, unmistakable intro. Stevie.

"And this one's for all the lovers out there!" The DJ's voice bounced through the reception hall as couples flooded the dance floor.

My glass froze halfway to my lips. The drink's bubbles popped against the crystal, silent beneath Stevie's voice now filling every corner of the room. *Seriously, universe?* This song? Tonight? Way to be subtle.

Cruz was still talking beside me, something about a client, but his voice faded to nothing as the music wrapped around me like a physical thing. Heavy. Inescapable.

Memory slammed into me like a surprise attack I should've seen coming. Us, barefoot in our kitchen at 2 AM, both of us in ratty sleep clothes, me in a bonnet. Riley's hands warm on my waist, spinning me like I was something precious instead of a disaster in mismatched pajamas.

Our song, though we'd never said it out loud.

My eyes found her instantly across the crowded room, like some magnetic pull I couldn't fight. Riley sat rigid at her table, fingers clenched around her water glass. The suit made her shoulders look broader, stronger. Made her look like everything I'd ever run from because I wanted it too much.

Our gazes locked, and the whole room dissolved. Just us. Just that goddamn song playing like our own private joke—except neither of us was laughing.

I saw the exact moment something in her broke. Her jaw tightened. Her eyes went hard in that way I knew too well—when she'd decided that enough was enough.

She stood up. And walked right out the side door.

No drama. No scene. Just gone.

I should have let her go. That would have been the smart thing to do.

But smart had never been my strong suit when it came to Riley. Actually, smart hadn't been my strong suit in general. More like "impulsive" and "self-sabotaging" were my superpowers. And there I went again, chasing her down like some rom-com stalker instead of letting sleeping dogs lie. Peak chaotic BG energy. Can't just let her walk away and process in peace, oh no. I have to make it *A Moment*, turn everything into high stakes drama because apparently I don't know how to exist at normal volume.

My bare arms prickled in the air conditioning as I crossed the reception hall, champagne abandoned like my common sense. My heart slammed against my ribs. Hands shook.

The rooftop garden looked like something I'd have saved on my wedding Pinterest board two years ago. String lights overhead, city skyline framing everything like some backdrop to a moment I wasn't ready for. The air smelled like rosemary and night flowers and stupid hope.

And there she was. Riley. Standing at the edge, hands on the brick wall, looking out at the city instead of at whatever mess I was about to make. The copper edge caught the moonlight, outlining her silhouette in a way that made my chest hurt. Not crying. Just standing there. Bracing.

Makes sense the universe would give her impeccable lighting for the moment she breaks my heart again.

The string lights in the ivy behind her blinked like warnings. *Stop.* Don't do this. But when had I ever listened?

I approached slowly, my heels sinking slightly into the fake grass. "Riley?"

She didn't turn. Didn't acknowledge me at all. Just kept staring out into the darkness, arms wrapped tight around herself like she was holding something in. Or keeping something out.

I stopped a few feet behind her, close enough to smell her cologne again. The night air swirled between us, cool against my bare shoulders, carrying the distant notes of our song from inside.

"I almost managed to stay inside," I finally said, the words tumbling out before I could stop them.

Riley's shoulders stiffened minutely. The only sign she'd heard me at all.

"You should've," she said, her voice flat.

I moved closer, the fabric of my dress brushing against my legs. "That song—"

"Don't." She turned then, the moonlight catching on her face. Her eyes were dark fire. "Don't pretend you've been carrying this all along. Not when I've been drowning in it by myself."

"I have been carrying it," I shot back, surprising myself with the force in my voice. "Every day. Every time I hear Stevie. Every time I see someone dancing in a kitchen."

"You sure had a funny way of showing it," Riley said. "Two years of silence. Two years of nothing."

"What was I supposed to do?" I threw up my hands. "You were different after. So shut down. I thought—"

"What else was I supposed to be?" The first real crack in her control. "You checked out, BG. Long before you physically left. I was trying everything to reach you, and you were just...gone."

My chest tightened like someone was slowly cranking a vice around my ribs. "I was scared." Understatement of the century. I was terrified. Of how much I wanted her. Of how easily she could destroy me just by deciding I wasn't enough.

"So was I." Her laugh was sharp, bitter. "But I still showed up. I still tried."

"You didn't show up," she continued, stepping closer. "That's how you've always dealt with anything hard. You just don't show up."

"I was there," I said weakly. "I was right there with you."

"Physically, maybe. But you weren't present. You were already planning your exit."

"That's not fair," I countered, feeling heat rise to my face. "I didn't know how to—"

"What?" She cut me off. "How to pick up the phone? How to answer a text? How to not leave me wondering if any of it was real?"

Every word cut deep. I wrapped my arms around my middle. "Of course it was real."

"Then why couldn't you fight for us?" she asked, her voice breaking slightly. "I was drowning, BG. And you watched."

The accusation hung in the air between us. We didn't need to say any of this. We absolutely needed to say all of this. Even the ugly parts.

My breath hitched, feeling my armor cracking apart. "I thought I was doing you a favor. Letting you move on to someone who deserved you."

"That wasn't your decision to make," Riley said. She looked annoyed. "You didn't get to decide what I deserved."

"I see that now," I admitted, the words catching in my throat. "I was trying to protect myself from how much I wanted us. How much it would destroy me if we crashed and burned."

"So you burned it down first?"

The words hit and I wanted to argue, to deflect, to make it about anything else. But I couldn't. Because she was right. I did burn it down first. I always did. Fuck, I really am that girl, aren't I? The one who runs before anyone can walk away.

"Yes," I whispered. The truth, finally. "God, what a cliché, right? Classic BG, unable to handle anything real."

Riley was quiet for so long I thought she might just walk away. When she finally spoke, her voice was quiet.

"I used to think that if I loved you hard enough, it would be enough. That eventually you'd stop running."

A heavy silence fell between us. The faint notes of our song had stopped. In the distance, a new melody started playing—something upbeat and celebratory that felt jarringly out of place.

"Shaye and I broke up," Riley said abruptly. "Two weeks ago."

Of course I'd imagined it. Wondered. Hoped. But hearing it aloud made everything tilt. "What? But I thought—"

I stared at her, stunned. Wait, seriously? Little Miss Perfect Singer could see Riley was still—? The universe has jokes. And apparently, killer timing.

"Riley, I—" My throat closed up before I could finish the thought. Riley didn't want perfect. She wanted *me*.

"She was right to end things." Riley said, cutting me off. "She knew I was elsewhere. But that doesn't mean I'm ready to—" She gestured vaguely between us. "This. Whatever this is."

"Where?" I asked before I could stop myself. "Where were you?"

She looked at me like the answer should be obvious. "With *you*. I was still with you. Ever since that fucking meeting—"

"I wanted forever," I blurted, the words hitting the air too fast to catch. "With you. I wanted it so badly it terrified me. I ran because I thought I'd ruin it." I let out a bitter laugh. "And then I did."

Riley studied me, her expression unreadable. "Tell me something. When that song started playing, what did you remember?"

My heart beat so loud I was sure she could hear it. "The kitchen. Us dancing."

"What else?"

My fingers automatically found a seam on my dress, fidgeting with the fabric. "You said...you wanted it to be our first dance."

Surprise flashed across her face. "You heard that? Because, I gotta admit, I've been telling myself I imagined that moment. That you didn't really hear me. That maybe we weren't on the same page after all."

The song was still playing inside, faint but unmistakable through the door I'd left open a crack.

"We were," I whispered. "I just couldn't—"

"Handle it. Yeah, I got that part." Her voice grew distant, clinical. "You know what hurts the most? I would have given you time. All the time you needed. But you didn't trust me enough to stay and work through it. You just left."

She turned away, and panic surged through me.

"Of course I heard it," I said, my voice breaking. "It was the most beautiful thing anyone's ever said to me. And I was too terrified to acknowledge it because it meant everything was real."

"And now?" Riley asked, her voice quieter. "What's changed?"

"I have," I said. The words felt both true and insufficient. "Two years of running from myself. From how I feel about you. From how badly I screwed up the best thing in my life."

"You hear our song and suddenly decide you're ready to feel something? That's not love, Beckham. That's nostalgia with convenient timing."

"It's more than that," I insisted, taking a step closer. "I never stopped feeling it. I just got better at pretending I didn't."

"'You left me to burn,' she said, each word measured and final. "And now you want credit for noticing the ashes."

Well, *fuck*. One sentence and my whole personality just laid bare. Classic BG: torch everything beautiful, then act surprised when you can't warm your hands on what's left.

"No," I shook my head. "I don't want credit. I want—" I stopped, searching for the right words. "I want you to know I understand what I did. What I lost. That I finally understand how much damage I caused by running."

"You didn't leave breadcrumbs," she said, softer now but somehow more devastating. "You gave me silence. Two years of nothing, and then that text after Deena's party. Like dropping a grenade and walking away."

Heat rushed to my face. "I meant what I said in that text. I did want you to be happy. I just didn't expect it to hurt so much."

"That's the problem," Riley said. "You never do. You act, then you're surprised by the aftermath. Every time."

I couldn't argue. That was my whole pattern: military brat logic. Jump first, deal with the damage later. Feel everything, process nothing.

"What do you want from me, Beckham?" Riley asked, fatigue creeping into her voice. "Because I can't do this anymore. I can't be your emotional safety net whenever you decide to feel something."

"I don't know," I admitted, the most honest thing I'd said all night. "I just know that when I heard that song, when I saw you walk out, I couldn't—" I swallowed hard, as my voice got weird and shaky. The words escaped and tumbled over themselves without a gut check. Fucking mascara stung my eyes. "I couldn't let you go. Not again. Not without telling you that I know what I threw away. And maybe...maybe I didn't want you to be over me. Cause I'm not over you. I tried, Ry. But I don't know how to be."

Riley looked at me for a long moment, her face softening almost imperceptibly. "I hear you," she said finally. "But I can't do this tonight. I just...can't."

The finality in her voice made my chest cave. This wasn't just about tonight, or the song, or even the text. This was goodbye. For real this time.

She turned to leave, and panic surged through me.

"Riley, wait—" My voice broke on her name, tears already burning tracks down my cheeks.

She paused at the door, her hand on the handle, not turning back. For a long moment, I thought she might not respond. Then, softly:

"Maybe next time...just knock."

The door closed behind her in a way that sounded like the end of everything. I stood alone in the garden, the distant sounds of the reception filtering through the walls, reminding me of everything I'd thrown away.

I exhaled, and it sounded more like a sigh than breathing.

Finally, I knew how it felt to watch someone walk away and realize they weren't coming back. No dramatic exit needed. No screaming match. Just that soft click of a door that might as well have been a goddamn vault slamming shut.

Peace without Riley? Yeah, right. That's like peace without oxygen. Technically possible, just not while you're still breathing.

Knock-Knock Jokes

Riley

My sunglasses didn't hide enough.

The hotel hallway stretched before me like a gauntlet I had to run, each step precise and measured. I'd perfected the art of controlled movement. No wasted energy, no unnecessary gestures. Just forward momentum. One foot in front of the other. Keep going until you're somewhere else.

My hand gripped the strap of my overnight bag, knuckles whitening beneath the pressure. The weight of it against my shoulder anchored me to the moment, kept me from floating away into the dangerous territory of last night's memories. The rooftop. The song. BG's face in the moonlight, more honest than I'd seen it in two years.

Maybe next time...just knock.

Had I really said that? Left that door cracked open when every instinct screamed to seal it shut? The words had slipped out before I could catch them—a betrayal from some hopeful part of myself I thought I'd buried.

The elevator arrived with a soft chime, empty and waiting. Small mercies. I stepped inside, pressed the button for the lobby, and watched the doors close on the hallway where I'd spent the night staring at the ceiling, replaying every word, every gesture, every painful truth we'd finally spoken aloud.

My reflection in the polished elevator doors looked foreign—a woman trying desperately to disappear. Dark hoodie pulled up, joggers, those oversized sunglasses hiding red-rimmed eyes. The uniform of someone running from her own shadow. I adjusted my posture slightly, straightening my spine, refusing to physically manifest the collapse I felt inside.

The lobby buzzed with wedding guests checking out, their laughter and animated conversations about the reception creating a chorus of normality that felt obscene against how raw I felt. I moved through them like a ghost, head down, following the path of least resistance toward the exit.

"Ry!"

Cruz's voice cut through the ambient noise, warm and familiar. I paused, calculating the energy required for this interaction. How convincing could my "I'm fine" be this morning?

I turned to find him and Sakia approaching, both looking remarkably put-together for people who'd been dancing until 2 AM.

"There she is," Sakia said, giving me a quick once-over. "You look like the inside of my hungover brain."

A laugh escaped before I could stop it, rusty and unrehearsed. "Thanks. I think."

"We're heading to that brunch spot on Bedford," Cruz said, his eyes studying me with that gentle perceptiveness that made him such a good friend. "Want to join? They've got those caramel banana waffles you like."

"Can't." It came out clipped and final. "Early shift tomorrow. Need to get back."

Sakia nodded, not pushing, though her eyes held mine a second too long. "You missed the sparkler send-off. Deena almost set Taj's aunt on fire."

"*Almost* being the operative word. But hey, no injuries and the happy couple are off." Cruz added. "They're headed to the airport now. Maui for a week."

"Good for them," I said, meaning it despite the hollow echo in my chest. At least someone's love story was working out according to plan.

A brief silence settled between us, heavy with the question no one was asking. I wouldn't be the one to break it. Wouldn't be the one to say her name. They looked at each other, and Cruz cleared his throat.

"She left early," Sakia finally offered, studying my face. "Like, way early. Before breakfast service even started."

I nodded once, face neutral. Of course she did. BG had never been good at mornings after. Especially difficult ones.

"I should go too," I said, adjusting my bag. "Traffic."

Cruz stepped forward, pulling me into a hug so gentle it almost broke me. "Call if you need anything," he murmured. "Even if it's just to not talk about it."

The kindness nearly undid me. I returned the hug briefly, then stepped back before emotion could rise to the surface.

"Drive safe," Sakia called as I moved toward the doors. "And Ry?"

I paused, not turning fully.

"It was good to see you both in the same room without the building catching fire."

I didn't have a response for that. Just lifted my hand in a small wave and pushed through the revolving door into the cool spring morning.

Outside, the valet brought my car around. I tipped him automatically, movements mechanical. The driver's seat welcomed me like an old friend—familiar, contained, mine. I adjusted the mirror, catching a glimpse of my own eyes behind the dark glasses. Eyes that had seen too much. That knew too much.

I started the engine, the quiet purr filling the silence. My hands found their place on the steering wheel. Ten and two. Control what you can control.

The hotel grew smaller in my rearview mirror as I pulled away. I didn't look for her. Didn't scan the entrance or the windows, hoping for one last glimpse. What would be the point?

But something had shifted, like tectonic plates beneath the surface. Imperceptible unless you knew exactly where to place your hand and feel the tremor.

I'd given her coordinates to a door I wasn't sure I wanted opened. Now all I could do was drive away and wait to see if she'd use them.

The Jackie Robinson Parkway curved ahead like a river flowing between the dense spring greenery that lined its edges. Sunday morning light broke through the trees in golden slivers, touching the hood of my car with fragmented warmth. The road was mercifully empty—just a few cars scattered across the lanes, everyone keeping their distance, as if by unspoken agreement.

I merged onto the I-678 North, fingers adjusting the steering wheel with practiced precision. My mind felt foggy, not quite processing at normal speed. Exhaustion or emotional overload—maybe both. I hadn't slept more than two fragmented hours, my body rigid on the hotel mattress, afraid to relax into the vulnerability sleep would bring.

My hand moved automatically to the radio, needing something—anything—to fill the silence. The soft click of the button echoed the sound of that door closing between us.

A morning talk show burst into the car's quiet interior, hosts laughing too loudly about some celebrity gossip I couldn't bring myself to care about. I changed stations. Pop music. Changed again. Classical. Again. Sports commentary.

Nothing fit. Everything felt abrasive, intrusive. I turned it off, leaving only the hum of tires against pavement and the subtle rush of air around the car.

Exit 19 approached. I signaled, checked my blind spot, shifted lanes. Mechanical movements. My body navigating by muscle memory while my mind circled around the image I couldn't shake: BG standing alone in that rooftop, moonlight catching the tears she was too proud to let fall. That look in her eyes when she'd finally said it out loud. *I'm not over you. I don't know how to be.*

Too late, I told myself. Two years too late.

But then why did I leave that opening?

I merged onto the I-278, the Triborough Bridge stretching ahead. Manhattan's skyline spread along the horizon, buildings catching the morning light. The city already awake and moving forward while I felt suspended between moments, unable to progress in any direction.

The soft vibration of my phone in the cup holder pulled me back to the present. I glanced down. Tangi's name lit up the screen, but I let it go to voicemail. Not ready. Not yet. The questions she'd ask, the concerned silences, all the probing—I couldn't handle it. Not with everything still so raw, so unsettled.

A delivery truck cut in front of me, too close, and I tapped the brakes, the sharp alert of danger clearing my mind momentarily. Focus. Pay attention. The habit of control reasserted itself, muscles tensing slightly as I adjusted my grip on the wheel.

The I-78 stretched ahead, carrying me closer to home with each mile. Home. The word felt hollow now. Just a place to keep my things. A space where I could close the door and not have to perform composure for watching eyes.

I caught my reflection in the rearview mirror and finally removed the sunglasses, squinting slightly at the brightness. The woman looking back had shadows under her eyes, a certain tightness around her mouth. She looked worn, weathered by a storm that had been brewing for two years.

My townhome came into view as I turned onto my street. Familiar brick. Familiar steps. Familiar emptiness waiting inside. As I pulled into my parking spot, everything—the wedding, the rooftop, those words hanging between us—settled more heavily on my shoulders.

I sat there with the engine off, hands still on the wheel, uncertain of what came next. For someone who'd spent two years hiding from her, I'd left a dangerous ambiguity between us. I couldn't even tell myself *why*.

I glanced at my watch, a simple, practical timepiece Pops gave me, and realized I'd been sitting in the car for nearly ten minutes. Time slipping away while I remained caught between moments, between decisions. Just like I'd been for years.

I didn't have an answer. Just questions that echoed in the silence, and a decision I couldn't undo.

The townhouse welcomed me with the same pristine emptiness I'd left behind. Everything exactly where it should be. Everything perfectly, deliberately in place.

I toed off my shoes at the entryway, sliding my feet into the house slippers I kept by the door. Never bring the outside, inside.

I stood in my own living room, staring at the space like it belonged to someone else. The navy throw blanket folded precisely over the arm of the couch. Books arranged by height on the coffee table. A single ceramic vase on the mantel—empty, collecting dust in my absence.

Moving through my own home felt strange, as if I were acting out the role of someone who lived here rather than actually inhabiting the space. I opened the refrigerator, surveyed its sparse contents, closed it again. Filled a glass with water from the tap, set it on the counter untouched.

My eyes caught on a small stack of mail I'd left on the kitchen counter before leaving for the wedding. I straightened the edges, aligning the corners perfectly, then set them aside. Wiped the counter clean where they had been.

My body felt heavy with an exhaustion that went beyond physical. I sank onto the couch, letting my head fall back against the cushions. The perfect order I'd maintained suddenly seemed pointless, almost laughable.

Who was all this precision for, when no one else ever saw it?

Without conscious decision, I reached for my phone. The message thread with BG was still open from last night, when I'd stared at her text for the hundredth time before the wedding

My fingers hovered over the keyboard. *Hey.* Delete. *I keep thinking about—* Delete. *Are you—*Delete delete delete. What would I even say that wouldn't just reopen wounds that had barely stopped bleeding?

The three dots appeared suddenly. BG typing, then stopping. Typing again. Then nothing. Just blank space where words should be.

I waited, breath caught, waiting for something that didn't come.

The screen dimmed, then went dark, my own reflection staring back at me from the black glass. I set the phone down on the coffee table, screen face-up, visible if it lit again.

Outside, clouds shifted, changing the quality of light filtering through my windows. The shadows in my living room lengthened, stretched, reconfigured themselves around the furniture, around me.

I sat perfectly still, watching them move across the hardwood floor. There were decisions to make. Boundaries to establish or destroy. But not today. Today, I just needed to breathe in this quiet, empty space that was mine alone.

The silence didn't ache the way it used to. It just felt...unfinished.

My phone lit up.

Knock, knock.

I'm not sorry for what I said. I miss you. When you're ready to talk, I'll be here.

It's Not Avoidance If It Pays Well

BG

I'D MASTERED THE ART of looking unbothered while internally combusting. Yet another soft skill for my résumé.

My brand strategy zoom call ended with Irina, bougie skincare mogul extraordinaire, gushing over my luxury line rebrand mock-ups. Her perfectly moisturized hands framed her face on my screen as she praised the "divine" rose gold against matte black palette.

At some point, her words blurred. "Elegant but grounded," she was saying. Or maybe had already said? I was staring at my own thumbnail in the bottom corner of the screen, wondering when I'd started looking this tired.

I flashed my professional smile, hard and perfect. "I'm thrilled you like the direction. The color psychology research shows this palette creates a luxury association while still feeling approachable. I'll send over the final renders by

Friday."

"You're a gem. Truly."

We exchanged a few more pleasantries—her asking about my weekend plans, me fabricating something that didn't involve staring at my phone like it was a bomb about to detonate—before signing off with air kisses.

The second her face disappeared from my screen, my smile collapsed like a cheap tent in a storm. I slumped back in my chair, rubbing my temples where the beginnings of a tension headache throbbed. My apartment fell silent except for the low jazz I kept playing as white noise while working.

The mock-ups were still open behind me. I stared at them for a moment—rose gold, matte black, perfectly aligned—then alt-tabbed away like they'd accused me of something.

Everything was polished. I was polished. And still, I couldn't stop checking my phone like Riley might suddenly remember how to want me again.

My eyes slid to my phone, sitting face-up next to my laptop. Thankfully, it hadn't magically grown thumbs and sent any panicked follow-up texts for her to ignore.

Screen still dark. No notifications.

I tapped it once to check if missed something. Nothing. Not a 'fuck you, Becks', not an invitation for lunch, not even spam emails offering to enlarge body parts I don't possess. I deliberately turned it face-down, like I was punishing it for disappointing me.

A week since the wedding. A week since that rooftop conversation. A week since I'd sent that text that made my stomach twist every time I thought about it.

Knock, knock.

I'm not sorry for what I said. I miss you. When you're ready to talk, I'll be here.

Simple words that felt like jumping off a cliff without knowing if there was water below.

My therapist said I needed to sit in the discomfort for a while to really digest what happened. To reflect. To me, I had been sitting in this so long, my ass had gone numb.

I stood up suddenly, my body protesting after hours of hunching over screens. My tea had gone cold—again. Third time today. The sunset was casting long golden rectangles across my hardwood floors, and I realized I'd been working since dawn without a real break.

My therapist would call this "avoidance behavior through hyper-productivity." I called it "billable hours."

In the kitchen, I dumped the cold tea and started fresh, watching steam curl from the kettle. My apartment was unnervingly quiet. Too neat. Too empty. I'd been keeping it immaculate lately, like I was expecting company that never came.

Back at my desk, tea in hand, I opened my sketchbook to work on concepts for another client—a boutique coffee shop wanting to expand into merchandizing. I needed to stay busy. Busy meant not thinking about Riley's face in the moonlight. Not replaying our conversation for the thousandth time. Not checking my phone every three minutes like a teenager waiting for her crush to text.

My hand moved across the page, creating precise lines. There was comfort in the control of it: the way the pencil responded exactly as I wanted it to, unlike everything else in my life.

A chime from my laptop startled me. Calendar notification: "Deena & Taj return from honeymoon next week."

I stared at it, a weird heaviness settling in my stomach. Once they were back, our friend group would inevitably start gathering again. Which meant awkward evenings where Riley and I would pretend we hadn't broken each other's hearts all over again at their wedding.

I closed the notification and forced my attention back to the sketch, my lines becoming firmer, more deliberate. This was fine. I was fine. I'd built an entire brand around being self-sufficient and emotionally enlightened. I'd posted Instagram carousels about healing and growth. I could absolutely handle a woman not texting me back.

Even if that woman was Riley.

My eyes drifted toward my phone again.

Dammit.

The buzzer sliced through my concentration like a chainsaw through butter, making me jump. Tea splashed onto my sketch—a tiny brown Rorschach test blooming across the pristine page.

"Shit," I muttered, blotting it with my sleeve.

I froze, heart suddenly racing. It was after 8 PM. Not the usual time for package deliveries or food I didn't remember ordering. My eyes darted to my phone automatically, as if it might explain this disruption.

Could it be...?

I approached the intercom slowly, trying to keep my breathing even. Trying not to let hope swell in my chest like the world's most disappointing balloon.

"Hello?" I aimed for casual but hearing my voice come out slightly higher than normal.

"Open up! We know you're in there!" Cruz's voice blared through the speaker.

My shoulders slumped with a complex mixture of emotions. Disappointment (which I refused to acknowledge), relief, irritation, and reluctant affection. I pressed the buzzer without responding, then took a quick glance around my apartment. Good thing I'd been keeping it pathologically clean.

By the time I opened my door, Cruz and Sakia were already in the hallway, loaded down like packhorses heading into the wilderness. Two bulging bags from Spice Jawn (my favorite Thai-fusion place), a bottle of wine in Sakia's hand, and what looked like a non-alcoholic option in Cruz's. Sakia was also balancing what I recognized as the distinctive pink box from Magnolia's Bakery. The one with those diabolical Biscoff chocolate cheesecake brownies I'm totes incapable of resisting.

"The cavalry has arrived!" Cruz announced dramatically, spreading his arms wide while somehow managing not to drop anything. "Please hold your applause."

"Your phone's been going straight to voicemail for two days," Sakia said, practical as always, her eyes scanning my face with that knowing gaze that always saw too much.

I crossed my arms, suddenly defensive. "I've been working. Some of us have deadlines."

"And some of us have Thai food getting cold," Cruz replied, pushing past me into my apartment without waiting for an invitation. Typical Cruz, but I couldn't help the tiny smile tugging at my lips.

"I have a deadline tomorrow morning..." I tried, even as they invaded my carefully ordered space.

Cruz beelined for the kitchen like he owned the place, immediately opening cabinets for plates. Sakia set down the wine and started looking for an opener, completely ignoring my weak protest.

"Where's the third musketeer?" I asked, glancing toward the door. "FaceTiming from paradise?"

"Deena doesn't know we're here, and she shouldn't." Sakia uncorked the wine with an expert twist. "She's hopefully getting her back blown out on a balcony somewhere."

"From your lips to God's ears!" Cruz called from the kitchen. I heard the familiar sounds of my cabinets opening and closing. "Girl, when was the last time you went grocery shopping? This fridge is giving 'abandoned hope' vibes. You're not hoarding MREs are ya, sweetie?"

I followed them into the kitchen, my resistance melting as I watched them move around my space with the easy familiarity that only comes from true friendship. There was something both irritating and deeply comforting about how they'd just decided I needed company and made it happen, whether I thought I wanted it or not.

Sakia poured a generous glass of red and pushed it toward me. "You ain't even gotta talk about it," she said quietly. "We're just here."

I looked between them—Cruz now unpacking containers of pad Thai and green curry, Sakia leaning against my counter with that calm, steady presence she's always had. The realization that they weren't leaving, that they'd come specifically to check on me without making a big deal about it, hit me with unexpected force.

My shoulders dropped about three inches, tension I hadn't even realized I was holding releasing all at once.

"Did you at least bring curry puffs?" I narrowed my eyes, finally giving in. It was the closest I could get to 'I fucking love you two.' But I knew they heard me just the same.

Cruz's smile was triumphant. "Double order. Extra plum sauce, just how you like 'em."

An hour later, my coffee table was covered in half-empty food containers, and my apartment smelled like lemongrass and garlic. We'd migrated to the living room, sprawled across my couch and floor pillows like we used to do in college. My rigid posture had gradually loosened. Possibly due to the wine, but more likely because of the company.

Cruz was mid-dramatic reenactment of his latest dating app disaster. Mr. DJ had ghosted him. "So he shows up twenty minutes late, wearing what I can only describe as 'finance bro goes to Burning Man'—like, khakis with a mesh tank top? And the first thing he says is—" Cruz put on a deep, douchey voice, "'Oh, you look different from your photos.' Which, excuse me? My photos are a documentary-level representation of this—" he gestured to his face, "—masterpiece."

Sakia snorted, nearly choking on her wine. "What did you do?"

"What could I do? I said, '*You* look exactly like your photos—that's the problem,' finished my drink, and left." Cruz shrugged dramatically. "Life's too short for bad fashion and worse manners."

I found myself genuinely laughing for the first time in days. Almost inhaled a mouthful of cheesecake brownie in the process. Amazing how friendship could temporarily override heartache.

"Speaking of disasters." Sakia reached for more pad Thai. Her face crinkled up. "This is gonna go left, but we gon' lean into it, okay? The new assistant at the salon flooded the back room yesterday. Left the sink running while she went to answer the phone."

"No!" Cruz and I exclaimed in unison.

"Oh yes. Picture three inches of water, all the towels ruined, and Mrs. Abernathy sitting there under the dryer, completely unbothered, asking if this was 'one of those new spa treatments she's heard about.'"

The conversation flowed easily, deliberately light and far away from wedding talk or anything Riley-adjacent. They were doing that thing good friends do—creating a safe space without acknowledging why it's needed. The ambush wasn't lost on me, but I was grateful for it, nonetheless.

My phone chimed suddenly from the coffee table. The sound was like a record scratch across our easy conversation. I tried to be slick about it, but my hand darted out so quickly I nearly knocked over my wine glass.

Just a notification from a work app. The disappointment must have been written all over my face because when I looked up, Sakia and Cruz exchanged a quick glance.

"So," I said too brightly, setting the phone back down harder than necessary, "tell me about this nightmare client of yours, Sakia. The one who wanted the blue-but-not-blue hair?"

She took the lifeline I'd thrown, launching into a story about a client who'd brought in seventeen different photos of "the exact blue" she wanted, each one a completely different shade. The moment passed, but I caught Cruz watching me with a gentleness that made my throat tight.

By the time they started gathering their things to leave, my apartment felt warmer, lived-in again. The empty spaces that had been echoing with my thoughts were now filled with remnants of their visit.

"This was really nice," I said, walking them to the door with genuine gratitude warming my chest. "Thanks for the ambush."

"What ambush? This was just friends having surprise dinner," Sakia said with mock innocence, pulling me into a hug. "But maybe charge your phone now and then."

I hugged her back tightly, breathing in the familiar scent of her shea butter hair products. "I'll try to remember that technology works better when it's not dead."

Cruz lingered after Sakia stepped into the hallway, his usually animated face settling into something more serious. "Have you heard from her?"

I hesitated, the question landing somewhere tender. Didn't dare tell them it took me twenty minutes of playing chicken with the send button before I reached out. And it took all the strength I had to not go on airplane mode again immediately after that.

"I texted," I admitted. "Ball's in her court now."

He nodded, understanding the significance. "That's brave."

Sakia nodded in agreement. "And new for you, girl. You're standing your ground *and* respecting her space. Growth, right?"

I shrugged, aiming for nonchalance and missing by a mile. "Or stupidity. Jury's still out."

"Look, I'm only gonna say this once because I love your indecisive ass," Cruz said, pulling me into a bear hug. "Real love? It doesn't wait around forever while you get your shit together. But it also doesn't give up on you becoming the person it knows you can be. So figure out which version of yourself you're bringing to this, Becks. Y'all are totally aggravating, but y'all taught me that."

He kissed my forehead, and I could only burrow into him to keep from ugly crying.

Sakia hesitated, then added, "You know, sometimes people need time to figure out what they want to say. It doesn't always mean..." She trailed off, leaving the rest unspoken.

"Either way, Becks, we're here. We love you."

"And Deena would be too," Sakia added from the hallway, "if she wasn't busy getting lei'd."

I groaned at the terrible pun, pushing them both toward the door, even as tears finally rolled down my cheeks. "Get out of my apartment with that joke immediately!"

Their laughter echoed in the hallway as I closed the door behind them. The click of the lock felt different now. Less like sealing myself in a fortress and more like simply closing a door.

I turned back to face my apartment, seeing evidence of friendship everywhere. Empty wine bottles on the counter. Cookie wrappers on the coffee table. The faint imprint of people who cared enough to nag me.

Evidence I was loved, at least by *my* people.

Almost without thinking, I picked up my phone. One more check. Still nothing.

Instead of returning to my desk and the half-finished sketches waiting there, I curled up on the couch with what remained of the wine. Without thinking, I'd grabbed my favorite mug—the one with "Trust Your Gut (Unless It's Being Dramatic)" printed in faded letters on the side. Riley had given it to me for my birthday three years ago, just before everything fell apart. She'd said it reminded her of me. Intuitive but overthinking. I ran my thumb over the worn lettering, a tiny connection to her that I hadn't been able to throw away despite my best efforts at exorcising her from my apartment.

It hurt less thinking about it. *Yay*. Progress.

I rolled my shoulders back and—*oh*. When had they migrated up to my ears? Riley used to call them classic stress shoulders, like I was perpetually bracing for impact. I let them drop, actually let them drop, and the relief was so immediate I almost laughed.

The thing about waiting, I learned, is that it didn't have to happen in isolation. Maybe that was the real growth. Not the grand gestures or dramatic confessions, but the quiet acknowledgment that I didn't have to white-knuckle my way through this alone, no matter the outcome.

My phone sat dark and silent on the coffee table. But suddenly, I didn't feel quite so much like I was holding my breath.

The text from Sakia came at the exact wrong moment.

Which, let's be honest, was pretty much every moment these days. I was lowkey stress-eating Corn Pops for dinner while refreshing my phone like it might magically conjure a response from Riley that didn't exist.

Pottery class tomorrow at 7! That place in Dumbo. You need to get your hands dirty with something that isn't your phone. Don't make me drag you.

I stared at the message, spoon halfway to my mouth. Pottery. Like, actual clay? The kind that required focus and patience and not checking your phone every thirty seconds to see if the woman you'd confessed your undying love to via text had maybe, possibly, thought about responding?

Fine, I typed back. *But if I make an ashtray, I'm blaming you.*

Deal. 7 PM sharp. Wear clothes you don't mind ruining.

Great. Another opportunity to be terrible at something new while my emotional life imploded in the background. At least clay couldn't ghost me.

The next evening, I stood outside Muddy Waters Studio, staring through the windows at people bent over pottery wheels like they were performing surgery. The whole place had that aggressively cozy vibe. Exposed brick, Edison bulbs, the kind of casual sophistication that screamed "we charge extra for authenticity."

I pushed through the door, immediately hit by the smell of wet earth and that brand of forced creativity that made my skin crawl. This was Sakia's fault. All of it. She probably thought getting my hands in clay would be "therapeutic" or some shit. My Reiki master would definitely call this grounding.

"BG!" Sakia waved from across the room, her usual composed energy slightly frazzled around the edges. "You made it!"

I approached the cluster of pottery wheels, noting the other students, a mix of couples looking disgustingly happy to be molding clay together and individuals who probably read about mindfulness in some wellness blog. Classic Brooklyn scene.

"Where's my wheel?" I asked, scanning the setup. "Please tell me I'm not sharing with someone who takes pottery seriously. I don't need that kind of negativity right now."

Sakia's expression shifted, just slightly. A flicker of something that might have been guilt if I didn't know her better. "About that..."

The door chimed behind me, and I turned automatically—then froze.

Riley. Standing in the doorway like she'd materialized from my most elaborate stress dreams. She wore dark jeans and an old button-down with the sleeves rolled up, looking effortlessly put-together in that way that used to make me want to mess up her hair just to see her laugh.

Our eyes met across the studio. Time felt like someone had hit pause on the entire universe except for my racing heartbeat. She looked just as surprised as I felt, which was either comforting or terrifying. I couldn't decide which.

"Tangi invited me," Riley said quietly, her voice carrying across the space with that controlled precision I knew meant she was fighting to stay calm.

"Funny thing about that," Sakia said, suddenly appearing at my elbow with Tangi beside her, both of those sly-ass mofos wearing expressions of barely contained mischief. "Seems like there was some miscommunication about who was inviting who."

I turned to stare at them, comprehension dawning like a hangover. "You didn't."

"We absolutely did," Tangi confirmed, her smile unrepentant. "And since we're both terrible at pottery, Sakia and I are going to partner up. You know, for safety reasons."

"Safety reasons?" Riley's voice had that edge it got when she was trying not to laugh.

"Clay can be very, very dangerous," Sakia said solemnly. "We might need adult supervision."

They were already moving away, gravitating toward wheels on the opposite side of the room like this had been choreographed. Which, knowing them, it probably had been.

Riley and I stood there, stranded in the middle of the studio like two people who'd been abandoned on a particularly craft-oriented desert island.

"I can leave," she said quietly.

"Don't." The word escaped before I could think about it. My cheeks burned. "I mean, you paid for the class. And our friends are clearly losing their minds, so we might as well..."

"Make ashtrays together?" Her mouth quirked up at the corner—not quite a smile, but close enough to make my stomach do that stupid flip thing.

"Speak for yourself. I'm making a vase. A very sophisticated vase that definitely won't look like a wonky cup."

Riley's laugh was quiet, but real. "Right. Very sophisticated."

The instructor—a woman whose paint-stained overalls and serene expression suggested she'd achieved enlightenment through clay and probably had strong opinions about mercury retrograde—clapped her hands. "Alright, everyone! Find your wheels and settle in. We're starting with centering."

Riley and I looked at each other. Centering. Because the universe was apparently a stand-up comedian with terrible timing.

We claimed two wheels in the corner, as far from our meddling friends as possible. Riley settled at the wheel to my left, I took the one on the right, and for a moment we just sat there staring at our respective lumps of clay like they might spontaneously combust and save us from this situation.

The instructor launched into her spiel about water and pressure and finding the center, but I was only absorbing every third word because the other two-thirds of my attention was laser-focused on Riley's proximity—the way she tucked her bottom lip between her teeth when she was thinking, the scent of her cologne cutting through the earthy clay smell and making my brain short-circuit.

"Gentle pressure," the instructor called out. "Let the clay guide you."

Let the clay guide you. *Suuuuuure.* Because that wasn't a direct callout to my entire approach to emotional regulation, which was basically "fight everything until it submits or explodes."

I pressed my palms against the clay, trying to mimic what I'd seen in movies. The clay was cold and slippery, spinning under my hands while I attempted to find some kind of rhythm. Next to me, Riley's movements were steady and methodical—of course they were—while mine kept skittering around like they'd forgotten their basic function.

My clay started wobbling ominously.

"You're fighting it," Riley observed quietly, not looking over but obviously aware of my struggle.

"I'm not fighting anything," I muttered, even as I squeezed the clay harder, trying to bend it to my will through sheer stubbornness. The wobble got worse.

"Becks—" she started, then stopped herself.

Too late. My clay collapsed completely, splattering wet earth across my jeans and the wheel.

"Shit," I breathed, staring at the wreckage.

Riley's hands stilled on her own perfectly centered clay. She glanced over at my disaster, then at my face, and something shifted in her expression. After a long moment, she sighed.

"Scoot forward," she said quietly.

"What?"

"Make room. Before you destroy what's left of the clay." She was already standing, wiping her hands on a towel.

I shifted forward on the stool, hyperaware of every sound as Riley moved behind me. Her body settled close, not quite touching but close enough that I felt the warmth radiating from her. When she reached around me to grab fresh clay, her arms bracketed my ribs almost like one of her hugs from behind, and suddenly my entire nervous system was throwing its own personal rave.

I was *that* starved. Almost pouted.

"Like this," Riley murmured, her voice soft near my ear. Her hands covered mine on the clay, guiding my fingers. "Feel the pressure, don't force it."

Her chest pressed lightly against my back as she leaned in to demonstrate, and I had to concentrate on breathing normally. The wheel spun slowly between us, clay taking shape under our joined hands, and for a moment everything else fell away except the warmth of her touch and the gentle pressure of her guidance.

Perfect angle to capture her lips between mine and cut off this whole separation bullshit. If I wanted to be bold, anyway.

She guided my hands to the clay, her fingers covering mine with that same gentle authority she'd always had. The clay responded immediately under our combined touch, rising and centering like it had been waiting for someone who knew what they were doing.

"There." Her breath was warm against my ear. "See?"

See. If only she knew what I was seeing—how her hands still knew exactly how to guide mine, how easy it was to fall back into this, how catastrophically not-over-her I was despite two years of aggressive therapy.

"This is trickier than Instagram makes it look," I managed, my voice slightly hoarse.

"Most things are." Her hands were still covering mine, still guiding the clay's movement. "But you'll figure it out. You always do."

The casual confidence in her voice hit me sideways. Like she still believed in me, even after everything. Even after I'd proven exactly how good I was at fucking up the things that mattered most.

The clay rose between our hands, taking shape under the gentle pressure. Not a vase, not a cup, just...something. Something we were making together, our hands moving in sync like they remembered how to do this despite everything.

"It's crooked," I observed, tilting my head to study our creation.

"Everything good is a little crooked," Riley replied, and there was something in her voice that made me look at her more closely. Something that might have been hope, if I was brave enough to name it.

Our eyes held for a moment longer than necessary. Long enough for me to remember what it felt like to be seen by her, really seen, without judgment or expectation. Long enough to remember why I'd fallen so hard in the first place.

The clay collapsed.

"Oh, fuck," I breathed, staring at the ruined mess between us.

Riley was already reaching for more clay, her movements calm and sure. "It's okay. We'll start over."

Start over.

Such simple words, but they landed like a promise in the space between us. Or maybe like an answer. Was this her way of responding to my text? Her own Riley way of knocking back? My brain immediately started spiraling through the possibilities. Was she talking about pottery or us? Did she mean start over as in "let's try this clay thing again" or start over as in "maybe we can figure out how to exist in each other's orbit without everything catching fire"?

Stop it, Becks. It's about clay. Just clay.

But the way she said it, soft and deliberate, made something flutter in my chest that had nothing to do with pottery disasters.

That old familiar urge to *know* things kicked up hard and fast. To push, to ask what she meant, to demand clarity on every syllable. The old BG would have blurted out something like "start over how exactly?" and turned this into a whole interrogation. We're talking pissed-off Stabler pacing around a table, here.

But sitting here, watching her hands work the clay with such gentle certainty, I made a choice: let it be what it was. To trust that whatever this was, pottery lesson, olive branch, or something else entirely, we were moving forward from being two hurt people yelling at each other on a rooftop.

And maybe that had to be enough for now.

Riley prepared the new clay, her hands gentle but confident as she shaped it into something workable. When she looked up and caught me staring, her cheeks flushed pink. "What?" she asked softly.

"Nothing," I said, but I didn't look away. "Just...thank you. For not leaving. When you saw me here."

Riley's hands stilled on the clay. "I thought about it," she admitted. "For about three seconds."

"What stopped you?"

She was quiet for so long I thought she might not answer. Then: "Seemed easier than making a scene. And we're both here now, so..." She shrugged, but there was something softer in her expression. "Might as well see if we can make something that doesn't fall apart completely."

My throat went tight. "We are pretty terrible at pottery."

"The worst," she agreed, but she was smiling now, and it was the real smile. The one that made the whole room brighter.

We bent over the clay again, our heads closer this time, our hands finding their rhythm more easily. The conversation flowed as we worked. Careful at first, then more natural.

The instructor paused at our tables, gave us a look, and thought better of it.

Thank goodness.

She told me about a difficult patient, I told her about a client who wanted their brand colors to "evoke the emotional essence of a sunset but also convey corporate trustworthiness." We laughed about our friends' obvious matchmaking scheme.

It felt normal. Like maybe we could do this. Be in the same space without everything combusting. Like maybe friendship was possible, even if nothing else was.

By the end of class, we'd both produced something that might charitably be called a bowl if you squinted and tilted your head. It was lopsided and had a weird thumb print on one side, but it was ours.

"Not bad for a couple of beginners," Riley said, surveying our works with exaggerated pride.

"Speak for yourself. This is clearly a masterpiece." I gestured dramatically at my wonky creation. "I'm calling it 'Bowl with Existential Crisis.'"

Riley snorted. "Perfect. Very avant-garde."

As we cleaned up, washing clay from our hands in the communal sink, I caught sight of Sakia and Tangi across the room. They were trying to look casual, but I could feel their laser beam eyes all over our corner of the studio.

"Think they're pleased with themselves?" Riley asked, following my gaze.

"Oh, they're absolutely smug as hell right now." I dried my hands on a paper towel, suddenly aware that class was ending and we'd have to figure out what came next. "But...this was nice. Even if they tricked us into it. Yet again."

Riley nodded and rolled her eyes. "It was."

We stood there for a moment, the easy conversation of the past hour crystallizing into something heavier. The reality that this was just a pottery class, not a reconciliation. That we still had two years of hurt between us and no idea how to bridge it.

"I should go," Riley said finally, reaching for her jacket.

"Yeah," I said, trying to keep the disappointment out of my voice. "Me too."

But neither of us moved.

"Beckham," she started, then stopped, shaking her head. "Never mind."

"What?" I pressed. "You can say it. Whatever it is."

Riley's eyes searched my face, like she was looking for something specific. "I got your text. The knock knock one."

My stomach dropped. Of course she had. "Riley, I—"

"I'm not ready to talk about it yet," she said quietly. "But I wanted you to know that I...I heard you."

I heard you. Not forgiveness, not acceptance, but acknowledgment. It was more than I'd expected and somehow exactly what I needed.

I swallowed around the lump in my throat, nodding. "Fair enough."

She nodded once, then headed for the door. I watched her go, noting the set of her shoulders, the careful control in her movements. At the last second, she turned back.

"Take care of yourself, Becks."

"You too, Ry."

And then she was gone, leaving me standing in a pottery studio that smelled like earth and possibility, holding the weight of everything we hadn't said.

Sakia appeared at my elbow, her expression carefully neutral. "So. How was that?"

I looked down at my misshapen bowl, still sitting on the wheel. "Complicated."

"The best things usually are," she said gently. Sakia nudged my shoulder. "My treat in exchange for a full debrief?"

"Your messy ass."

As we gathered our things and headed out into the Brooklyn night, I found myself thinking about Riley's words. Let the clay guide you. Maybe that applied to more than pottery. Maybe sometimes you had to stop fighting and just...see what wanted to happen.

Worth the Wait
Riley

I COULDN'T OUTRUN MY thoughts.

But God knows I was trying.

My feet hit the dirt path in perfect rhythm—one-two, one-two—each impact sending a jolt up my legs that grounded me in the physical. The late morning light warmed my skin, April sun finally finding its strength. Sweat gathered along my spine, soaking into my running shirt.

I pushed harder. Three miles already, and I still hadn't reached that empty mental space I was chasing. You know the one—where your body takes over and your brain finally, mercifully shuts the fuck up for twenty blessed minutes.

No such luck. BG's text from this morning still played on a loop.

Made it through the workweek without punching a single vendor. Personal growth?

Three weeks since the wedding. Three weeks of these messages since I knocked back. Casual, almost friendly. Small talk via text between people who used to know each other's bodies by heart. My response had been equally light: *Proud of you. Did you light a candle or just drink wine and threaten God?*

Her reply came back almost instantly: *Both. Simultaneously. Multitasking queen.*

I'd laughed despite myself, then immediately felt guilty about it. As if allowing myself even that small moment of connection was a betrayal of...what, exactly? My own boundaries? The distance we'd both maintained for two years? The righteous anger that had kept me lighting up an entire borough all by myself after she left?

My pace increased unconsciously, feet pounding harder against the packed earth. My lungs burned, heart pounding against my ribs. Faster. Clearer. I just needed to run a little faster, push a little harder, and maybe then I could outpace the confusion that had taken up residence in my chest.

I didn't hear Tangi's approach until she was practically beside me, falling into stride.

"Morning, speed demon."

My head turned, surprised. Tangi wore her usual running gear—black leggings, a faded Trina tee, braids pulled back. Her breathing was controlled, but I could tell she'd pushed to catch up with me.

"What are you doing here?" I asked between breaths. "Did Taj tag you in to babysit this time?"

"I plead the fifth on that part. But I texted you." She matched my pace without visible strain. "When you didn't respond, figured you were either dead or doing your impression of the Flash."

I slowed slightly, the companionship making me aware of how fast I'd been going. "Sorry. Phone's on silent."

Tangi glanced sideways at me, not saying anything, but her expression spoke volumes. I knew that look. It was the "I'm-not-going-to-push-but-I-no-ticed-you're-being-weird" look she'd perfected somewhere around sophomore year of college.

"Nice day," she offered instead, giving me space.

"Yeah."

We ran in silence for a while, following the winding path through the park. Trees in the first blush of spring green created dappled shadows across our path. The familiar rhythm of our matched strides felt unexpectedly comforting. A body conversation without the pressure of words.

When we reached the small lake at the park's center, I finally eased to a stop, more for Tangi's sake than mine. My own lungs were burning, legs trembling slightly, but I wasn't ready to admit I might have been pushing too hard.

"Water?" Tangi pulled a bottle from her running belt, offering it to me.

I took it gratefully, suddenly aware of how thirsty I was. The cool liquid was a shock against my parched throat.

"You've been out here a while," she observed after I'd handed the bottle back. Not a question. "Your shirt's soaked through."

I shrugged, stretching my arms overhead to ease the tension in my shoulders. "Needed to clear my head."

"Seems like it's getting pretty crowded up there lately."

I shot her a look, but there was no judgment in her expression. Just patient understanding. I sighed, some of the defenses I'd been maintaining crumbling.

"Yeah," I admitted. "It is."

We walked to a nearby bench, both of us silently agreeing to take a break. The wood was sun-warmed beneath my legs as I sat, stretching them out in front of me. A family of ducks paddled across the lake's surface, leaving tiny ripples in their wake.

"Cruz is meeting up with his mom today," Tangi said, breaking the comfortable silence. "That gallery opening she's been talking about for months."

"Right," I nodded, grateful for the neutral topic. "The one with the sculptures made from recycled electronics?"

"That's the one. He's been dreading it. Apparently the artist is his mother's ex-student who's had a crush on Cruz since high school."

The normalcy of the conversation eased something in me. "Poor Cruz."

"He'll survive. Just means he'll be extra dramatic at the next brunch."

I smiled despite myself, imagining Cruz's theatrical retelling that would surely follow, with New York hand gestures, wide eyes and dramatic pauses. Tangi always knew how to create space—when to push and when to just sit with me in the quiet.

We watched a jogger pass, a golden retriever trotting happily at his side. Birds called from the trees overhead. The world continuing as it always did, indifferent to the chaos in my head.

"I'm texting with BG," I said finally, the words coming out in a rush.

Tangi nodded, her expression carefully neutral. "I figured something was up."

"You did?"

She gave me a gentle side-eye. "Ry, you nearly dropped your coffee when your phone pinged during brunch last weekend. Then looked at it like it might bite you."

Heat crept up my neck. "Was I that obvious?"

"Only to someone who's known you since you were afraid to ask that cute TA for extra credit." She bumped my shoulder with hers. "So, texting, huh? How's that going?"

I sighed, leaning forward to rest my elbows on my knees. "It's fine. Normal. Casual."

"Casual-casual or 'I'm-pretending-this-is-casual-but-I'm-actually-dying-inside-overthinking-every-word' casual?"

The accuracy of her assessment made me laugh, the sound unexpected even to my own ears. Tangi was the queen of being the little sister who liked to pretend she was the big sister. "That obvious too?"

Tangi smiled, stretching her legs. "You forget I've seen every stage of Riley Benson in love, from infatuated co-ed to heartbroken professional."

"I'm not in love," I protested automatically. The words felt hollow even as I said them.

"Didn't say you were." Tangi's voice remained gentle. "Just noting that I know your patterns."

I picked at my running shorts, avoiding her eyes. "It started after the wedding. Just...checking in. Nothing serious."

"And?"

"And nothing. We text sometimes." I swallowed. "It feels nice. And terrifying. Both at once."

Tangi didn't press further, giving me space to continue or not. Around us, the park was coming to life—families spreading blankets on the grass while dad manned the grill, an impromptu frisbee game starting on the open field beyond the lake. Normal people living normal Saturday lives, not tangled in the wreckage of relationships they'd both destroyed and missed desperately.

"She makes me laugh," I admitted quietly. "Even now. After everything."

Tangi nodded, understanding that simple statement and all it carried.

"I don't know what I'm doing, and you *know* me. That bugs the hell out of me." I continued. "Cause I don't know if this is...if it's closure or reopening old wounds or something else entirely."

"Maybe you don't have to know yet."

I glanced at her, surprised by the response. Tangi, usually the first with advice, ready with practical solutions, was giving me permission to navigate this uncertainty at my own pace.

"I keep waiting to feel angry again," I said. "For all the hurt to come rushing back. But then she'll text something about threatening God while lighting candles and I just...I laugh. And then I feel guilty for laughing."

"Why guilty?"

I struggled to articulate the feeling. "Because it feels like, like I'm betraying my own boundaries. Like I spent two years building this wall, and now I'm just letting her walk right through it because she made a joke about multitasking?"

"Maybe the wall served its purpose," Tangi suggested. "And maybe it doesn't need to be there anymore."

We fell silent again, watching a young child feeding the ducks despite a nearby sign prohibiting it. The simple joy on the kid's face as the birds gathered around made something twist in my chest.

"What if I mess it up again?" I asked, voicing the fear that had been lurking beneath all my reluctance.

Tangi paused for a long moment, weighing her words. When she spoke, her voice was softer than usual, but firm with conviction.

"Then you mess up again." Tangi's tone was matter-of-fact. "And you figure it out from there. Like the rest of us messy humans."

I stared at her, slightly stunned by the directness. No promises that everything would work out perfectly. No guarantees. Just the simple reality that life involves risk, and that's okay.

"When did you get so frustratingly wise?" I asked, only half-joking.

"Probably around the time I stopped trying to micromanage my life. Toddlers have a way of undoing your plans and being irritatingly cute and cuddly later so you can't be too mad." She stood, stretching her arms overhead. "Ready to finish this run? Or do you need more time to brood attractively on this bench?"

I snorted, rising to my feet. "I don't brood."

"Mmhmm. Tell that to your furrowed brow." She tapped her finger between my eyebrows. "You'll get wrinkles."

We started jogging again, taking a more leisurely pace this time. The frantic energy that had driven me earlier had dissipated, replaced by something calmer, if not more certain.

"I'm not telling you to forgive her. I'm not telling you to try again." She looked straight ahead at the lake, giving me the privacy of not having to meet her eyes.

"I'm saying—if she makes you happy, and she's trying again and *you're* trying again? You're allowed to want that."

A pair of ducks took flight from the water, wings cutting through the air with purpose. Tangi let the silence stretch before adding:

"You don't need my blessing. But for the record—I don't think choosing her again makes you stupid. I think it makes you brave as hell."

Tangi's words settled between us, unexpectedly profound in their simplicity. I studied my hands, not trusting my voice yet. A gentle breeze rippled across the lake's surface, carrying the distant sound of children's laughter from the playground.

"You have a knack for saying what I want you to say, and also what I don't want you to say. How do you do that?" I finally asked, aiming for lightness but landing somewhere closer to vulnerable.

Tangi shrugged, a small smile playing at the corners of her mouth. "I have my moments. Usually between making terrible dating choices and yelling at reality TV contestants."

That pulled a genuine laugh from me. "At least you're consistent."

"Someone has to be."

We cooled down, the conversation settling around us like the dappled sunlight through the trees above. A realization formed slowly, like muscles relaxing after tension: BG was being brave as hell, too.

Each text she sent was a small act of courage. Reaching across the void I'd maintained, risking rejection each time. She'd always been the one to dive headfirst into feelings while I calculated risks from the shore. But now she was doing it differently: patient, giving me space, letting me set the pace. This wasn't the impulsive BG of before. This was someone who'd learned from our past, too.

And what had I been giving her in return? The same distance that used to make her freak out. The same measured responses that probably felt like rejection to someone who'd spent her childhood watching people withdraw before they left. BG was putting herself out there, being vulnerable in her texts, and I was...what? Managing the situation? Processing my feelings in isolation like that was somehow more mature?

Shit.

Maybe my emotional regulation wasn't the strength I'd convinced myself it was. Maybe it was just another way of running.

But this time, somehow, we were both still here. Still texting. Still trying, despite our patterns threatening to derail us again.

There was comfort in this—in rebuilding the type of friendship that didn't demand immediate resolution or perfect answers. That allowed space for uncertainty.

"I should head out," Tangi said eventually, checking her watch. "Meeting Sakia for that pasta-making class she's been obsessing over. I think the new boyfriend is coming, too."

"Making ravioli like we're in culinary school?"

"Excuse you! They're 'handcrafted pasta parcels,' according to the website."

She stretched her arms overhead. I did side bends, muscles already feeling a bit looser.

"You good?" she asked, her expression telling me she'd understand if the answer was no.

I considered the question, all its layers and implications. "Not entirely," I admitted. "But I'm working on it."

Tangi nodded, satisfied with the honesty. "That's all any of us can do."

She bumped my shoulder, a gesture that contained decades of friendship and understanding. "Text me later?"

"Yeah," I promised. "Go make your fancy ravioli."

"Parcels!"

Her laughter lingered in the air as she jogged away, leaving me alone with my thoughts once more. But they felt lighter somehow. More manageable. Like naming them aloud had robbed them of some of their power.

I turned back toward the path, the morning stretching open before me.

The rain started just after four in the afternoon.

Not the dramatic, thundering kind that suited my mood earlier in the week. Just a steady, persistent patter against the windows that had continued for hours, turning the city streets slick and emptying the sidewalks of all but the most determined pedestrians.

I stretched out on the couch, wearing the old shorts I'd had since school. The television murmured in the background—some home renovation show where impossibly photogenic couples transformed disasters into showplaces in forty-two minutes plus commercials. I wasn't really watching.

My phone sat on the cushion beside me, screen dark. I hadn't checked it in seventeen minutes. I knew because I'd been counting.

The day had stretched long after my morning run with Tangi. Her words still echoed in my head.

She thought I was being brave. Not stupid. Brave. The word felt foreign, ill-fitting. Was I brave? Or just stuck in the same pattern, circling the same wound, unable to let it properly heal?

Outside, the rain continued its steady rhythm, a soundtrack to my thoughts. I picked up my phone, unlocked it, and found myself opening our message thread before I could talk sense into myself.

Rain's back. City's trying to remind us it's still winter-adjacent.

I pressed send before my brain could veto it at the last second. Simple. Neutral. A door barely cracked open.

The reply came almost instantly, as if she'd been waiting with her phone in hand.

April in New York: like a wet paper bag with commitment issues.

A smile tugged at the corners of my mouth despite everything. The easy humor that had always been there between us, even now, after all this time.

Dinner plans faring better than the weather? I texted back.

Bold of you to assume I had plans. Currently debating between eating a crusty loaf with cheese standing up over a counter or crackers with peanut butter in front of the TV. The height of sophisticated adulthood.

My smile widened. *Nutritional powerhouses, both options. Very balanced.*

Better than that time you thought ramen and pickles counted as dinner.

The memory hit with unexpected warmth. The disastrous attempt at cooking (at my insistence) during our third month together, when I'd been too exhausted after working too many hours ten days straight to realize how bizarre the combination was. BG had laughed until she cried, then ordered us Thai food while I sulked in mock offense.

That was a culinary experiment, I replied. *You just weren't sophisticated enough to appreciate it.*

Mmhmm. Is that what we're calling sleep-deprived hunger decisions now?

The banter felt so natural, like slipping into a favorite sweater I'd forgotten I owned. The careful distance I'd been maintaining these past weeks seemed to evaporate with each exchange.

What about you? she asked. *Treating yourself to a gourmet feast of microwaved leftovers?*

Pasta. With actual vegetables. I'm practically a grown-up now.

Impressed. And slightly suspicious.

I smiled, setting the phone down to adjust the throw blanket across my legs. The rain had picked up slightly, drumming against the windows with more insistence. I found myself grateful for it—for the cozy isolation it created, the way it made the world beyond my walls seem distant and unimportant.

When I picked up my phone again, a new message awaited.

You always hated the rain. Except that one time.

My fingers paused over the screen, the reference landing with precision. I hadn't expected her to mention it. To acknowledge that particular memory so directly.

It came anyway, uninvited but not unwelcome.

Bushwick. Early spring, five years ago. We'd been at that dive bar with the surprisingly good Amy Winehouse cover band—some indie outfit whose name I couldn't remember now. What I did remember, with perfect clarity, was stepping outside to find the skies had opened during our hours inside.

"Shit," BG had laughed, her hand flying to cover her already dampening locs. "Where did this come from?"

We'd huddled under the narrow awning, watching the downpour, knowing it was too heavy to wait out. Neither of us had thought to check the forecast. Neither of us had brought an umbrella.

"My jacket's useless in this," I'd said, looking down at my thin windbreaker. "But it's better than nothing."

We'd been dancing around each other for months by then. Kinda friends but something *more*, both of us aware of the current running beneath each conversation, each lingering touch. Neither willing to be the first to name it.

"On three?" BG had suggested, eyeing the distance to the subway entrance.

But I hadn't moved. Something about that moment—her profile in the neon glow of the bar's sign, raindrops catching in her locs, the slight flush on her cheeks from the two beers she'd nursed all night—had crystallized a certainty I'd been fighting for weeks.

I'd reached out, my fingers finding her cheek. Her eyes had widened slightly, questioning, hopeful.

"Worth the wait," I'd whispered, and then I'd kissed her.

Slow. Certain. The kind of kiss that changes the air between two people forever. Her hands found my waist, pulling me closer as the rain soaked us both to the skin. I remember the taste of her—warm beer and promise—and how neither of us cared about the storm around us, suddenly secondary to the one between us.

Now, in my living room, my eyes stung with the memory's clarity. The certainty I'd felt then was so foreign to the hesitation that had drove every interaction since the engagement party. Since her text. Since I'd finally admitted, at least to myself, that two years of distance hadn't diminished what I felt for her at all.

I never stopped feeling. I just got better at surviving the silence.

I stared at my phone, at her words on the screen.

My thumb hovered over the keyboard as I considered my response. The truth, I realized suddenly, was that I hadn't really hated rain—I'd hated uncertainty. And in that moment outside the bar, drenched but completely sure, there had been no uncertainty at all. Just clarity. Just us.

The rain could've kept falling, could've turned the whole city into an ocean, and I'd still have been right there, holding her, finally brave enough to want what I wanted without apology.

I'd never stopped loving her. And this fear of ruining it again? That wasn't big enough to outweigh the love anymore.

I opened the chat.

What's your address?

There was a pause. Then the bubbles started up again as she typed it in.

You okay?

She didn't say *why*. Didn't ask why now.

And somehow that made it easier.

I'm good. Wanna see you. Be there soon.

I didn't wait for her response. Didn't need to. The certainty I'd felt that night in the rain was back, settling into my bones with a rightness I couldn't deny.

I pulled on sweatpants, grabbed my keys from the bowl by the door. I didn't bother with an umbrella.

The rain was still falling, steady.

But this time? I didn't mind.

Turns Out, We Had a Lot of Catching Up to Do

BG

THERE WAS A BUZZ from the intercom that made my stomach drop.

Not my Postmates delivery guy with his signature double-buzz pattern. Not Cruz forgetting his key for the billionth time. A single, steady buzz that sent my heart ricocheting around my ribcage like a pinball machine gone haywire. My insides threw their own little rave, butterflies moshing around like they'd been mainlining espresso and bad life choices.

I hesitated before pressing the intercom button. "Hello?" My voice cracked, betraying me instantly.

"Hey, it's me." Riley's voice, even through the static, unmistakable.

I knew before she'd even spoken. My spiritual advisor would call this "intuitive recognition." I called it pure panic.

My finger hovered over the buzzer button for a second too long before I pressed it. I heard the distant click of the building's front door unlocking downstairs. Now the countdown began. Sixty-seven steps up to my apartment. I'd counted them once during a particularly bad anxiety spiral.

My hand lingered on my own doorknob like I was eighteen again waiting for a prom date, not a grown-ass woman with an impressive collection of crystals for emotional regulation that were clearly failing me right now. I took a breath. Opened the door.

And there she was.

Riley. Soaked to the skin, rain running down her jacket and dripping from her hair. She looked like something out of a dream and a memory all at once—solid and impossible. Her eyes were bright against her rain-damp skin, that perfect dark brown that had lived rent-free in my head since Deena introduced us.

"Hey," she said softly.

For a second, I couldn't move. Couldn't breathe. Couldn't do anything but stand there like an idiot while my brain short-circuited. Where was all that witty banter when you actually needed it?

"You showed up," I finally managed, barely more than a whisper. As if saying it too loudly might make her disappear. Or maybe make her real. I wasn't sure which scared me more.

Her eyes didn't leave mine. "I couldn't not."

Everything in me fractured and reformed at once. Like being broken open and put back together, but better this time. Stronger in the broken places. Like emotional kintsugi, but with less gold and *way* more gay panic.

For weeks I'd imagined this moment in loops—what I'd say, how I'd keep it together, how I'd pretend I wasn't still half in love with her. I'd rehearsed in front of my bathroom mirror like a job interview from hell. "Yes, I've grown tremendously during our time apart. No, I don't still have all your texts saved in a folder labeled 'emotional self-harm.'" But none of that mattered now. None of it fit. She was here. Really here. Not texting. Not waiting. Not running.

Just...here. Standing in my doorway, dripping on my welcome mat, looking at me like I was the answer to a question she'd been asking for years.

And I wasn't scared anymore. Okay, that's a lie. I was terrified. But not of her. Of how much I still wanted this.

"I missed you," I said, my voice raw with everything I'd been holding back. No performance. No deflection. No BG's Greatest Hits of Avoidance Tactics. Just truth.

Her breath hitched. "Say it again."

I stepped closer, heart pounding loud enough that the neighbors could probably hear it through the walls. Mrs. Petrovich would be filing a noise complaint any minute now. "I missed you. I love you, Ry."

Her hands slid to my waist, grounding me when I felt like I might float away or possibly combust on the spot.

"Dammit, Becks. I love you, too. Never, ever stopped. *Don't* leave me again," she leaned her forehead into mine.

"I won't," I said. "I promise." And for the first time in forever, I knew I could keep it. Me, Beckham Grace Adams, queen of the Irish goodbye, actually promising to stay put. Growth? Or temporary insanity? The jury was still out.

Her hands tightened on my waist, and that was all it took.

I crashed into her like a wave breaking against rock. Inevitable, unstoppable, slightly dramatic but I couldn't help it. My fingers tangled in her rain-soaked curls, pulling her closer, closer, until there was no space left between us.

Her mouth opened over mine, hungry and desperate. This wasn't the scared, tentative reunion I'd imagined. This was two years of longing compressed into a single moment—messy, urgent, and absolutely necessary. Like oxygen after holding your breath too long. Her tongue swept against mine and I made a sound I didn't recognize. Needy. Starved for reconnection.

Riley walked me backward until my shoulders hit the wall, never breaking the kiss. Her body pressed against mine, hot through damp clothes. I gasped as her cold hands slid under my shirt, fingertips leaving trails of electricity across my skin. My nipples hardened instantly, pressing against the thin cotton of my tank top. The contrast of her rain-chilled hands against my overheated skin made me shiver, not even gonna lie.

Always opposites, always perfect.

"Right here," I breathed against her mouth, unable to wait any longer, unable to imagine moving even an inch away from her. Not my most eloquent moment, but whatever. Eloquence could wait. This couldn't. I was already wet, already aching, my body remembering what my mind had tried to forget.

Her eyes darkened, understanding immediately. We'd always communicated best like this—with touches, with looks, with the silent language we'd built between us. The one dictionary I'd never thrown away. She paused, just for a second, her forehead touching mine, and I could feel her trembling with restraint.

"You sure?" she asked, even as her hands were already tugging off my shorts. Even though I was already arching beneath her, already desperate for her to move.

"Please, Ry," I managed, already helping her, both of us clumsy with need and urgency. My hands, usually so steady with a stylus or brush, fumbled like I'd never undressed before. Like we were doing this for the first time instead of the hundredth. She pushed my panties aside. The first brush of her fingers against me made my knees buckle. I was soaked, embarrassingly so, like a teenager making out with her crush for the first time.

The wall was cold against my back, but I barely noticed, consumed by the heat of her touch. Riley's hands remembered me perfectly. Exactly where to touch, how much pressure, when to slow down and when to quicken. My body had spent two years forgetting, but it all came rushing back in an instant, like muscle memory for the soul. She circled my clit with just the right pressure and I bit down on her shoulder to keep from crying out.

"I missed this," she whispered against my throat. Rough, desperate, like she was confessing something sacred. "Missed you. The way you sound, the way you feel."

My fingers dug into her shoulders, anchoring myself as sensation threatened to overwhelm me. Everything was too much and not enough, too fast and not fast enough. Two years of absence collapsed into this single, perfect moment of presence. Past and future disappeared, leaving only now, only us, only this.

"Look at me," Riley whispered, her voice rough with need, and she had the nerve to say this while inside of me. Her wet t-shirt rubbed against my stomach, but I didn't give a single fuck. Even pulled up my tank so I could feel more of her against me. Skin to skin, finally. Her nipples hard against mine, both of us burning despite the rain still clinging to our clothes.

I lifted my gaze to meet hers, and something cracked open inside my chest. This was Riley—my Riley—the woman I'd walked away from, the woman who somehow found her way back to me. And now she was here again, deep inside me like she had never left. There was nowhere to hide in that gaze, no escape route, no way to hold back the flood of everything I'd been running from. Her fingers moved deeper, finding that spot that made spots explode behind my eyelids.

Don't look away. Don't you dare look away now.

Our rhythm intensified, breath coming faster, Riley's name falling from my lips like a prayer. My nipples rubbing against hers. I felt myself climbing toward something that felt bigger than pleasure, bigger than desire. Something that broke me open. My thighs trembled, muscles tightening as the pressure built. I was close, so fucking *close*.

When it hit, it shattered me completely.

The release tore through my body in waves, but it was the emotional dam breaking that undid me. I arched off the wall. Riley buried her face into my neck and *moaned*. The orgasm left me breathless, my whole body seizing up like I'd touched a live wire. Tears spilled hot and fast down my face, my body shaking with sobs I couldn't contain. Two years of grief, of regret, of emptiness—all of it pouring out at once in the only place I'd ever felt truly seen.

Not now, not like this, I thought, but my body betrayed me. And there I was, having an emotional breakdown mid-orgasm like the world's most clichéd romance novel heroine. Cruz would never let me live this down if he knew. Thank God he wasn't here.

"Becks," Riley whispered, alarmed, trying to pull back.

"No," I gasped, my fingers dug into her shoulders, desperate and clinging. I pulled her closer to me, needing to feel her heartbeat against mine. "Don't go. Please." My voice sounded foreign to my own ears—stripped bare, desperate, no coolness to hide behind. My body said what my words couldn't—stay, stay, stay—every muscle tense with the fear she might slip away again.

Riley's thumb brushed the tears from my cheeks, her own eyes glistening in the dim light. "I'm not going anywhere," she promised, voice thick with emotion.

"I've been...so alone," I confessed, the words ripped from somewhere primal and honest. "Even when I wasn't alone, I was alone. Without you." No metaphors, no pretty language, no Instagram-worthy quotes about growth and authenticity. Just the truth I'd been running from for two years.

Riley pressed her forehead to mine, our breath mingling. "I know," she whispered. "Me too."

My hands framed her face, my body still trembling with aftershocks. "I won't run again," I vowed, the words carrying the weight of a promise I finally understood how to keep. "Not from this. Not from you." The most terrifying and most honest thing I'd ever said.

The Riley from before would have asked how do I know? Would have needed reassurance, proof, guarantees. Signatures. Fingerprints. But *this* Riley, the one who rebuilt herself without me, she just watched my face, searching for something. And whatever she saw there must have been enough, because she kissed me with a tenderness that broke me all over again.

I'm a fucking hurricane. Always have been. But Riley, she's the eye of the storm. The only place I've ever felt calm enough to just...be.

"Good," she said. "I figured I had to rush over here before you changed your mind on me again."

She wasn't a wall anymore, and I was grateful, finally. Her kiss tasted of salt and forgiveness and coming home.

My fingers found the hem of her shirt. "Not a chance. Bedroom, now, you." I said, tugging it up and over her head, fighting to get it off like it had personally offended me and needed to be punished. Classic BG—zero patience, maximum desire.

Before it hit the floor, her mouth was on mine again. She kissed me like it was breathing, like it was the only thing keeping her alive. I recognized that desperation. Had felt it churning inside me for months, intensifying every time I scrolled past a picture someone tagged her in.

I pulled her toward the bedroom, almost tripping over our clothes, falling into each other with helpless laughter that turned into gasps and sighs as we stumbled forward like we were drunk on each other. It was ridiculous and perfect—this ungraceful, urgent dance toward my bed.

"Can't walk," I half-laughed, half-moaned, clutching at her like some romance novel heroine about to swoon. "Forgot how your kisses make my knees malfunction."

"Then don't," she said, and her lips were on my collarbone, and I thought I might collapse right there, in my own bedroom, fully endorsed by my spiritual advisor who'd tell me this was "surrendering to the universe" or whatever.

My legs would buckle any moment, and had it not been for the bed behind me, this would've ended with me in a heap on my own bedroom floor, giggling and explaining myself to a very confused EMT. I pulled her on top of me, needing all her weight on me, like a security blanket made of perfect muscle and soft skin.

Her breathing was ragged, deep and hard, punctuated by small, sweet sounds that I'd replayed in my head during countless sleepless nights. Her skin was slick beneath my touch, her body impossibly warm despite the rain she'd walked through to get to me. She was everywhere, all I could see and feel, as I traced her with my hands—down her shoulders, her breasts, her stomach, lower. When I felt how wet she was, I thought I might lose it all over again.

This was Riley in my bed. Not just some fantasy I'd conjured to torture myself at 3am. Real and solid and wanting me as desperately as I wanted her.

My hand trailed dipped even lower, found her clit, circled it slowly. Her body twitched and she let out a deep, almost wounded noise that made me want to give her everything, all at once. I'd spent two years trying to forget the sounds she made. I never wanted to forget them again.

"Keep going," she gasped, her voice choked and urgent, eyes fluttering closed. I could've come again watching her just like this. Unguarded. Unrestrained. All mine, again. The most beautiful thing I'd ever seen, unraveling under my touch. My mouth found her breast because apparently I'm greedy like that, and when I sucked her nipple, she made this broken little sound that made my thighs clench together. She got even wetter under my touch, and honestly? Peak performance on my part.

I touched her again, feeling her rocking slick against my fingers, teasing and drawing it out until she was shaking, until she couldn't take it anymore. I'd always been good at this. At reading her body, knowing exactly what she needed. The one language I'd never lost fluency in.

Riley's hand found mine with that desperate energy I remembered, dragging me inside like we had unfinished business. Which, let's be real, we absolutely did. My thumb ran lazy eights around her swollen clit, and she shuddered like she'd been holding it together with duct tape and prayer. When my fingers finally sank into her wet heat, fuck, she was so tight around me I nearly lost it right there.

"There you are," came out before I could think about it, and honestly? We were both there. Finally. We had both spent way too long pretending this wasn't inevitable, and here we were proving that some things don't stay buried. It was terrifying and perfect and I was definitely going to overthink this later, but right now? Right now felt like coming home to a house I thought had burned down.

"Please," she gasped, as I found the rhythm that pushed her over the edge. I bit my lip a little, loving the way she fluttered and clenched around my fingers.

She buried her head into my shoulder, trembling body arched, and I watched her come apart with a rawness that left me breathless and aching. She was beautiful, impossibly so, and I wanted to hold this moment forever, to keep it inside me, to live in it. To build a little shrine to it in the corner of my heart where I kept all my most precious memories.

"Becks," she moaned, and I swallowed the sound with a kiss that was almost desperate in its intensity. My name in her mouth like that was a revelation, a religion, a homecoming.

I slowed, gentled, touching her softly now, tenderly, feeling her pulse around me, on top of me, everywhere. Her eyes were closed, her breath coming in shallow, uneven gasps, her skin damp and flushed against mine. She looked completely undone, and I felt a surge of pride knowing I'd done that—I'd made the always-in-control Dr. Riley Benson fall apart.

"Goddamn," she said, a dazed, post-coital wonder in her voice.

"Yeah," I said, and we both started laughing, overwhelmed and out of breath and so full of each other that it felt like spilling over. This was the part I'd missed most: the easy laughter, the joy that always followed. The way we could be completely wrecked and still find each other funny.

She rolled to the side, pulling me with her, keeping me close. Her fingers traced my arm, my shoulder, my face, like she was memorizing me, like she was making sure I was real. I recognized the gesture—I'd done the same to her countless times. Like we both still couldn't believe we'd found each other again.

I wasn't done. Not by a long shot.

Her eyes were bright and hungry as they drifted down my body, landing on my slick mound. She licked her bottom lip, and I could see from the way her chest was rising and falling that she wasn't done, either. It had been too long. Years of fantasizing during lonely nights, of imagining this moment and then punishing myself for imagining it.

Riley pushed me onto my back and shifted lower, pressing soft kisses down my stomach. When her tongue traced a slow, deliberate line along my slit, I nearly came undone all over again. "God, I missed how you taste," she murmured against me, and it caused my hips to buck involuntarily. Like magic, my legs parted for her.

She gave me another slow lick, then another series of quick licks, teasing and light, like she was reacquainting herself with my taste. Tiny shocks followed her tongue with each lick. Her lips curled around my clit, sucking. She hummed against my clit and I swear the vibrations made my toes curl and my thighs squeeze together.

When I started squirming away from the intensity, Riley hooked her arms under my thighs and pulled me back to her mouth with a moan, holding me exactly where she wanted me. The casualness of it, like of course I belonged right here, to her, under her—*god*, why was that so hot?

She held me right there, and kept going while I shook and gasped. My fingers tangled in her curls, hips grinding to meet her mouth, torn between pulling her closer and pushing her away because it was too much, too good to stop, too—

This time, the orgasm rolled through me slower, deeper, like waves lapping at the shore. I came with a soft cry, my back arching as the pleasure spread through every nerve ending. But Riley didn't stop. She kept her mouth on me, gentle now but persistent, until I was shivering and oversensitive with twitching legs.

A wicked thought formed in my head and before I could talk myself out of it, I knew exactly what I wanted. What I needed.

"Wait," I gasped, tugging gently at her hair. "Wait, I—"

She looked up at me, lips glistening, and the ache between my legs suddenly felt different, deeper. I needed more than this. I needed all of her. For a second she looked confused, maybe even hurt, until she saw the look on my face. Recognition dawned slowly, followed by that familiar smirk I'd missed so damn much. "Oh," she said, understanding completely.

I was already off her and pulling the drawer open. The same drawer where I'd kept it all this time, unable to throw it away even when I'd purged every other reminder of her from my bedroom.

She watched, knowing exactly where my mind had gone, how badly I wanted her in me, fully. That was always the thing about Riley—she could read me like no one else, could anticipate what I wanted before I even knew I wanted it.

"Couldn't wait, could you?" she said, low and amused, placing small kisses against my hip.

"Not even a little," I admitted. "Never was good at patience. You know that." I'd always been the impulsive one, the one who couldn't wait, couldn't slow down. She'd been the steady one, the anchor. But not tonight. Tonight we were both desperate, both needy.

"It's all good to go, pinky swear," I said, holding up the strap, watching her watch me. "And I *know* you still remember how to use it." Like riding a bike. A very specific, very intimate kind of bike that made my entire body flush with anticipation.

She propped herself up on her elbows, gaze burning through me. Her fingers worked the buckles with that same precise care she used for everything. Methodical, sure, like she was adjusting a stubborn joint instead of getting ready to wreck me completely. The anticipation was killing me, but I couldn't look away. Didn't want to miss a single second of this.

I bit my lip, heart hammering, and watched her fasten the harness around her hips. Riley's eyes never left me, her focus so intent it made me shiver. She reached for me, and I couldn't get back to her fast enough, couldn't get close enough, couldn't get enough. Two years of deprivation making me greedy, desperate.

"Come here, then" she said, and I was already there, already on top of her, already kissing her like I needed her to breathe. I tasted myself on her lips. Her hands found my waist, steadying me, grounding me, and for a moment we just stayed like that. Me straddling her, the toy pressing against my entrance, both of us breathing hard, both of us knowing exactly where this was going but taking a beat to savor it. The feel of her beneath me, solid and real and mine again. She flipped us around with a strength that shouldn't have surprised me but still did.

The room spun as we rolled, as she pinned me to the sheets, as she pushed inside me with a single, smooth thrust that left me gasping. No hesitation. No uncertainty. Just pure, perfect connection. Fuck, I'd forgotten how good she was at this. How she filled me just right, like my body had been custom made for hers.

She was everywhere again, filling me, surrounding me, overwhelming my senses. Her weight pressed me into the mattress and I thought, yep, this is how I want to die. Pinned under Riley Benson with her inside me. Every nerve ending lit up as she moved slower, deeper, fuller than my fingers could ever manage, than anyone else had ever been. I moved with her, against her, pulling her closer, needing more, always more. This is how we'd always been—never satisfied, always hungry for more of each other. The eternal "not enough" that somehow was everything.

"Ry," I cried out, and she swallowed the sound, her hand finding my clit, her thrusts coming faster, out of control. Jesus Christ, the woman still had magic fingers. Two years and she remembered exactly how to make me lose all good sense. Like she never forgot. She was absolutely *soaked* against my thigh, and I grinned against her mouth. I loved this—loved when she lost herself in me, when all that control and restraint slipped away.

"I know, baby. I know," she murmured, her voice rough.

She was right there with me, kissing the words from my mouth, shaking and breathless and lost. Sweat dripped from her onto my chest and I didn't give a damn.

Her curls stuck to her forehead, and I couldn't resist brushing them back, needing to see her face when she came apart for me all over again.

The careful, composed Dr. Benson disappearing completely, replaced by this raw, desperate version of herself that only I ever got to see.

"This is what I missed," she gasped, her rhythm becoming erratic, eyes locked on mine with an intensity that made my breath catch. "Not just this—you. All of you. The way you say my name when you can't think straight."

Her gaze pinned me in place, the same look that used to make me want to bolt for the nearest exit. Relentless. Cutting through two years of my fake ass "I'm totally fine without you" performance like it was tissue paper. Now it just made me want to surrender completely to whatever she saw in me that I'd never been brave enough to see myself.

The base of the strap hit her just right with every thrust. Hit us both just right. I felt myself come again, harder than before, arching, as it shot through me. I probably made sounds that would've embarrassed me if I'd had any brain cells left to care. Legs locked around her like I was trying to keep her inside me. Her name was the only word I knew, and I said it over and over again, until the syllables blurred together and I was undone beneath her. Complete surrender. Something I'd only ever been able to give to her. Riley followed right after, crying out against my neck, her whole body shuddering as she came.

She held me, moved with me, until we both collapsed, until there was nothing left but the mingling of our breath and the pounding of our hearts. A perfect tangle of us. Love rewritten in sweat and laughter and skin.

"Fuck," I said, the word a wonder, a benediction. The most eloquent thing I could manage in my completely demolished state.

Her head rested on my chest, and she grinned against my skin. "Missed this."

"Missed everything," I said, my fingers threading through her hair, holding her close. I'd missed her smile, her laugh, the way she always knew what I was thinking. I'd missed the way she made me feel safe enough to be exactly who I was, without performance or pretense.

We lay tangled in each other, the world still and quiet around us, the storm outside finally easing to a light, steady patter. Riley's weight was heavy and perfect on top of me, her body flush against mine, her breathing softening into something like peace. For the first time in two years, I felt still inside. Calm. Like my body finally remembered how to exist without constant motion, without running.

"You know what this means, right?" I murmured against her hair.

"Hmm?" She sounded half-asleep, completely content.

"We're going to have to tell all our friends they were right." I groaned dramatically. "Dee is going to be absolutely insufferable."

Riley laughed, the sound vibrating through both our bodies. "Worth it," she said simply.

And it was. It really, really was.

Welcome Home

Riley

TWO YEARS OF WRONG alignment, corrected in an instant.

The spring light caught in the restaurant windows, refracting gold across the sidewalk as we approached. My fingers were intertwined with BG's, her palm warm against mine, our steps falling into rhythm. Something we'd been practicing all month without realizing it.

My heart thumped, steady but quick. A controlled acceleration, like during my morning runs when I pushed just past comfortable. This wasn't just brunch. This was our announcement without words. Our reemergence as *us*.

"You okay?" I asked, my thumb tracing circles on the back of her hand. Her pulse sped under my fingertips. Familiar territory, finally reclaimed. "Your pulse is racing, Becks." A physical assessment—something I couldn't turn off, even outside the clinic.

"Professional assessment, Dr. Benson?" BG kept her voice light, but I caught the slight tension in her shoulders.

I smiled, feeling the joy of her gaze again. "Just an observation."

I breathed in, trying to center myself. Four weeks since I'd shown up at her door in the rain. Twenty-eight mornings waking up next to her. Nights apart wouldn't do it for us anymore. Countless moments relearning each other—her rushing off to product photoshoots, me coming home late from the clinic, both of us tired but making time, anyway. The work of two people determined not to lose each other again. Three Sunday mornings of salt and pepper omelets.

At least *these* ones came without crushing regret and podcasts. I'll take it.

Last night, she'd fallen asleep with her head on my chest, the playlist in her headphones soft in the background. Songs that reminded her of us that no longer carried the time and ache of what we lost. I'd stayed awake, listening to her breathe, cataloging her weight against me, the perfect alignment of her body with mine. Might've even kissed her forehead when she snuggled closer. No adjustments needed.

Our couples' therapist would be proud of how far we'd come from two people who couldn't just enjoy each other's company again without creating chaos somehow.

Now, standing outside the restaurant, I felt every muscle in my body tense with anticipation. The glass door reflected us—BG in her flowing spring dress that caught the light, me in my tailored shirt and jacket that she'd helped me pick out, saying the color brought intensity to my eyes.

"Ready?" I asked, squeezing her hand once. The contact grounded me, steadied my breathing.

She nodded, her eyes bright with a nervousness she wasn't bothering to hide from me anymore. No performance. No deflection.

We stepped inside, warmth and the scent of coffee washing over us. The host's smile was kind, professional, but her eyes flickered to our joined hands before she led us toward the private section in back. My throat tightened as we rounded the corner.

The circular table was already surrounded by familiar faces. Tangi gesturing wildly mid-story. Taj sipping her black coffee, short hair perfectly styled. Cruz with a sparkling water, phone in hand while pretending to listen. Sakia nodding along, amused. Deena leaning forward, elbows on the table, completely engaged, her untouched orange juice sitting nearby.

Deena noticed us first. Her eyes dropped to our linked hands, then lifted to my face. There was a moment—just a heartbeat—where surprise registered, her eyebrows lifting fractionally. Then her expression softened into something knowing, something warm. Something that said finally without a word.

The conversation ebbed as we approached, awareness spreading around the table like ripples in water. Tangi's sentence trailed off mid-word. Taj set down her mug, a knowing smile playing at her lips. Sakia's smile widened. Cruz looked up from his phone, eyes darting between us, comprehension dawning slowly then all at once.

The silence lasted three seconds—I counted them in my head, an old habit from measuring therapeutic stretches.

Then Cruz's voice cut through: "Well, look who finally figured their shit out!"

The table erupted in laughter. The tension in my shoulders released as BG's fingers tightened around mine, anchoring me in place.

"Only took you what, two years?" Tangi added, pulling out the chair beside her for BG.

"And countless hours of refereeing and coordinating, don't forget." Taj chimed in, raising her coffee mug in a mock toast, her eyes carrying a warmth I hadn't seen in months.

BG rolled her eyes but couldn't hide her smile. "You all think you're so clever."

"But we *are* though," Deena said, winking at me, one hand resting subtly on her stomach. "And observant. And patient."

"*Very* patient," Sakia agreed, raising what looked like a mimosa.

As we took our seats, the weight of their acceptance wrapped around us, more comforting than I'd anticipated. No interrogations. No surprised questions. Just this easy slide back into the group as if the configuration had always been inevitable.

BG settled next to me, her knee pressing against mine under the table—deliberate, grounding. I watched her from the corner of my eye, noting the subtle signs only I would recognize: the way she twisted her rings when nervous, the slight rhythm her foot tapped against the floor, the extra brightness in her laugh. But beneath the nerves was something else. A steadiness I hadn't seen before. Her smile reached her eyes in a way it hadn't two years ago, unguarded and real.

Tangi excused herself to the restroom, and BG fell into easy conversation with Sakia about a gallery opening. I followed Tangi with my eyes, knowing what was probably coming. I tried to talk her out of it with my eyes, but she fixed me with a raised brow that didn't invite pushback. Understood.

Two minutes later, as BG was accepting a menu from the server, Tangi appeared at her side.

"Need your help with something," Tangi said, gesturing vaguely toward the hall.

BG glanced at me, questioning. I nodded slightly, keeping my face neutral.

They stepped away, just far enough for privacy but still within my sightline. I watched as Tangi's expression turned serious, her stance protective—the big little sister energy I'd grown to respect over the years. I couldn't hear the words, but I could read Tangi's body language as clearly as text: *If you hurt her again...*

Then, like sunlight breaking through clouds, Tangi's posture softened. She pulled BG into a tight hug, her face breaking into a wide smile. BG's eyes found mine over Tangi's shoulder, relief evident in her expression as she mouthed "thank you" to me. Something loosened in my shoulders, a knot I hadn't realized was still there.

When they returned to the table, the atmosphere had shifted subtly. Lighter somehow, as if the last piece had clicked into place. The server arrived with a tray of drinks. Mimosas for most, a mocktail for Cruz, orange juice for Deena that she barely touched. Conversation flowed as easily as the drinks, plates passed family-style across the table.

I watched Becks move through our circle with a grace that seemed effortless. She'd always been charismatic, always the center of any room she entered, but this was different. There was no performance to her joy now, no calculated reactions. When she laughed at Cruz's terrible jokes, it was genuine. When she asked Sakia about her new project, she listened with complete focus.

She remembered exactly how I took my coffee, sliding a mug toward me without breaking her conversation with Taj. Her fingers brushed mine in the exchange, lingering just a second longer than necessary. These small touches weren't for show. They were quiet reminders, private anchors between us.

"All I'm saying," Cruz was insisting, gesturing with his fork, "is that Mercury retrograde is a valid excuse for at least sixty percent of my bad decisions."

"That's convenient," Taj countered, "since Mercury is retrograde for like a third of the year."

"Exactly my point!"

Tangi threw a napkin at him. "Your point is bullshit, and we all know it!"

Sakia chimed in, her voice dry as desert sand: "Fascinating how your retrograde-related disasters always seem to involve dating apps and dark-skinned dudes, though."

"Listen, I have a type, though! Nothing wrong with that. Everybody has a type, Kia. Even if *your* type looks suspiciously like Aaron Pierre..."

Sakia gasped.

As laughter rippled around the table, I noticed Taj and Dee exchange a look. Something meaningful, something planned. Taj nodded slightly, and Deena cleared her throat.

"Since we have everyone here," Deena began, her fingers automatically finding Taj's, "there's something we wanted to share."

The table quieted, attention shifting. Taj's smile was small but impossibly bright.

"We're having a baby," she said simply.

A little mental math, and suddenly, the vendor fiasco all made sense. Sneaky as *hell*, both of them.

I raised an eyebrow at Taj, the corner of my mouth lifting slightly. "Interesting timing. This wouldn't happen to be the same 'client' who had that emergency the day you two abandoned us with the vendor meeting, would it?"

Taj's eyes widened slightly before her mouth quirked into a guilty smile. Deena pressed her lips together, barely containing her laughter.

"Scheduling conflicts," Deena offered with exaggerated innocence. "*Very* unfortunate."

"Very convenient," BG countered, but couldn't keep the warmth from her voice.

Their matchmaking had been transparent, but I couldn't fault the results.

"All *I'm* saying," I laid hands against my chest, "Is that Riley is a perfectly gender-neutral name. Just putting that out there."

Taj and Deena raised eyebrows at each other, then back at me.

The announcement landed like a stone in water, a moment of perfect stillness before the ripples of joy spread outward.

"I'm gonna be an auntie!" Tangi's squeal was probably audible three blocks away. Cruz almost knocked over his water reaching to hug them both at once. Sakia's usual composure broke into a genuine grin.

Becks was on her feet immediately, arms wrapping around Deena, words tumbling out about astrological signs and nursery colors. I watched her face light up with authentic happiness for our friends—no calculation, no performance, just pure joy.

In the midst of the celebration, I watched them all. This patchwork family we'd built. Cruz dramatically offering to be the "cool uncle" while Tangi insisted she had dibs on godmother. Sakia quietly promising design help for the nursery. The easy back-and-forth of people who had chosen each other, who had built something lasting together.

Across the commotion, BG's eyes found mine. Even with the noise and movement between us, it felt like we were in our own pocket of stillness. Something passed between us: understanding, acknowledgment, possibility. The look held all our history and all our future at once.

She disentangled herself from the group hug and made her way back to me, sliding into her seat with that grace that had first caught my attention years ago.

Her shoulder pressed against mine, an alignment that felt inevitable.

"What are you thinking about?" she asked quietly, just for me.

I took a moment, feeling honesty and the new brightness between us return after so long. "How different this feels. How right."

Her hand found mine under the table. "It is right," her voice was steady with certainty. Then, lower still: "Love you, Ry. I never stopped."

The words settled inside me, familiar and new all at once. I leaned forward, drawn by the gravity between us, and kissed her, soft and brief, but never hesitating.

Around us, our friends erupted in cheers and wolf whistles, the sound supportive rather than teasing. Not mocking our reunion but celebrating it, lifting it up as something worthy and real.

"Welcome home," I whispered against her lips.

BG smiled, that real smile that reached her eyes and crinkled the corners. We hadn't gone backward, hadn't tried to recreate what was lost. We'd built something new instead. Something honest and hard-won.

We hadn't returned to the past. We'd chosen this present, deliberately and fully. Together, finally, exactly where we were always meant to be.

Anything but Tangerine (Epilogue)

BG

THE THING ABOUT HOSPITALS is they always smell like they're trying too hard to be clean. Like that industrial-strength disinfectant is working overtime to convince you everything's sterile and safe, when really it just makes you hyperaware of all the *not-clean* things lurking underneath.

I'm spiraling about hospital smells. Classic BG.

Riley's hand finds mine as we navigate the maze of hallways toward the maternity ward, her fingers automatically threading through mine like they've been doing it for—well, longer than I'm going to calculate right now because I'm already spiraling about disinfectant and I don't need to add math anxiety to the mix.

"You good?" she asks, because she knows me. Knows my spiral face, knows when I'm about to disappear into my own head about something completely ridiculous.

"Just thinking about how hospitals smell like lies," I say, which makes her laugh—that surprised bark of laughter that means I've said something simultaneously weird and accurate.

"Only you would philosophize about institutional cleaning products on the way to meet our goddaughter."

Our goddaughter. The phrase hits different now, doesn't it? Now that we're an *us* again, now that there's this small circle of white gold and amber around my ring finger that I keep forgetting is there until I catch the light and remember, *oh right, we're doing this thing. We're actually doing this thing.*

The waiting room is chaos in the best possible way. Tangi's sprawled across two chairs, her three-year-old son Malik building some kind of architectural nightmare out of waiting room magazines while she scrolls through her phone. A few other family members are scattered around—people I recognize but don't know well enough to name.

"Finally!" Tangi says when she spots us, like we're late to our own party. "I was about to send a search party."

"Traffic was insane," Riley says, which is Riley-speak for *BG made us stop at three different places because she couldn't decide between the stuffed elephant, the musical mobile, or the onesie that says 'Future CEO' and we ended up getting all three.*

Malik looks up from his magazine fort. "Auntie BG! Auntie Riley! Did you bring presents?"

"Malik," Tangi warns, but she's grinning.

"Actually," I say, crouching down to his level, "the baby was so excited to meet you that she picked out a special present just for you."

His eyes go wide like I've just revealed the location of buried treasure, which, let's be honest, is exactly the reaction I was going for. "The baby picked it out?"

"Mmhmm," I say seriously, handing him a small wrapped box. "She told us you might like to color her some pictures." Inside are crayons and a coloring book because I remember being three and how the world felt like this giant canvas just waiting for you to make your mark on it.

I catch something in my peripheral vision. Riley's hand pressed to her chest, this soft expression on her face that I'm too focused on Malik to fully process right now. But there's something there, something warm and wondering that makes my stomach do this little flip.

"Y'all bought the whole store, didn't you?"

"Just half of it," Riley says dryly when Tangi eyes our overstuffed gift bag, hefting it like evidence of our complete lack of restraint.

The truth is, we went a little overboard. But when your best friend has a baby and you're standing in some baby store holding tiny socks that are somehow smaller than your thumb and Riley's making that face she makes when she's trying not to cry in public? You buy the socks. You buy *all* the socks.

"Sakia sends her love and these," Tangi says, gesturing to a bouquet of balloons tied to her chair—silver and pink and one shaped like a teddy bear that's somehow managing to look judgmental. "She's covering someone's shift but she'll be by in a few."

"And Cruz?" Riley asks.

"Flowers," Tangi says, and we all laugh because of course Cruz sent flowers. Cruz who communicates in bloom language, who probably spent an hour researching what specific flowers mean 'congratulations on your tiny human.'

"Plus this," Tangi adds, holding up what might be the most beautiful handmade teddy bear I've ever seen. It's small enough for tiny hands to grasp, soft enough to love to pieces, and somehow perfectly imperfect in that way that screams *Cruz made this with his entire heart.*

Malik abandons his coloring to investigate the bear. "It's soft," he announces, like this is breaking news.

"Everything Cruz makes is soft," Tangi says, and there's something in her voice. This warmth, this *knowing*. Like he gets it, the way Cruz pours himself into everything he creates. The way love looks different for different people.

A nurse appears like they do in those hospital tv shows. Suddenly, efficiently, with that particular brand of controlled urgency that makes your stomach flip even when you're not the one being attended to.

"For the Muhammad family?" she asks, and we all turn toward her like flowers following the sun.

"That's us," Tangi says, speaking for the group.

"Congratulations," the nurse says, smiling. "Mom and baby are doing great. We can take the next two visitors back now."

Tangi looks at us with this knowing smile. "You're up next. Everyone's been waiting for you two."

My heart does this silly flutter thing. Everyone's been waiting for us. Riley and me. The godparents.

Riley squeezes my hand and I realize I've been holding a nervous breath.

We follow the nurse down another maze of hallways, and I can feel Riley's nervous energy radiating beside me like heat.

The door to room 310 is cracked open, and through it we can hear quiet voices, soft murmurs of family getting acquainted with their newest member.

The nurse knocks gently. "Your next visitors are here."

"Send them in!" comes Deena's voice, tired but bright with joy.

And then we're inside, and Deena's sitting up in the hospital bed looking exhausted and radiant and somehow exactly like herself, and Taj is standing beside her holding this impossibly small bundle wrapped in hospital blankets, and my throat goes tight because *holy shit, they made a person.*

"Everyone," Deena says, her voice soft with something I don't have words for, "we'd like you to meet our daughter."

She pauses, and Taj grins, looking between us with barely contained excitement.

"Riley Grace Muhammad."

The room goes quiet except for the sound of my heart trying to beat its way out of my chest.

Riley Grace.

Riley Grace Muhammad.

Riley sucks in a sharp breath beside me, her hand tightens in mine, and I know she's got to be feeling the same thing I'm feeling—this overwhelming rush of *holy shit* and *we love you* and *what did we do to deserve this honor* all at once.

"Riley Grace," Riley repeats, and her voice cracks just slightly on the Grace part.

"We figured," Taj says, grinning, "if we're gonna give her the best possible namesakes, they might as well be you two. And Little T forbade me from naming her any variation of *Tangerine*."

I'm crying. Of course I'm crying. Standing in this hospital room that smells like antiseptic and new beginnings, watching my chosen family introduce me to the newest member, watching Riley's face as she looks at this tiny person who shares her name, and I'm crying like the emotional disaster I've always been.

"Come here," Deena says, reaching for us. "Come meet your goddaughter."

We approach the bed like we're approaching something sacred, which maybe we are. Taj carefully transfers the baby to Deena's arms, and she looks up at us with this expression that's pure wonder.

"She's perfect," I whisper, because what else do you say when you're looking at a miracle that weighs seven pounds and two ounces?

"She's got your nose," Riley observes to Taj, which makes her beam with pride.

"And Little T's stubborn chin," Taj adds, looking down at the baby with this expression of pure wonder.

"Riley Grace," I say, testing the name out loud. "RG for short?"

"Absolutely not," Deena says immediately. "We are not starting nickname chaos on day one."

But she's smiling when she says it, and baby Riley Grace chooses that moment to make a small sound. Not quite a cry, not quite a coo, just this tiny announcement of her presence in the world.

"She likes the sound of her name," Deena says, because she's already completely gone for this kid, which is exactly as it should be.

Riley pulls out her phone. "Can we...?"

"Obviously," Deena says. "But I look like I just birthed a human being, so make sure you get my good angle."

"You don't have a bad angle," I say, which is true. Deena exhausted is still more beautiful than most people on their best day.

We crowd around the bed—this ridiculous, wonderful, chosen family of ours—and Riley takes approximately fifty photos while baby Riley Grace sleeps through her first photo shoot like the little pro she's destined to be.

"Can I...?" Taj asks, moving toward the bed, and Deena immediately shifts to make room, transferring the baby carefully back into Taj's arms.

Watching Taj hold her daughter they both created—because that's what this is, even though the biology is complicated and beautiful and modern in ways that would have blown my grandmother's mind—is watching someone fall in love in real time. Her whole face transforms, goes soft and fierce and protective mama all at once.

"She's going to be so loved," Riley says quietly, and there's something in her voice that makes me look at her more closely. Something soft and wondering and maybe a little scared, like she's seeing a future we haven't talked about yet.

"The most loved," I agree, and when I say it, I'm looking at Riley, not the baby, because sometimes love isn't just about the person in your arms. Sometimes it's about all the people who are going to help you love them.

A gentle knock interrupts the moment, and the nurse peeks her head in. "Sorry to interrupt, but we need to rotate visitors now. Hospital policy."

"We should let Nia have her turn," I say, even though every fiber of my being wants to stay in this room and stare at this perfect tiny human for the rest of the day.

"Thank you for coming," Taj says softly, looking between Riley and me with this expression that's somehow both exhausted and radiant. "It means everything that you're here."

"Wouldn't miss this for nothing, T. Love y'all."

"We'll be back," I promise, though I'm already mentally calculating when visiting hours end and whether we can sneak back in somehow.

We head back toward the waiting room, and as we walk down the hallway, Riley leans over to whisper in my ear:

"We're going to be amazing at this."

"At what?" I whisper back, even though I think I know.

"All of it," she says, and her free hand—the one that's not holding mine—briefly touches the ring on my finger. "The godparent thing. The family thing. The forever thing."

And yeah. Yeah, we are.

In the waiting room, we find Malik showing Sakia his finished coloring page, a rainbow that somehow extends off the paper and onto the magazine it was resting on. The family members are passing around phone photos, everyone smiling and cooing over the images.

"How is she?" Tangi asks immediately.

"Perfect," Riley and I say at the same time, which makes everyone laugh.

"Completely perfect," I add. "And her name is Riley Grace."

The waiting room erupts in a chorus of "awws" and "that's so sweet" and I watch Tangi's face light up.

"Riley Grace Muhammad," Riley says, and I can hear the wonder still lingering in her voice.

As family members start heading back for their turns with the baby, Tangi gathers Malik's art supplies. "Baby, let's clean up so you can thank your new cousin tomorrow."

"But I want to thank her now," he protests.

"Tomorrow," Tangi promises. "She's going to be here tomorrow too. I'm sure she'd love you to thank her with a gift?"

Riley catches my eye over Malik's head. *Tomorrow.* Like this isn't just a one-time visit, like we're going to be part of this little girl's life for all her tomorrows.

Baby Riley Grace made that small sound when we were in there, like she was agreeing with us, like she knows she's been born into exactly the right amount of love and chaos and joy.

Welcome to the world, little one, I think as we settle into the waiting room chairs, watching our chosen family take turns falling in love with their newest member.

The Space We Make (Bonus Epilogue)

Riley

THE KEY TURNS IN the lock with more resistance than usual, my fingers stiff from gripping the steering wheel too tight during the drive home. I pause in the doorway, shoulders rigid with the accumulated tension of eight hours spent coaxing reluctant joints back into place.

Two cardboard boxes sit stacked near the entryway. BG's art supplies and the collection of crystals she swears help with "energy alignment." We'd laughed about it when she moved them in three weeks ago, me teasing her about turning my minimalist space into a "spiritual marketplace." Now they just look like what they are: evidence that she's here, that she's staying, that this is ours again.

The smell hits me before anything else. Garlic and herbs, something simmering on the stove that makes my chest loosen just slightly. Home. Not just the physical space, but the presence that makes it feel alive.

"Ry?" BG's voice floats from the kitchen, warm and questioning. She always knows when something's off. Used to make me want to hide, that intuitive radar of hers. Now I'm learning to be grateful for it.

I drop my keys in the ceramic bowl by the door. My work bag follows, hitting the floor with a soft thud that speaks to how completely drained I am.

"In here," I call back, my voice coming out flat and tired.

She appears in the doorway, wooden spoon in hand, an apron tied around her waist that reads "Kiss the Cook" in faded letters. It was a housewarming gift from Cruz years ago that I'd banished to the back of a drawer. Somehow she'd excavated it and claimed it as her own, wearing it with the same confidence she brought to everything else.

Her smile falters slightly when she sees my face, those amber eyes doing their quick assessment. But she doesn't pepper me with questions, doesn't immediately try to fix whatever's written in my posture. Growth, for both of us.

Instead, she just crosses the space between us and kisses me, soft and sure, tasting faintly of the sauce she's been testing. Her free hand finds my cheek, thumb brushing once against my skin before she pulls back.

"Rough day," I say simply. Not a question, not a detailed explanation. Just acknowledgment of the obvious.

She nods, understanding layered in that single gesture. "Want to try what I'm making? I might have gone overboard with the oregano, but I think I saved it."

This is how we do it now. The small offerings, the gentle redirections toward comfort without demanding I perform okay-ness I don't feel. She's learned not to take my silence personally, and I've learned not to disappear entirely when the world feels too heavy.

I follow her to the kitchen, noting how she's somehow managed to use every pot I own despite making what appears to be a simple pasta sauce. Controlled chaos—her signature. She dips a clean spoon into the simmering pot, blows on it carefully, then holds it out to me.

The taste hits exactly right. Rich enough to satisfy, complex enough to distract, and exactly what I need without knowing I needed it.

"It's good," I tell her, meaning it. "Really good."

"Yeah?" Her whole face lights up, pleased in that way that makes something tight in my chest ease. "Go shower. It'll be ready when you come down."

I nod, already moving toward the stairs. Halfway up, I pause, looking back. She's returned to the stove, stirring with one hand while adjusting the heat with the other, completely absorbed in the task. The sight of her bopping around in our kitchen still catches me off guard sometimes. The rightness of it. How had we ever questioned this?

"Becks," I say softly.

She looks up, eyebrows raised in question.

"Thank you."

She winks. "Always."

The shower runs hotter than usual, steam filling the bathroom until the mirror fogs completely. I stand under the spray longer than necessary, letting the heat work at the knots in my shoulders, the tension I've been carrying since the moment my patient started crying in my office this morning. Sixty-two years old, rheumatoid arthritis advancing faster than we'd hoped, afraid she'd never be able to hold her first grandchild without pain.

Some days the weight of other people's bodies, other people's fear, settles into my bones and refuses to leave. I can feel the beginning of a headache threading behind my eyes, that familiar tension that starts as a whisper and builds to a shout if I don't catch it early.

I towel off methodically, the rough cotton scratching against skin that feels too sensitive. My nighttime routine unfolds automatically. Moisturizer applied in careful strokes, hair wrapped in the silk scarf BG bought me last month, teeth brushed with more attention than they probably need.

When I'm finished, I pull on soft sleep shorts and an old t-shirt, then sit on the edge of our bed and just breathe. The house is quiet except for the distant sounds of BG moving around the kitchen—cabinet doors closing, water running, the soft clink of dishes. The familiar rhythm of home—our home again—finally, around us.

The mattress dips slightly behind me, and I don't need to turn to know she's there. Her presence soothes something in my nervous system.

Her lips find the top of my head, soft and warm through the silk. Then her arms come around me from behind, crossing over my chest, holding me against her without words. She's changed into a slip nightgown. Soft cotton that smells like her, still my favorite scent in the world.

For a moment, we just breathe together. Her chin rests on my shoulder, and I can feel her pulse against my back, steady and sure. Real.

"One of my patients," I say finally, the words barely above a whisper. "Progressive arthritis. She asked me if she'd ever feel normal again."

BG's arms tighten slightly, understanding immediately. She knows about the cases that follow me home, the ones that lodge themselves under my skin and refuse to leave.

"What did you tell her?" she asks, her voice soft against my ear.

"The truth. That normal is going to look different, but different doesn't have to mean worse. That we'd work with her rheumatologist to find ways to manage the pain, to maintain mobility, to help her adapt." I lean back into her warmth. "She cried for twenty minutes. Happy tears, mostly, but still."

"You gave her hope."

"I gave her reality. Sometimes that feels like the harder gift."

BG's hand finds mine, fingers interlacing. "Both things can be true."

The rightness of her response shouldn't surprise me anymore, but it still does. Still makes something ease in my chest that I didn't know was clenched. We taught each other this: how to hold opposing truths without breaking. How to sit in the space between healing and hurting. It took us six years and a *spectacular* implosion to get here, but we got here.

"Dinner's probably ready," she murmurs, but makes no move to let go.

"In a minute." I rub my thumb across her hand.

She hums agreement against my neck, and we stay like that—her holding me while I hold the weight of the day, both of us exactly where we need to be.

After a moment, her hands shift, one moving to cup the base of my skull while her thumb finds the spot just behind my ear. She starts with gentle circles, and I feel some of the tension I've been carrying begin to loosen. Her fingers know exactly where to press, how much pressure to apply, years of watching me work the knots out of my own neck have taught her my body's map of stress.

"Better?" she asks softly, her thumb working along the curve of my ear.

I lean into her touch, eyes closing. "Getting there."

Her other hand moves to my shoulder, kneading the muscle there with practiced ease. She works methodically, the way I approach my own patients—with intention, with care, with the knowledge that healing happens in layers. Down my arms, smoothing away the day's tension with each stroke. The ring on her left hand is a comfort.

When she presses a soft kiss to my shoulder, barely there through the cotton of my t-shirt, something in me shifts. Not quite desire, not quite relief, but something in between. Something that feels like coming home to my own body after a day of existing outside it.

Another kiss, this one at the junction of my neck and shoulder. Then another, trailing up toward my ear. Her breath is warm against my skin, and the headache that's been building begins to recede.

I turn my head slightly, catching her eye, and she pauses—checking in without words, making sure this is what I want and not just what she's offering. It's such a small gesture, but it's everything. The way she always gives me space to choose, even in moments like this.

I answer by turning in her arms, my hand finding the back of her neck as I catch her lips with mine. The kiss is soft, unhurried, tasting of the oregano she's been testing and something that's purely her. She melts into it, her arms tightening around me, and for the first time all day, I feel completely present in my own skin.

Her hand slides across my stomach, the motion casual but deliberate, and when her arm brushes against my breast through the thin cotton, my nipple responds immediately. The sensation shoots straight through me, and suddenly I'm kissing her harder, my breathing becoming shallow and uneven. The stress of the day transforms into something else entirely—this need, this want that only she can answer.

BG pulls back slightly, her lips curved in that teasing smile I know so well. "Is this your new stress management technique, Dr. Benson?" she murmurs, but her voice is already rougher than it was moments ago, her own breathing unsteady. Her hand doesn't stop moving, fingers tracing lazy patterns across my ribs, and I can feel the slight tremor in her touch that means she's just as affected as I am.

"I'll have to run some tests," I manage, my voice barely steady. "Let you know if the treatment is effective."

She laughs, low and warm, and the sound vibrates against my neck as she leans in to nibble my ear. The gentle scrape of her teeth sends electricity shooting down my spine, and any remaining tension from the day dissolves completely. There's only this—her mouth on my skin, her hands mapping my body, the way she makes everything else disappear until there's nothing but us and this moment and the heat building between us.

This would normally be the point where BG gets impatient, where she'd climb into my lap and take what she wants with that beautiful urgency of hers. But she doesn't. She keeps her touches light, her kisses soft and exploring, like she's determined to pull me back into my body one gentle caress at a time. The restraint is driving me wild in the best possible way.

When I can't take it anymore, I catch her hand and guide it under the hem of my shirt, tugging the fabric up. She pulls back just long enough to meet my eyes, checking in one more time, and when I nod, she helps me pull the shirt over my head and lets it fall to the floor beside us.

Her mouth finds my collarbone, trailing soft kisses along the ridge of bone, and when her fingers gently tug at my nipple, I can't hold back anymore. I pull her into my lap, my hands tangling in her locs as I capture her mouth with mine. The kiss is deeper now, hungrier, and I feel the soft brush of her locs against my bare shoulders, tickling my skin in a way that makes me shiver. She settles against me perfectly, her weight grounding me even as everything else spins away.

BG gently pushes me back onto the bed, and I let her guide me down, my head hitting the pillow as she follows me with her mouth. She trails kisses across my chest, down to my stomach, each touch deliberate and unhurried. When she pauses at my breast, taking my nipple into her mouth with gentle suction, I arch beneath her, my body responding with an intensity that surprises me. Heat pools low in my belly, my skin hypersensitive to every brush of her lips, every sweep of her tongue. The stress of the day has transformed completely—all that pent-up tension redirecting into pure want, pure need for her touch.

Her nails drag lightly across my lower stomach, and the sensation pulls a moan from deep in my throat. The sound seems to surprise us both, raw and needy in the quiet of our bedroom. I reach for her, my hands finding her face, pulling her mouth back to mine with an urgency I can't contain anymore.

BG's hands move to the waistband of my sleep shorts, her fingers hooking into the fabric and tugging them down. When I lift my hips to help her, the movement is too eager, too desperate, and I feel heat flush across my cheeks at my own transparency. But BG just smiles against my mouth, that knowing look in her eyes that says she loves seeing me lose my carefully maintained control.

She kisses her way down my body, her tongue tracing patterns that make me arch beneath her. The anticipation builds with each touch, each pause, as she holds me right at the edge of everything I need. When her fingers finally find me, slipping between my legs to discover how wet I am, we both exhale sharply.

"Your turn," I breathe, tugging at her nightgown, desperate to feel her skin against mine.

She grins, catching my wrists gently. "I'm not done with my treatment yet, Dr. Benson," she murmurs, her voice thick with desire and mischief. "Patient care requires my full attention."

She moves lower, pressing soft kisses along my hipbones, then down to my thighs. Her mouth is gentle but insistent, and when she kisses the sensitive skin there, my legs fall open for her without conscious thought. When her tongue finally touches me, sliding between my folds, I gasp her name, my hands fisting in the sheets as need cancels out every other thought.

BG knows exactly how to take care of me, her mouth working with a patience and skill that makes my whole body sing. She's literally eating the stress from my body, one lick at a time.

The pleasure builds slowly, deliberately, until I'm moving against her, my hips finding their own rhythm. When I look down and catch her eyes, dark with desire and fixed on my face, something inside me breaks open completely. I ride the waves of sensation she's creating, lost in the connection between us, until the pleasure becomes too much and I throw my head back, crying out as control snaps. Orgasm slams into me in waves that seem to go on forever.

BG slows her movements but doesn't stop, her tongue gentle now as my body shudders through the aftershocks. Each soft touch sends little sparks through my oversensitive nerves, drawing out the pleasure until I'm trembling beneath her.

I tug her back up to me, needing her mouth on mine, needing to taste myself on her tongue as we kiss deeply. My hands find her hips, still bracketed between my thighs, and when I push against the fabric of her nightgown, I can feel how wet she is too, the heat of her arousal even through her underwear.

I press my thigh up against her, and she gasps into my mouth as her hips roll forward instinctively. "Come on," I whisper against her lips, my hands guiding her movement. "Need to take care of you."

She hesitates for only a second. The heat in her face gives her away, even before she angles her hips and presses down, dragging herself against the flex of my thigh. Her hands brace the mattress on either side of my shoulders, arms corded and trembling. The nightgown is loose on her, so thin I can see the dark shadow of her nipples, hard and begging for my mouth.

I pull at the hem of the slip, get it halfway up before she lifts her arms and lets me peel it off her body. Her skin is radiant, the kind of brown that holds onto sunlight even on a rainy day, and still dusted with the faintest shimmer from that body butter she loves. I kiss a path from her throat to the hollow between her breasts, feel her shudder each time my lips graze her skin. She makes a sound—half sigh, half plea—when I take her nipple into my mouth, swirling my tongue around the tight bud, then biting down just hard enough to make her gasp.

"Ry," she breathes, god, and hearing my name in her voice is the only prayer I ever need. "God, please."

I don't tease her. Not tonight, not when her whole body is trembling and her hips stutter against me like she might fall apart if I don't hold her together. I catch her ass in both hands, fingers digging in, guiding her, letting her ride the pressure and rhythm she needs. The fabric between us is an afterthought; her underwear is already drenched, practically melting against the heat of her center. I wedge my thigh higher, flexing, while she grinds against me.

"You need something, Becks?" My hand grazes the line where her panties slip, skin hot and soft. I let my thumb circle there, slow for a moment. She nods.

I drag my palms up her back, feeling the fine tremor beneath her skin. She's shaking, just a little, and it lights me up from the inside. My hands pass over her ribs, the soft give of her waist, the heat at the small of her back. Her pelvis moves in tight, urgent circles, pressing her against the muscle of my thigh, slick heat leaving wet marks against my skin. I want her so much it's almost laughable and desperate. The way she kisses me—open-mouthed, tongue greedy—turns me molten.

Her breathing is shallow, frantic. I can tell she's close, even before her fingers slip down to guide herself harder against me, chasing the friction. I bite lightly at her neck, mouthing at the place just below her ear, fingers ghosting the back of her neck right at her hairline, and she goes rigid for a second, hips jerking. Then she's moving faster, grinding in short, stuttering thrusts, the rhythm relentless and perfect.

She comes with her forehead pressed to mine, her whole body shaking while she makes these noises that drive me nuts.

Her body bucks, goes taut, and then BG is melting, too. A liquid, boneless collapse. We stay fused for a moment, her chest stuttering against mine, her weight a beautiful sweaty sprawl across my chest. She sags onto me, heavy and wild-eyed, lips parted as if she's forgotten how to shut them. I smooth the damp locs from her face and kiss her forehead. She lets out a sound, soft and undone, and burrows closer. I wrap my arms around her, tight, refusing to let even an inch of air exist between us. Never again.

The warmth of her calms me, makes the world small and manageable. I press my nose into her hair, still fragrant with whatever oil she'd run through it earlier, and just breathe her in. Her heartbeat is a wild thing, but for once, it's not the only one out of control.

Eventually, she shifts. Just enough to look at me, eyes bright and amused, mischief returning as the aftershocks fade. "Feel better?" she says, voice lazy, almost slurry.

I nod. "I'd prescribe another round, but we should probably eat before we both pass out."

She laughs, the sound low and satisfied, then props herself up on one elbow.

Her gaze flicks down my body before returning to my face, and I know she's storing the image for later, for the next time the day breaks her instead. "Give me a minute. Then I'll feed you, Dr. Benson."

BG slides off me with exaggerated care, like I'm china teetering at the edge of a shelf, and I catch her wrist before she can reach the floor. She looks back, slanted smile in place. The look she gives me is so open it's almost uncomfortable, like she's holding my heart up to the light and finding it beautiful, anyway.

"Stay," I say, softer than I intend. "Just another minute."

She folds back onto the bed, curling her body around mine like we're built to fit this way. Her fingertips trace lazy, aimless patterns on my stomach, and we lie together in the dusk, the world outside fading into nothing but our own small universe. I don't know how long we drift like that. Me pulling back from the edge of sleep, BG humming something tuneless and sweet in my ear, her hands always moving, as if she can keep me from unraveling if she just holds on tightly enough.

Eventually, the smell of dinner creeps back in, mingling with the sweat and us and the faint lingering trace of body butter on her skin. BG snorts when my stomach growls, a low, embarrassing rumble in the quiet.

I don't let go until she's laughing softly, until the air between us is light again. She sits up, tidies her hair, then grabs my discarded shirt and pulls it on, grinning when it hangs almost to her knees. "Yours looks better on me," she says, and she isn't wrong.

I watch her move around the room, collecting our nightclothes, smoothing the bedspread, all with that easygoing grace that makes me want to memorize her. The last rays of sunset leak in through the blinds, painting her skin in gold and shadow. I could watch her forever. I probably will.

THE END

Also By L.M. Bennett

Other Series

Competing Desires is the Las Vegas-based trilogy of love and rivalry in the worlds of Championship Poker, Mixed Martial Arts and Racing. High angst, action-packed, firecracker slow burn sports romances. Titles in the series include:

Bad Beat

Pit Stop

TAP OUT

CONNECTED STANDALONES:

THE ART OF GOING Rogue

Love Cynics Anonymous is a series of loosely-interconnected stories about young women who are avoiding love, but find it anyway. Some even manage not to mess it up. Sweet and spicy, slow burn romances. Other titles in the series include:

Corked!: An Enemies-to-Lovers Short (no spice)

Lesbian Speed Dating: A Short Story (no spice)

(re)twist – A [Hendrix/Fatima] Short Story

The Cynic's Christmas Conundrum: A Novelette

The Connoisseur's Christmas Courtship: A Holiday Novella (McKenna's Story)

Bespoke: A Novella

String Theory: A Valentine's Day Novelette (no spice)

Crushed: A Novelette

You Were Almost Home